MW00326027

# UNTIL MY NAME IS KNOWN

TELL OF MY KINGDOM'S GLORY SERIES BOOK 1

## SONYA CONTRERAS

Bull Head Press

# UNTIL MY NAME IS KNOWN

Copyright ©2015 by Sonya Contreras

All rights reserved.

No part of this book may be reproduced or transmitted in any form or by any means, electronic or mechanical, including photocopying, recording, or by any information storage and retrieval system without the written permission of the publisher, except where permitted by law.

All Scripture quotations are taken from Holy Bible, New International Version. Copyright ©1973, 1978, 1984 International Bible Society. Used by permission of Zondervan Bible Publishers.

*Until My Name Is Known* is a work of fiction. Although retelling the Scriptures' events as closely as possible, the real people, events, establishments, and locales are used fictitiously. All other elements of the novel are drawn from the author's imagination.

Published by Bull Head Press Squaw Valley, California Paperback: ISBN 978-0-9907237-0-7 eBook: ISBN 978-0-9907237-1-4

Library of Congress Control Number 2014915693

Study Guide is available upon request at www.sonyacontreras.com.

Cover design by Kirk DouPonce of DogEared Design Content edited by Marcy Weydemuller Copy edited by Katie Vorreiter Font: Felix Titling, Bell MT, and Constantia

Printed in the United States of America.

 Created with Vellum

*To Lydia Luree Kreidler, my mom,*
*who showed me God.*

# CONTENTS

## UNTIL MY NAME IS KNOWN

*They will tell of the glory of Your kingdom... so that all men may know of Your mighty acts.*

— PSALM 145:11-12

*But I have raised you up for this very purpose, that I might show you My power and that My Name might be proclaimed in all the earth.*

— EXODUS 9:16

# CHAPTER 1

$Z$ ipporah paused, stirring the lamb stew bubbling in a pot over the fire outside her dry-mortared dwelling. She smelled the dried rosemary as she crumbled it to add to the stew.

"Is that Father?" Gershom pointed to a lone figure running down the hillside.

She looked where her son pointed. Her heart pounded. Moses was returning home early. What was wrong?

"Zipporah!" he yelled as he panted for breath.

She dropped her spoon. "Gershom, stay with the baby." She raised her ankle-length tunic to run.

When she reached Moses, she clutched his arm. "What is it? Where are the flocks?"

She looked into his eyes gleaming with a fire not his own. His face flushed with color, not just from running.

"God appeared unto me!" Moses grabbed her waist and swung her in circles. His beard tickled her neck.

She squealed.

He laughed. He smelled of sheep, dust, and sunshine.

Zipporah grabbed his shoulders as he continued to twirl her. "Moses, stop! You're making my head spin."

His demeanor grew somber. He stopped twirling her, suddenly

serious. "I saw the Lord, the Lord God Almighty. He spoke to me."

"What do you mean? No one sees God and lives." She touched his flushed face. Was he feverish?

He gently lowered her feet to the ground. "He gave me a mission." He put his arm around her waist and guided her toward their house. "I saw a light flickering like a star. I went to see. It was a bush on fire, but without ashes. Yet it burned. I drew closer."

Fire brought death in pastures where rains fell only in the rainy season. Zipporah smelled for smoke. His cloak did not smell of smoke. Had he dreamed this bush? She touched his face again; it was warm, not hot. "Weren't you afraid?"

He took hold of her hand. "I took off my cloak to smother the flames if it spread. A voice from the bush called me by name. I fell before His presence."

She studied his eyes. She could almost see the reflection of the bush that burned.

Moses stared into the distance. "Who am I but a shepherd, a watcher of sheep and goats? My unworthiness filled me as the voice spoke, 'Do not come closer. Remove your sandals for you are on holy ground.' I knelt before His presence."

Zipporah looked at his feet. "Your sandals. Did you leave them at the bush?"

Moses appeared not to have heard.

Zipporah squeezed his arm.

He started walking, still holding her hand. "I covered my face. I feared to look at Him. The Lord spoke, 'My people suffer in Egypt. I hear their afflictions. Go to Pharaoh. Bring My people out of Egypt.'"

Her heart raced and her legs felt weak. Zipporah whispered. "Pharaoh will kill you. I cannot lose you, Moses. This God can save His people without you."

Moses squeezed her hand. "The Lord assured me that the men who would kill me are dead."

They reached the house but stayed outside. Zipporah took baby Eliezer from Gershom.

Gershom gave Moses a hug. "You are well?"

"Yes, my son. All is well."

Zipporah jiggled Eliezer on her hip as she stirred the stew trying to clear her thoughts. This God might say Pharaoh would not kill Moses, but the entire world knew Pharaoh's power and control. Moses ran from Pharaoh forty years ago. Could she believe this God would protect Moses now? If Moses obeyed, who would watch the flocks that had grown under his care? How safe would she feel away from her father's land?

Zipporah said, "Why must you go? What do you care of the suffering of *those* people?"

"*Those* people, Zipporah, are *my* people. Remember, I killed that Egyptian overseer because he whipped *my* brothers. You can't imagine doing nothing while watching your own people suffer. I saw the agony of my people. I can't forget it." He took the spoon from her hand and put it into the pot, then gathered the baby from her arms. "God calls me to obey."

Her breathing quickened. Her voice trembled. "Why you, Moses? God can find someone else."

He squeezed her shoulder. "I asked God the same thing. He didn't tell me why. It didn't seem to matter to Him what I'd done. Instead, He told me who He is. 'I Am that I Am. The Lord, the God of your fathers.'

"This God promised Abraham a nation like the stars in number, Zipporah..." He sighed and handed the baby to Gershom. "This God of Abraham is sending me. He will be remembered from generation to generation. He will lead His people to their land."

Zipporah stirred the fire under the stew. Her insides felt like the sparks that flew around her. Why would this God tell her husband to leave everything that she valued? Why would Moses want to obey? "You left your first wife. Why would God want you?"

She grabbed her spoon, trying to call back her words.

Moses's face paled, as he stepped from her.

Why did she spout such words?

Moses swallowed several times.

Could she persuade him not to go? She approached him.

Moses held her face toward his own.

She did not look into his eyes.

He waited.

She met his eyes, seeing the hurt but also his resolution. She wilted. She would yield, and already hated herself for it.

He squeezed her shoulder. "The Lord commands. I must obey."

Could she accept this Lord that called her husband to his death? Thoughts tumbled through her mind like bubbles in her boiling stew. She wanted to shout them at Moses but instead willed herself to calm down. Zipporah would not convince him if she were angry. Breathing deeply, she slowed her thoughts. She stroked his beard gently. "You trust this God too much."

"I trust this God too little. Or I wouldn't question."

"This peace, this confidence that you have..." She shook her head, unable to finish. How could he obey? Throwing back her shoulders, she resigned herself. "Sit, eat. We must tell my father." Keeping her hands busy, she lowered her head and did not meet his eyes.

Before settling to eat, Moses tucked her head to his chest. He smoothed her head covering away and stroked her hair. "Oh, Zipporah," he whispered. "This is what I was meant to do."

"Sheep are enough for me." Her shoulders trembled. "Why would the Lord take you from me?"

"God is with me. He will do great things. What more can I do but obey?"

The next morning, Zipporah finished packing their blankets, and cooking vessels. Glancing to the hillsides that surrounded their rock dwelling, she wondered if they would ever return to her lands, her home. She knew where to gather herbs after the spring rains came. She had watched the lambs gallop across the rolling hills.

With a sigh, she massaged the back of her neck as if she could rub away thoughts that threatened to topple her. Would her father allow Moses to leave? Maybe she would not have to leave, if her father did not bless their departure. She threw her shoulders back and clung to that thread of hope.

Eliezer began to cry.

She cradled him. "You hate to leave too, little one."

Gershom burst through the doorway, stirring the air. "Father comes with the goats."

"Settle, Gershom. You disturb Eliezer." She directed her focus to the baby, at least outwardly, tucking her memories of her land into her heart where they would stay protected.

Moses came inside their dwelling. "Ready?"

Zipporah sighed. Could she ever be ready to leave her homeland? Her husband's countenance still glowed with excitement and purpose. Could she keep him from fulfilling his mission?

Moses squeezed her shoulder. "We'll leave shortly."

He handed Gershom a small bundle. "Here, son, carry this to the donkeys."

Gershom lifted the offered bundle with great effort and followed Moses who carried more skins.

Zipporah could hear Moses speaking. She rose to listen from the doorway.

"You must calm down, Gershom. Your mother needs quietness. This move is hard for her."

"Why's it hard?"

Zipporah strained to hear Moses's response. "Sometimes, we value what we have more than we should. We struggle to give it to God when God asks us."

Gershom plopped his bundle by the donkey with a grunt. "What does God want from us?"

Moses finished tying the bundles onto the donkey. He squatted before Gershom to look him in the eye. "Your lamb you raised without its mama, could you give it to me when time came for its meat?"

"Does God want my lamb?" Gershom's voice rose in pitch.

Moses patted Gershom's back. "No, but we must give whatever He wants." Moses glanced at Zipporah in the doorway. He stood and smiled.

Zipporah returned his smile with a wobbly one of her own. Looking one more time around the inside of the dwelling, she whispered, "So many memories."

Moses came behind her. "We've only begun the memories God has planned for us."

Nodding, Zipporah tore her gaze from her house.

Moses settled her on her donkey with Eliezer in her lap. Taking the reins from Moses's offered hand, she raised her head covering over her dark hair. She kicked the donkey to start. The dirt rose to meet her, filling her nose with the smell of pasture, flocks, and home. She heard the goats and sheep shuffling behind her, settling into their order. Ewes called to their lambs to stay close. If only she could stay close to her family, too.

When she came to the first rise, she turned back for a final view. The hills rolled beneath a cloudless sky of blue. Her stone home blended into the brown landscape as if it were nothing. Would her memories also disappear? Her gaze lingered on the sheep following them. She knew nothing but desert life. Things stayed the same. Her life was here.

Egypt's city life frightened her. How would she live with another people? Would these people accept her? She was dark skinned, Moses light. How would she even talk to them? Would her sons adopt their ways?

She hugged Eliezer close. He squirmed and fussed at the constraint.

She turned her gaze away from her hills and set her head forward. This God of Moses must change her heart if she would be ready for this mission.

After a day of traveling, they approached the land belonging to Jethro, Zipporah's father. Zipporah heard him shush his dog's barking as their flocks approached his watering pool.

Jethro embraced Moses, kissing each cheek, and then faced Gershom. "Who do we have here?"

"Grandfather, it's me, Gershom."

Jethro bent to one knee and pressed the boy to his chest. "Could this be the little boy whom I last saw? You've grown to be a man in one night."

Zipporah dismounted from the donkey, jolting Eliezer as she did. "Father."

Jethro stood to hug her and Eliezer. "My desert flower, you grow dearer with the days." He stepped back to tickle the baby's foot. "This is Eliezer? If only the pastures could grow as fast as he."

Zipporah saw Naima, her mother, running to meet them.

Naima hugged her. "It's been too long. This is Eliezer? How quickly he grows! You feed him well."

"Could that man who stands beside my husband be my little Gershom?" Naima asked.

Gershom thrust out his chest and stood taller. "I've lived four cycles of the harvest. I'm almost a man."

They laughed.

Reaching the dry-mortared stone house, Jethro settled on cushions around a raised table. "Sit, Moses. Tell me, how are your flocks?"

Conversation ensued. Preparations for the meal began.

When the evening meal was prepared, Jethro requested the blessing. He dipped his flatbread into the bowl in the center of their circle. He dug chunks of *chevon* with his bread before dipping it in a paste of cheese and herbs. Once he prepared his, Moses, as the respected male guest, followed. The women finished, helping Gershom fix his flatbread.

No serious news was shared until the meal was completed. The finishing blessing over the meal was spoken. Jethro settled against the cushions. He held his wine vessel in his hand and relaxed in the growing dusk.

Snuggling against his father's side, Gershom nestled his head on Moses's lap and closed his eyes.

Jethro drank. "You have prospered. My flock thrives under your care. Yet something brings you here. Speak what is on your heart."

Moses hesitated. "I wish to return to my people."

Eliezer fussed and wiggled. Zipporah settled in the darkened corner to soothe him.

Jethro drank from his cup in the silence. Her father was a man who weighed his words. "Zipporah is not from the tribe of Israel —why risk her and the children becoming slaves in Egypt?"

"God desires to free all Israelites."

"All Israel hopes for that, but until then, won't your family be in danger?"

Moses grabbed Jethro's arm in his enthusiasm. "God's time for deliverance is soon. He has told me to lead them."

Zipporah strained her eyes from the corner to see her father's expression over the glow of the fire. Would he forbid them from going? Her father's long pause gave Zipporah hope. She closed her eyes and took a calming breath. They might not leave.

Moses's voice broke the silence. "God called me from a bush that burned but was not consumed. He promised protection. He gave me a mission."

Jethro looked to his cup, which was apparently empty because Naima hurried to fill it for him.

She offered Moses more.

He shook his head.

Jethro drank. "Tell me what He said."

Zipporah could not mistake the excitement in her husband's eyes. His countenance glowed as his words came with speed.

Resting her head against the wall, she sighed in defeat as Eliezer settled in her arms. Moses could convince anyone of anything. Didn't he change the minds of shepherds so long ago when she first met him?

She and her six sisters had fought with other shepherds over water. As the men pushed her flocks away from the well, Zipporah sucked in her words, her face growing hot.

She heard a voice, rich with Egyptian accent command, "What's going on?"

The speaker's rich linen garb and recently shaven face and head spoke of an Egyptian ruler with power. His height threatened even these herdsmen. She looked for his caravan. None was visible.

Zipporah watched without word as the shepherds measured Moses against their strength before retreating.

"You can't wait your turn?" Moses stepped forward to uncover the well. The huge stone over the water hole moved easily in his grasp. "Allow the women to go first." Dipping the water buckets, he filled the sheep's trough.

Her sister nudged her. "Shut your mouth; you'll catch a frog."

Zipporah forced herself to direct the sheep with her rod. Her shaking hands and clumsy movements further frustrated her. What was wrong with her? What power did this man have over her that made her heart flutter and her hands tremble? Why did she feel useless in his presence?

Zipporah sputtered to thank him but could not find her voice. Lowering her eyes, her face flushed with heat.

Her sister rescued her. "You would honor us by eating with our father."

Moses helped lead their flock home. He married Zipporah thirty years later, after his first wife died.

Zipporah pushed her head away from the wall and listened.

Eliezer turned in his sleep as she held him. She covered him with a goatskin against the cooling night air. Her focus returned to the present.

Her father spoke. "You have my blessing. May God be praised. I do not envy your mission. But I wish to see God's power."

Zipporah's heart sank. Her father had granted permission. She would leave her homeland and live with a people not her own. Swallowing, she tried to dislodge the lump in her throat.

They stayed the night and rose early.

Naima squeezed her. "Moses is a great man. His God will favor you."

Zipporah could not speak. She nodded but wondered if she believed it.

Naima hugged her grandsons. "Oh, little ones, may our God protect you."

Jethro clutched his daughter. "Zipporah, my flower of the desert, may your home be where your husband is. You will see God in the days to come." Dropping his arms from Zipporah, he placed his hand on the head of each grandson. "Gershom, your name 'alien,' may you find your true home. Eliezer, may your smallness bring you closer to the greatness of the Lord of your father."

Jethro grasped Moses's shoulders. "I give you fresh donkeys and servants to speed you on your way. Accept my blessing for your journey. May you find favor with our God."

Moses helped Zipporah and his sons onto donkeys and they started for Egypt. Moses held the staff of God in his hand.

Long ago, Moses had told Zipporah of Lot, Abraham's nephew. Before the Lord destroyed their city, Lot and his family fled. Lot's wife looked back, turning into a pillar of salt. As Zipporah watched her father's homeland grow dim, she, too, could feel her heart torn in two.

Moses reached across her donkey and patted her hand. "The Lord knows. If He sees the Israelites' suffering, He knows your suffering, too."

She nodded, blinking back tears. Moses was taking her from everything that she held dear. Was she losing Moses to this mission? Clutching Eliezer closer to her bosom, she determined not to forsake her own customs. She bit her lip to keep it from trembling and raised her chin. She adjusted Eliezer to straddle ahead of her on the blanket. She would remember her people and keep her memories. No God would take them from her.

The day grew hot under the sun's penetrating power. Sand sifted through their clothes and coated their mouths with grit. With the donkeys' plodding gait, Moses reviewed the Lord's words from the burning bush.

God showed Moses signs of His power.

Moses obeyed when God told him to throw his staff. It became a snake. Without the staff in his hands, he was defenseless, and exposed. When God told him to grab the snake by its tail, he stepped forward, believing God. That snake turned back into his staff.

The donkey faltered over an animal burrow. Moses tightened his grip on the reins.

He studied his staff now in his hand, the sole protection of a herdsman. He had killed many snakes with his staff. Each nick in the wood contained a story of God's past protection.

God would convince Pharaoh with his shepherd's tool. Egyptians disdained shepherds. God would show His power to Pharaoh by using something unclean in Pharaoh's eyes. Moses smiled as he thought of the humor of his God.

The donkey's gait settled back into a rhythm. Moses fell into the cadence as he considered the next sign God had shown him at the burning bush.

God told Moses to put his hand in his cloak. When he removed it, it was white.

Moses had seen leprosy once in his life. In his upbringing in Egypt, he had observed a leper village on the outskirts of the land. His stomach rolled as he stared at people without arms or legs; most had no fingers and toes. Their white skin was like the snow on the far distant mountains during the rainy season. Leprosy wore away the flesh to leave nothing. Moses had observed and grown sick. He turned from their village to look no more.

When Moses removed his hand from his cloak at the bush that burned, he clasped it with his other hand. The contrast between the white skin and his sun-browned hand made him nauseous. His hands shook. He forgot the burning bush.

God's words broke through his fears. "Put it back into your cloak."

He did, remembering he was before God. When he removed his hand again, it was whole, like the other. He breathed deeply, gratefully. God wasn't ready for him to die, yet.

Could God take him—a murderer, a fugitive from the former pharaoh's wrath, and elevate him to lead His people? Moses nodded. His return to Egypt would bring many surprises. God would do great things.

Moses glanced at Zipporah. How was she managing? Her troubled looked nagged at his heart. He was dragging her to the most powerful city in the world. She had never left her father's land. If he had not promised himself that he wouldn't leave his family for anything, he'd let her stay with her father until this mission was finished.

Memories of his first wife, Tharbis, were bittersweet. After fleeing from Egypt, he never saw her again. Her princess status would not permit her to live in a desert, hiding from civilization. Nor could he return to Egypt to meet his death. They lived apart. Moses mourned the separation. On news of her death, Moses grieved over his loss. His actions could not be undone. Her death also brought him a feeling of release. The killing he had committed would no longer bring suffering to another.

He promised himself when he married Zipporah that they would never be separated. Now he questioned his promise. Was Jethro right about the danger of his family in Egypt? Would they be safe?

Zipporah's words still stung, "You left your first wife. Why would God use you?" Could he obey God with Zipporah with him?

That was another problem. Gershom was four seasons old, Eliezer was six cycles of the moon; both were long overdue for circumcision. When Moses suggested Gershom's need for circumcision at his birth, Zipporah had almost sent Moses into the desert without water. When Eliezer was born, Moses repeated his request. She would rather cut off his manhood than hurt her babies. Moses had conceded. Now thoughts of God's people brought the subject of circumcision to his mind again. His request would send Zipporah spitting snake venom. Moses laughed, but it died quickly. He had better not laugh while she smoldered and stewed. How could he obey and make Zipporah understand?

Moses glanced at Zipporah. Deep furrows creased her brow. She never complained of the hardships of a shepherd's life; she knew nothing else. She roamed her father's hills gathering fresh herbs for their table and their illnesses. She thrived in the desert's space. How would she manage in a city, confined by people and streets? What was best?

Moses watched her.

Her focused look reminded him of when she tried to tame Gershom's energy and could not.

Moses pulled on the reins and waited for her to come beside him. "You're doing well?"

She kept her head down. "Yes."

The tension between them crackled. What could he say to ease her thoughts? If he ignored the tension, it would not go away. He would rather face all the wrath of Pharaoh, than Zipporah's disapproval. "What troubles you, my precious desert flower?"

Zipporah lifted her eyes. A ray of light shining from them gave Moses hope. She looked relieved to talk. "Why must you obey? Why can't you be happy with sheep? Weren't you fine with sheep after running out of Egypt like a mouse from a hawk?"

"Zipporah." Moses took a deep breath. "I was fine with sheep until God commanded me to leave. Do you want me to disobey God?"

"Why does He want you?"

"I don't know, but He does. Can't you support me?"

"Do I control whether you obey or not?" Zipporah pulled back on the reins of her donkey.

Moses blurted, "I need to obey. And that also means we need to circumcise the boys." He was immediately sorry for his timing.

"Not that pagan custom." She hissed. "You won't change my mind about that savage ritual. No, Moses..." Her voice trembled as her tone deepened. "My sons are mine. I may be going with you to *your* people, but I am *not* a part of them, nor will my sons be." She raised her chin. Moses stared into her cold, hard eyes.

"Zipporah, what happens if I don't obey God? I don't want His anger for our sons."

"These are my sons. No cutting will take place unless I allow it, and that will be over my buried body."

Moses saw her face turn pale and her lips tremble. What could he say to undo her promise? He started to speak, but closed his mouth. Would God kill her so he could obey?

"Zipporah, do not ask for that. God brought you into my life to help me be the man that I am. This mission is not my doing but God's. This mission is yours, too. I can't do my part without your help. I must obey my God. I do not know how to make both you and God happy. Tell me how." He searched her face.

She bowed her head. Her silence was her answer.

He pulled away from her donkey and kicked his donkey's sides to take the lead. Why was obedience so hard?

They approached a lodging tent at dusk. Zipporah drained from the desert's heat. Her lips were dried and burned. The wind blew sand through her loose clothing, coating her skin with grit.

Moses dismounted. "We will stay here tonight."

They spoke no more of circumcision, but the subject sat between them like a camel in the cooking tent. Zipporah had no answer, short of letting Moses perform the procedure. She felt her insides tighten into a ball and wished they did not have to spend the night with others.

Moses lifted her off the donkey, then handed her Eliezer. He whispered in her ear, "I love you." He turned to hail the owner of the lodging.

"Please don't leave me," she called, but he was gone.

The host offered cool water to wash. Moses dipped his entire head in the bowl and splashed water up his arms.

Zipporah wished that she could submerge her entire body, but instead splashed water on her face and arms. The water refreshed more than she could have imagined. She settled in the shadows at the back of the tent with Eliezer and Gershom. Gershom remained quiet, watching the new surroundings.

Moses ate with the host. They conversed of news and ideas as they scooped lamb chunks from the serving dish placed between them on a low table. They used the flatbread to gather pieces from the thickened stew. Moses raised his vessel toward his host. "This wine is from Egypt?"

"Can you taste the delicate flavor? You heading there?"

After Moses's nod, the host eagerly shared his news. "To Egypt, eh? Pharaoh Merenre Nemtyemsaf II is in power now. What a name. The pharaoh before him ruled over eighty years, they say. He created a kingdom none could conquer. I've heard his successor is more arrogant than even he could be. He has made an image of himself for every household to worship. Can you imagine having such worship?" He belched, as was the custom.

Zipporah trembled. Was this the Pharaoh Moses must confront for his people? She drew her cloak tightly around her frame. Her insides knotted like a halter on a stubborn donkey. Her father, a priest of Midian, worshiped the same God as Moses. She saw no need to depend upon Him as they did. He was just a faraway God with no interest in her. As Moses sought to obey this God, he slipped farther from her reach.

Could she trust this God to protect Moses from Pharaoh? She gained much information from the innkeeper, but it did little to calm her heart about the trials soon to test her very beliefs.


The stars rose high in the night before the host stopped talking and directed them to their tent.

Moses assigned a night guard with his servants, knowing that both mountain lions and animals with two legs wanted his possessions. Afterward he entered the sleeping tent. He was grateful for Zipporah's sheltered life that left her ignorant of the treacheries of man. How would city life affect her innocence?

He settled beside her on the pallet of skins. What should he do about circumcision? He sighed. Circumcision was required of every Hebrew. He had allowed Zipporah to sway him from obedience. He needed to obey God. But could he do it, if it meant her life?

Zipporah awakened from a restless sleep by a bright light. She squinted to see its cause.

The Angel of the Lord stood at her feet. His presence filled the room with his brightness. His eyes penetrated her being, as if he could see her thoughts. His countenance shone with holiness. His stature exuded strength. In his hand, he held a drawn sword.

She shook in his commanding presence and trembled at his low, deep voice.

"Circumcise Gershom, My son, so he may serve Me."

Zipporah clutched her throat, trying to breathe. The air closed around her.

The Angel's voice split the silence again. "Circumcise My son or I will slay you."

She looked for Moses.

He sat still, swallowing.

Why did Moses not do something? Zipporah screamed, "Save our son!" She grabbed him and shook him.

"You must allow this, Zipporah."

In her panic, she paused. She vowed her death, if she would circumcise. Moses did not want her death. She could read the struggle in his eyes.

"He'll kill my babies!" Zipporah whimpered.

The angel stepped forward with his sword aimed at Gershom.

Keeping her eyes on the angel, she felt for the knife that Moses kept by his head for protection at night.

She threw the skins off her son and lifted Gershom's loincloth.

With one quick, precise slice, she cut off the foreskin and then threw it into Moses's lap. She crawled to Eliezer and did the same, heedless of the wailing. As the scent of blood struck her nose, she winced. She ripped part of the hem of her tunic to tie around their cuts to stop the blood flow.

The room darkened. She glanced to where the Angel of the Lord had stood.

He was gone.

Her shoulders sagged; her strength was gone. She gathered Eliezer into her arms, squeezing him tightly. She pulled Gershom to her side. Her whole body shook. Her sons could be dead now. She gulped air to calm down.

Moses knelt in front of her. He reached for Gershom with trembling hands. "Zipporah, give me Gershom. I'll hold him." His voice quivered.

She looked into his face. It was white. She hissed, "You're a bloody bridegroom to me. Get out of my sight."

Moses walked out of the tent and into the night.

She cradled her two sons to her breast. She crumbled against the cushions, squeezed her eyes shut, and cried.

What kind of God did Moses serve? Why did He demand such a bloody practice? How could she protect her sons and her husband from the dangers of the world, when she could not even protect them from this God? What did this God want from her? She looked at her sons, whimpering in her arms and lap. What would this God do to them if she continued to fight? Would He stop at nothing to make her obey? She struggled into the night with her thoughts.

Moses's pale face returned to her memory. She had moved in anger and terror protecting her sons from this God. Her anger, now spent, left emptiness. She controlled nothing. She looked for Moses to return, but he did not. She waited without comfort.

I n the coolness of the morning, before the stars finished shining, Moses loaded the donkeys for travel. He had walked the remainder of the night. He should have obeyed a long time ago. He caused the Lord to visit in the night. If he had obeyed at their sons' births, Zipporah would not be hurting now. What a mess he had made by disobeying.

Last night, he would have obeyed the angel's command, but for Zipporah's vow. Now, he resolved to obey, but he could not have Zipporah interfering. He would send her home.

Zipporah stood waiting, her cloak wrapped tightly around her against the morning chill.

"Zipporah," Moses said, hoping she would look at him.

She did not.

"Zipporah, I'm sending you back to your family. The boys will heal faster. I won't endanger you or the boys any further with any disobedience on my part."

Zipporah looked up, but her eyes stayed guarded.

Moses finished tying the bundles onto the last donkey. He straightened the blanket where Zipporah would sit. He fidgeted with the reins. "I'll send back all the servants but Jaden. Stay there until I contact you." He reached to hold her, but instead dropped his arms.

During the night, she had been furious with him. When Moses glanced into Zipporah's face, her tear-filled eyes broke his resolve. He stepped toward her.

She threw her arms around his neck and hid her face in his chest. "Moses, I'm sorry. Your God wins. I must obey so you won't be killed."

He kissed the top of her head. "You will be safe. The time will be short. The Lord will come near to you and become your God. Let Him."

They stayed like that until he felt her body calm. He broke her hold and removed her arms from his neck. He lifted her onto the donkey and handed her the reins.

He motioned for the servants to bring the other donkeys to mount. He hugged Gershom to his breast and whispered in his ear, "You're my son. You will soon be home in the country God has given our people. Your flesh will heal. Remember to obey. The Lord has set you apart to be great."

Gershom squeezed Moses tightly. "Last night, I saw God, just like you did, Father. Does God have a mission for me too?"

Moses gulped down the lump in his throat. "Yes, Son. Your mission right now is to obey your mother. Then you'll be able to hear what the Lord tells you." Moses hugged Gershom before placing him on a donkey and handed Gershom the reins.

Moses took Eliezer from a servant and smelled deeply of his baby smell. "Your blessing will come from being with the Lord's people. You will do well." He lingered as he held him. Then with resolution, he handed him to Zipporah.

Moses took her hand in his and looked into her face. "I love you; I'll send for you when I can." Then he motioned to the servants to begin.

He watched his family retrace the path they had taken the previous day. Before she went over the first rise of a hill, Moses saw Zipporah turn back. He raised his arm to give the final parting for a long time.

# CHAPTER 2

OLD KINGDOM EGYPT 2451 B.C.

"Lay the lad on the table. Prepare a fire. Heat the blade." The *swne* commanded his servants as the stretcher entered his house. His skills as a doctor would be tested again.

Aaron guessed that the boy had not seen more than twelve cycles of the harvest.

The boy lay still. Sweat beaded his face. His hands clenched the edge of his loincloth.

Aaron's eyes lingered on the boy's leg. The flesh was crushed below the knee. The bone protruded from the flesh like a sharpened dagger.

Aaron adjusted the leg to its normal position, watching the boy as he did.

The boy tensed, his lips whitened, his jaw clenched, but he admitted no sound.

Aaron swallowed. When would the Egyptians stop using the Israelites as if they were animal dung? When would the suffering of God's people end?

He inspected the side table, containing scissors, a second knife, strips of linen, honey, bread covered with a hair-like growth of black and green, and vials of tonic. His servant Mack had anticipated all that Aaron would need. Aaron nodded. *"Toda raba."*

Glancing at the fire, normally dormant in the heat of the season, Aaron noted his blade gaining the heat's power. Fig and date wood piled beside the fireplace would feed lingering flames to prevent chills from the boy.

Aaron breathed deeply of the warmed air. Would the boy live? Only the sovereign Lord knew.

He paused, noticing the empty chair pushed in a corner. "No family?"

One man by the stretcher answered. "His father begged to come, but the statue must be carried to the temple for the priest's blessing."

Aaron shook his head and bit his lip to keep from speaking. He took the tincture of *belladonna* from the side table.

Growing the bush in his garden, Aaron guarded it lest a stray child taste the sweet black berries. Three berries could kill a child. For cases like today, the pain-relieving qualities would more than redeem the risk. Once harvested, Aaron extracted the medicinal qualities with the skill that brought his name to the Hebrews' mouths when trouble came.

Now it would soothe the lad into sleeping. He dropped several drops into the boy's mouth.

The boy licked his dry lips and grimaced.

Aaron patted his arm. "It doesn't taste good but will help."

The boy nodded, his eyes staying closed.

Aaron smoothed back the boy's dark hair from his cool yet sweaty flesh. His color appeared pale, almost bluish. Aaron moved his hand to the boy's neck, pressing lightly against the channels that carried life to his head. The faint beat fluttered, showing signs of weakness. Aaron watched his chest as he breathed with great effort. The swne felt the twitch under his fingertips.

The lad jolted his legs off the table. "Father, help me! I cannot move…" His legs relaxed back onto the table.

"*Shalom*, my son. Be still. May the sovereign Lord's care over you reach where no man can touch and heal all your wounds." Aaron looked again to the blade in the fire. Its color reflected the red of the flames. He retrieved the blade from the flames and moved back to the table where the lad lay.

Mack held down the boy's upper legs.

Aaron turned to the servant who stood by the stretcher. "Can you keep his chest still?"

The man's face paled, but he nodded and moved to brace the boy's trunk.

Before touching the leg, Aaron dropped a few more drops of the tincture into the boy's mouth.

The boy did not lick his lips this time. His eyes remained closed.

Aaron nodded to those who held the boy.

They returned the nod. They were ready.

Aaron shifted the handle of the blade in his hand for a better hold.

A crackle from the fire as wood shifted interrupted the silence of the room, sending sparks up the chimney.

Aaron breathed deeply again and struck below the knee.

The boy arched his back off the table, jerking his leg. The men held tightly and kept him from thrashing. The cut limb fell to the floor with a thud. His screams echoed around the walls of the small room before the boy passed into the state like sleeping.

Aaron seared the blood flow by holding the heated knife against the stump. The room filled with the smell of burnt flesh. Aaron laid the instrument on the side table. Breathing deeply through his mouth, he avoided the smell. He glanced at the servant holding the boy's chest.

The servant let go and wiped his hand over his sweaty forehead. He stepped back, apparently unsure what he should do.

Aaron massaged his fingers, sore from clutching the knife. "You have done well. It's never easy."

Aaron felt the boy's neck to find if he still lived. Faint movement beneath his fingers told him life remained.

The fire crackled. Aaron jumped. He rubbed the back of his neck and raised his shoulders to stretch out the tension.

Dropping his arms, he examined the wound. The blood had stopped. Wiping a thick layer of honey infused with healing herbs over the stump, he asked, "How did it happen?"

The servant, diverting his eyes from the legless stump, spoke. "Pharaoh required a new image for his temple by the Nile. While the men delivered the statue, the cart's wheel collapsed. To protect the sculpture, the boy braced the cart—"

"And caught his leg under the cart," Aaron finished and sighed.

Mack handed Aaron the bread covered with blackened hairs.

Aaron broke pieces from the offered bread and added it to the honey covering. "His name?"

"Amos." Amos meant burden carrier. He would not carry heavy burdens again.

Mack handed the linen wrap to Aaron.

The swne wrapped the wound to keep the bread and honey in place as the wound healed. When finished, he covered the boy's body with a sheet to prevent chilling. "Keep cooling cloths around the leg but not on the end. The redness of the flesh will carry the evil away. But don't wrap too tightly, it'll bring pain."

Mack nodded, dipping linen strips in a clay vessel filled with water. He wrapped the cloths around the now shortened leg.

Aaron studied the still figure. May the God of Abraham be pleased to work His miracle.

A fter Aaron finished treating his patients, he paused under the shade of his garden's fig tree. He mused about his doctoring skills. He barely touched the needs of his people. Even with his own wife, Aaron had felt helpless. The Lord had not spared her from suffering or death. What did the Lord expect of him?

He stepped on the mint growing between the stones of the path. Bending to pick a stem, he crushed the plant in his hand. He smelled deeply as the mint filled the air with its power to relax.

He used many of his herbs for tonics and poultices, but he only helped healing. The Lord controlled the outcome.

When he was young, Aaron became a swne through Moses's appointment. Moses, holding a place of power in Pharaoh's palace, placed many Hebrews in high places to help others see their God.

Aaron had often discussed with Moses how to remove their people's afflictions. Aaron alleviated some suffering, but much required a miracle.

On that fated day when Moses ran through Aaron's open gate, Aaron had been harvesting garlic. Its smell hung thick in the air.

Aaron saw Moses's pale expression and his trembling lips. "What is it?"

Moses glanced behind him before drying his sweaty hands on his white tunic. "Aaron, I must flee." He licked his lips before continuing. "I've killed an overseer."

"*Oy vey*, Moses!" Aaron had once witnessed a slave stumble under a burden. The overseer motivated with his whip until the man could not stand. Aaron had turned from the sight, sickened by the back that held no flesh. He felt powerless to help. He could understand Moses killing the overseer. He sighed.

Moses raised his hand to stop any words. "He lies deep in the sand where no beast will find him. But our people will report me."

"Why?"

"Two of our people were fighting. I interfered." Moses lowered his voice to whisper. "They saw me kill the overseer yesterday. I can't be reported to Pharaoh. Too many wish me dead."

Aaron knew too well the jealousies in Pharaoh's court over Moses's position and leadership. His position gave him rights, but Pharaoh spared no one from his wrath if Moses's rivals swayed Pharaoh. Aaron embraced Moses. "Flee quickly. Shalom, my brother. May our God protect you and show you His way."

"A way to end our people's suffering," Moses added before he slipped from the garden and out of Aaron's life.

Could that have been forty years ago?

Aaron squeezed the mint still in his hand. He breathed deeply. Its power to refresh was gone, just like his ability to bring healing to a people burdened by pain.

Mack approached, interrupting his thoughts. "Ptah, Amos's master, wishes to speak with you. He waits by the fountain."

Aaron turned his steps toward his trees brought by merchants from faraway lands. He quickened his pace and found Ptah sitting on the stone bench by the fountain. "Ptah, welcome!" Aaron extended his arms for a welcoming embrace.

"In peace, good Swne. How is my servant? Is he ready to work?"

Aaron guided Ptah with a hand on his back as they began to walk. "Amos's leg was crushed. I removed his leg below the knee. He needs much sleep to fight the evil. If he wins over the evil, he must fight for the will to live."

Ptah nodded. "Should I send a priest?"

"The priest may help you." Aaron shrugged. "But for a Hebrew, nothing but the Lord can help him."

"I'll tell his family to pay you."

Aaron swallowed. He directed Ptah to the gate. "His father knows of the injury?"

"He was there. He begged to leave. Why can't Hebrews just do their job?"

Aaron coughed into his hand.

Ptah looked into Aaron's face and blushed. "Well, most Hebrews. You work, good Swne." Ptah fidgeted, trying to undo his words.

Aaron remained silent.

"But the blessing and feasting at the temple was worth it." Ptah smiled with pride.

Aaron bit back his retort. Did the Egyptians think the Hebrews weren't human? Ptah would send Amos to the stone quarry. *If* he healed. Aaron massaged his neck.

They came to the gate.

"May you hear only good things." Aaron sent Ptah on his way.

The suffering of God's people never stopped. Aaron's help was like one drop in the great Nile. Did it even make a difference?

A fter dinner, Aaron returned to Amos's side. A young maiden sponged his head and body with cool cloths.

"Does he waken?" Aaron placed his fingers on the boy's neck.

The maiden trembled. "It's as if he has left his body."

"Place your fingers here on his wrist." Aaron waited for her to comply. "Can you feel the movement?"

She concentrated, then nodded.

"That assures me that he lives. His color is turning from pale to flesh. That helps me know the Lord is at work in his body."

Her fingers lingered on the wrist, then grasped the hand and squeezed it. A smile took possession of her face. Tears filled her eyes. "My brother will live?"

Aaron nodded. "He fights. But he wins." Aaron dropped belladonna and poppy seed tonic into Amos's mouth.

Amos's face contorted to reject the bitter potion.

Aaron pointed to Amos's reaction. "That is another sign that he will make it." He laughed and lifted Amos's shoulders to offer a swallow of water.

Amos swallowed and licked his lips.

"Hand me that other blanket. His flesh feels cold."

The girl covered him in spite of the warm temperatures in the room.

Aaron heard a low, commanding voice.

"Go, meet Moses."

He looked at the maiden, but she remained unmoved. He moved to look down the hall. All was dark except for the single candle at the entryway. Aaron turned back into the room. Again, he heard, "Go, and meet Moses."

Aaron walked toward the window flooded by the moon's rays. *Lord, by tomorrow, I will be on my way.*


E arly the next morning, before the sun's rays fell on his back, Aaron left Egypt with his servants. Their path entered a pass between mountains surrounded by boulders. Highwaymen would gladly relieve them of their burdens, not to mention their lives.

Resting his hand on his dagger sheathed at his side, Aaron nodded to his servants. He saw them touch their daggers. Some drew them.

The shelter of the mountains kept the sun's direct heat off their backs. Hours later, they passed through the mountains. Now their backs warmed with its direct heat. Aaron wiped his brow with his cloak sleeve.

A rasping *ffff* sound startled him. He turned in his saddle to see Zimran, his servant, lean over his horse and slice the head off the horned viper.

The others circled the writhing, headless snake.

Aaron nodded to Zimran. "Toda raba, I didn't see it." He breathed deeply and searched for other snakes.

After replacing his sword in its sheath, Zimran wiped his palm on his tunic. "I fear the spitting cobra more. Have you ever seen it fly through the air?"

The others shook their heads.

"It appears from nowhere. The only thing you see is its black neck against the sand."

Aaron knew of nothing to treat the horned viper's venom. "Let's be alert."

Aaron motioned his servant Zimran to come beside him as they nudged their horses. "I think that Moses went to Midian. You are from there?"

Zimran responded with a nod.

"How should we prepare ourselves?"

"My people are mostly herdsmen with little. We fight for water or better herds."

"Why were you taken?" Aaron questioned into the forbidden territory of a servant's past.

Zimran shrugged. "Merchants steal for more possessions. Once I became a possession... there's no freedom in Egypt."

Aaron nodded. He hesitated before asking, "Would you stay, if you could?"

"You mean in Midian?" Zimran asked. "When I came with

you… You treat me as an equal, not a servant." He looked down and did not answer.

"The choice is yours. I grant you freedom, without the penalty of an escaped servant."

Zimran studied Aaron's eyes, even though, he should not, as a servant, directly look at him.

Aaron added, "While I search for my brother, you could find your family."

Zimran's entire face lit with enthusiasm. "Oh, yes, master, that would be… that would be beyond my wildest dreams!"

"Let's find Moses, so you can live out your dreams." Aaron chuckled. "How soon will it be?"

"Not soon enough," Zimran said, "Within three days' light."

"Why don't you lead the way?" Aaron fell behind Zimran, pleased at his plan.

The days passed. God blessed them, directing their steps. As their journey ended, Aaron lifted his baritone voice in songs of praise. He could not contain his smile. He would see his brother soon.

At a well, while all the servants refilled their water skins, Zimran called to Aaron, "Master, I'll fill your water skin."

Aaron was looking to the east. "How much longer?"

Zimran handed Aaron a filled water skin. He reached for Aaron's empty skin, tied to his saddle. "Hard to wait?"

Aaron rinsed his mouth, spitting out the grit, before swallowing a mouthful of water. "It's been forty years since I've seen Moses."

The servants passed figs, raisins, and salted dried beef from their saddlebags as their horses rested. They submerged their heads and dunked their arms in the water. Their break was short, and soon they moved again.

Aaron's desire to see his brother deepened as the hours passed. The gait of his horse seemed too slow for him. He must show restraint. The desert killed men who hurried.

Had Moses changed? Would he have an answer to their people's suffering?

He glanced ahead at his servant and smiled. Zimran's face beamed like a child awaiting his father's blessing. Aaron did not know what prompted his impulse to grant freedom, but he felt that his time remaining in Egypt was short. He did not want his faithful servant in the wrong hands.

Before stopping at midday, Aaron noticed that Zimran could hardly sit on his horse.

Aaron finally asked, "What ails you? Do you want to stop?"

"No, my Master. We are close to my father's land. I seek my family."

"Your family?"

"I had a wife and one son, land, and a good-sized flock of sheep and goats. I've been gone seven years."

"How did you become a servant?" Aaron asked.

"Sheep were missing. I went to search for them. A merchant lured the stragglers and caught me." He shrugged his shoulders. Men were captured all the time. They brought a good price in Egypt where men died daily under heavy toil.

Aaron could not imagine being a slave. What men did to gain more wealth was evil. He wished to stop all suffering.

They continued in silence. His morning's exuberance mellowed at the reminder of his people's sufferings. "How much farther?"

"My father's land should be over the next mountain." Zimran paused, tilting his head toward a dog that approached, barking. He jumped from his horse to meet it. Kneeling, he called in a language unfamiliar to Aaron.

The dog approached warily.

Zimran grabbed it hugging it in a rolling wrestle.

The dog's alarming bark changed to happy yips. In spite of the different language, Aaron understood the endearments of a master reunited with his dog.

Aaron stayed mounted on his horse. He heard yelling and watched several herdsmen investigating their dog's alarm. Within moments, they rushed to Zimran, surrounding, shouting, and embracing him. Aaron could see their resemblance.

Zimran had found his family. When he finally broke free of their embrace, he pointed to Aaron and spoke something in their language.

His family's eyes narrowed. One, who looked to be the oldest, murmured.

Zimran laughed. Shaking his head, he responded.

Aaron watched their expressions turn from scowls and distrust to welcome.

Zimran turned to Aaron, "I said that you were my master. They would not accept you until I mentioned your promise of freedom. They welcome you to their fire."

Aaron and his men followed the herdsmen to their campsite. They staked their horses to graze while Aaron and Zimran's brothers settled around the fire.

They commenced to eating. All took from the stacked flatbread, dipping into the community bowl of goat cheese. Conversation stopped until their hunger was satiated. Afterward, they lounged with their water skins. The dog lay at Zimran's feet, not taking his eyes from his master. Zimran interpreted as the men talked.

Zimran's brother Hanoch asked, "Where're you headed?"

"I search for my brother who's been gone forty years."

Hanoch nodded. "I remember a family with seven daughters. One married a foreigner from Egypt. He stayed more than thirty years before marrying Jethro's daughter."

"Could that be your brother?" Zimran asked Aaron.

Hanoch studied Aaron, "The resemblance is there. He's taller than you."

Aaron nodded. "Moses stands tall."

Abraham was their ancestor. Jethro, a distant relative by Abraham's second wife, Keturah, seemed a likely choice for Moses to flee. "That would be the right time. Where's their land?"

"Their land borders our neighbor's. Their father is a respected priest."

Aaron nodded. A priest from a descendant of Abraham would worship the One and Only God. The Lord had led Moses to descendants who would worship the true God.

Aaron requested directions, noting landmarks.

In a lull of conversation, Aaron asked, "Zimran, how close are we to your home?"

Zimran's eyes twinkled. "Just beyond the ridge."

Aaron stood, motioning his servants to prepare the horses.

Hanoch patted Zimran on the back as he saddled his horse. Zimran's eyes shone. Zimran would not be returning with him. He was home.

Aaron smiled. It was good they had rested the horses at midday, for the pace that Zimran set for the group would have taxed a less rested animal.

Soon, Zimran kicked his horse into a gallop.

About to caution him not to tire his horse, Aaron glimpsed a lodging ahead protected against the hillside. He let Zimran gallop, but slowed the pace of the others.

Aaron watched Zimran leaped off his mount before he even stopped. He rushed toward a woman by the house and they flew into each other's arms. Aaron slowed his men. Indeed, Zimran had found his wife.

Aaron's eyes misted. He thought of his own wife Elisheba. How would it be to hold her again? How many years had she been gone? He blinked. He shook his head.

Aaron's group slowly moved toward the couple. Another servant grabbed the reins of Zimran's rider-less horse.

As they approached, Zimran's wife stepped from his embrace.

Aaron could not help but smile. What a roaring fire there would be in Zimran's tent tonight, regardless of the amount of animal dung that fed the cooking fire.

Zimran turned to Aaron, his face shining his pleasure "Praise the gods. She lives."

"May God be praised," Aaron answered.

An awkward silence followed. Women did not converse with

men. Aaron glanced around for a distraction. Taking his water skin from his saddle, he drank. Dismounting from his horse, he glanced across the pastures.

A boy, perhaps eight seasons of the harvest, ran toward them. He yelled something.

Aaron saw Zimran's attention torn from his wife's face as he heard the lad's cry.

Zimran's wife responded, reassuring.

Zimran took several faltering steps toward him. "Epher."

The lad slowed to a walk. He tightened his hold on a small knife and scrutinized the men.

Aaron watched the lad's courage and protective nature as he approached the strangers near his mother.

Zimran's eyes gleamed with pride.

Aaron could sense the boy's scrutiny.

Zimran's wife spoke softly.

Epher finished the remaining distance, appearing cautious, studying Zimran's face as if to see recognition.

When his son came within several *cubits*, Zimran broke from his wife's side, knelt down, and extended his arms to his son. He crushed him to his chest.

Aaron wiped his face with his sleeve. He glanced at the other men from the corners of his eyes. They watched the distant hills. Some swallowed deeply.

Zimran uttered blessings to his gods. He wiped his face on his cloak before turning to speak to Aaron. "You're most welcome to stay at our tent tonight and eat of the night's meal."

Custom demanded eating at their fire before leaving, but Aaron desired to journey farther before dark. Aaron glanced at Zimran's family, finally reunited. Zimran needed time with his family without a group of men. "Zimran, my beloved servant, we will move on."

Zimran hesitated, and then spoke quietly to his son and wife. He returned to his horse to remount.

Aaron stepped forward, touching Zimran's shoulder. "Your

service is over. I cannot be so cruel as to separate you from your family. You are granted freedom."

Zimran searched Aaron's face without speaking.

Aaron grabbed his shoulders and shook him. "You stay here."

Zimran remembered his place and lowered his eyes. "You are a master worthy of the God you serve. You show me His grace and mercy, but I must fulfill my agreement to lead you to your brother."

"God will show me the way. We will move on. You, I command to stay."

Zimran chuckled. "A more difficult command you could not give me. You showed me your God when you bought me and as you set me free." They embraced, no longer as master and servant but as friends. They walked back to the others arm in arm. Zimran embraced Aaron again before Aaron mounted his horse.

"May your God lead you to your brother, as you brought me to mine."

Aaron adjusted his reins in his hands, and raised his arm. "He will indeed."


A s the sun was sinking behind the horizon, Aaron tightened his cloak against the coolness of the desert.

Two figures in the distance approached on donkeys.

Aaron nodded to his companions. Even in the shadows, he would not guess them to be merchants, for their loads were light. He heard them call a greeting in Egyptian. He responded. The greeting made him wonder at the man leading, for he was not an Egyptian yet he spoke with no accent. He dressed like a shepherd, as did his servant. He held a staff. Would it be safe to camp with them? It would soon be too dark to continue.

"May God be praised! Is it Aaron?"

Aaron looked again at the approaching man. He was tall, broad in shoulder, cloaked in soft goat leather, and wore tough rawhide sandals. His face, though darkened by the sun, held the look of Aaron's father, no longer living. "Moses?"

The man dismounted from his donkey.

Aaron slid from his horse to embrace him. "Moses, God is good. He led our steps to you."

Aaron felt between them not just the bond of family and heritage, but of a mission that God had begun for them and their people.

# CHAPTER 3

B adru hurried from the temple of the most important god, Amun-Ra. He was the highest priest, second only to the great Pharaoh Merenre Nemtyemsaf II in responsibility for the spiritual welfare of the Egyptian people. Badru had been priest for part of the reign of Pharaoh's father, Phiops II, and had served him well.

Today, he offered incense to the gods to ensure the purity of the gifts. He gazed into the flames, beseeching the gods' favor.

As he stared, the flames turned from blue to green to red without the special agents he would normally cast into the flames. The fire grew without fuel. The flames possessed power of their own.

He fell before the fire, bruising his knees on the tiled floor.

A voice, deep and strong, spoke. "Beware of one who seeks to take all the power of Egypt from Pharaoh." The voice ended as quickly as it began, the fire dying with it.

Badru covered his head with his arms, shaking prostrate on the tile floor. Should he warn Pharaoh? Would Pharaoh kill him, though he was just the messenger from the gods?

Badru rose and rushed out of the temple. He ran through the

dirt streets toward home. He thought only of what the vision would mean for him.

A distant voice broke through his ponderings. "Badru! Wait!"

He turned to see another priest, one who knew nothing of casting spells or analyzing the stars, but who had served in the temple for three months. Badru drew a breath and released it before speaking. What could he want now? "Yes?"

He gestured toward Badru's garb. "Are you well?"

Badru looked down. He had run from the temple in the leopard skins worn only for worshiping the gods. After sacrificing, the priests changed into spotless white linen tunics. He had left behind even his cloak for the chill of the evening. His feet were still bare from presenting the gifts before each god. They bled from running through the stone drainage channels in the middle of the road.

Badru stuttered and coughed. "I must get home. I don't feel well."

The assistant studied Badru and nodded.

Badru resumed his flight through the slave quarters where mere huts housed families.

He continued through the artisan section of town. Their larger mud-brick buildings served for both living and business. One street, where carpenters built furniture for noblemen using mahogany and cedar transported from faraway lands, held smells of sawdust and oils. On another street, sounds of clanging and pounding told of silversmiths working into the evening to form statues of gods. The scent of heated metal filled the air.

Badru entered the section of town where the noblemen and court officials lived. Castle-sized houses loomed on platforms that prevented moisture from seeping through the painted mud-brick walls. Badru entered his house. He noticed not the servant who washed his foot to cleanse away the evil.

He staggered into his inner chamber where his wife and son were playing a game of *senet*. He paused in the doorway to catch his breath. What would the vision mean for Egypt?

"Badru, what's wrong?" Sacmis stood and approached her husband.

Their son stared at his father.

Sacmis escorted Badru to a chair. "You look faint. Sit down." She clapped her hands, demanding drinks for both of them.

Badru sat breathing deeply, staring in front of him. When the drink came, he sipped.

Sacmis tired of waiting. "Badru, tell me."

He drank again from the jar, trembling in his hands. His fingers shook. He dropped the jar, spilling the contents down his leopard skin and his bare legs.

Sacmis shouted in alarm. She clapped her hands again and a servant appeared. "Clean this up."

Badru remained silent, staring straight ahead.

Sacmis waited for the servant to leave. She paced as she waited. "Badru, tell me."

He mumbled in a voice so low she had to sit beside him to hear. "I saw a vision. A betrayer of Egypt will steal her power."

"What will you do?"

His shoulders hunched and he shook his head.

Sacmis stood by his chair, bracing his arm. "Stand up."

She motioned for her son to grab his other side. "We'll take him to bed," she whispered, as if Badru was not there.

They escorted him to his chamber. "Rest awhile and then a warm bath will relax you," Sacmis said. "Everything will be fine."

Once Sacmis situated Badru in bed, she directed her son to follow her from the room. "Not a word to anyone. Pharaoh could kill us for treason, blaming us for Egypt's ruin. Send for Aaron, the Hebrew swne. He will not spread rumors. I'll decide what to do next."

Why had Aaron not returned from his journey to find Moses? Mack, Aaron's servant, hurried to the priest's home in Aaron's stead. Why had they called for a Hebrew swne? Egypt had many swnes.

When Mack entered the house, he heard nothing—as if death walked before him. He followed a servant through the dark entryway and hallway to the master's bedroom.

Mack paused before entering the chamber. His eyes adjusted to the well-lit room, where a bed stood in the center. He saw the chief high priest, his pale, flabby flesh blending with the white linen sheets draped over him.

As Mack approached the bed, he felt the heat of the room. He pulled at the waist of his tunic to allow himself to breathe and noticed the flames in the fireplace in spite of the warm evening. Moisture in the air attested to a recent bath.

Placing his basket of supplies on the floor by a table containing candles, offerings, and statues, he smelled the strong musk incense. The smell reminded him of the bucks in his father's flocks of goats. His nose wrinkled at the memory. He looked at the window, wishing for a breeze. There was none. All he saw was the blackness of a moonless night.

The silence deepened. Mack studied Badru. The priest did not open his eyes. Mack felt Badru's forehead. His flesh was cool and sweaty. Mack turned at movement by the door.

Sacmis walked to the other side of the bed. "You have come."

Mack responded, "In peace." He gestured to Badru.

"He saw a vision concerning Pharaoh." She opened her mouth to continue speaking, but then closed it tightly.

Mack's eyebrows lifted at what was unsaid. Why had they not called another priest who would worship for the high priest's health? What had the chief high priest seen?

If the vision foretold evil, they would have sent for a magician. Priests pled for mercy from the gods; magicians did not plea, but demanded results. The vision must have foretold evil. Were they afraid at who might know of the dream? Why else would they call for Aaron?

A weight settled over Mack's *ka*. If he did not make this chief priest well, would the gods and Pharaoh curse him? Was this a test? Had he come here to his own death? He knew Aaron's God, but he had much to learn. Aaron's God would give him peace.

Mack took a deep breath. He rubbed his hands together before touching Badru's chest and arms.

Badru did not move.

Mack leaned over him to feel his breath on his cheek. Could a man die from a vision?

Mack took a tonic of coriander, poppy seed, and honey from his basket of supplies. He dribbled several drops into the priest's mouth.

Badru grimaced.

Mack reached for the vessel by the table. "Wine?" He looked to Sacmis. At her nod, he propped Badru's shoulders and coaxed some into his mouth, watching him swallow.

Mack listened again to Badru's labored breathing. Allowing time for the tonic to work, Mack massaged Badru's body with oil infused with lavender.

Sacmis watched silently.

Badru grunted but said nothing.

Sacmis slipped out of the room.

Mack looked to the door when she left. What kind of vision had the priest seen? His wife had watched him like a falcon eyeing a mouse's hole. Turning to extinguish the noxious incense, Mack breathed deeply. He was no longer watched. He massaged Badru's shoulders. His cool flesh moved easily in folds under the pressure of his hands. Mack applied more pressure to reach the deeper flesh.

Badru sighed under the pressure. "No betrayer will steal Egypt's power…"

Mack continued to massage but lowered his head closer to Badru's ear and whispered, "What betrayer?"

Badru's lips stayed open but no words came.

Mack rolled Badru onto his back and skillfully applied pressure to loosen tightened flesh. What betrayer? Was this the vision? He reached the bottom of the priest's back and circled outward.

Badru mumbled, "No betrayer will take Pharaoh's power."

Mack moved closer to Badru's head. "What did you see?"

Badru's eyelids quivered. "The flames grew with power, the

colors changed like one who would consume—death was present. Whose?" He shuddered and grew quiet. His eyes closed again.

Mack finished the massage, covering Badru with the light sheet.

The fire had died down. The room would grow cooler. Mack found his way outside. He breathed deeply of the cool air. He would not feel at peace until he spoke to Aaron. Had he done the right treatment? Would the priest recover? Treating Hebrews was one thing: if they died, no one cared who could do anything. But the chief high priest, if something happened... Mack could neither change what he had done, nor heal Badru. He must place this in the Lord's hands and work to leave it there.

The next morning, Sacmis sat beside Badru on his bed. She waited for him to awaken as she considered the vision.

Badru opened his eyes, reached for her hand, and smiled. "*Ra* shines again. We have hope."

"Sacmis, hand me my amulet with the scarab. I need its power and protection."

She found the charm of a beetle overlaid in silver on the table beside him. She placed it on his wrist, leaving her hand over it.

Badru looked into her face. "Was the vision yesterday just a bad dream?"

She shook her head. "Wishing will not make it so. Egypt is in danger."

Badru whispered, even though they were the only ones in the room. "How should I tell Pharaoh?"

"With a banquet, inviting all the high officials and Pharaoh..."

Badru put his hand over hers on his amulet. "I knew you'd protect my position. Make the plans."

She nodded but not so confidently as before. She controlled Badru. She knew his thoughts and could control his actions. But Pharaoh... He disturbed her. His arrogance dominated all his decisions. That made him unpredictable and volatile.

She squeezed Badru's hand and left to plan the banquet. She

would host it tomorrow, Pharaoh willing, when Ra began his battle with the evil of the darkness at sunset. May the gods soften Badru's message and protect his power.

S acmis invited the Pharaoh to the banquet. He would not dine at just anyone's house; high-ranking officials must meet his requirements. He had not been in power long enough to acquire a full harem, but he had married Nitocris, his sister. Sacmis requested her presence.

Sacmis would invite Pharaoh's vizier, along with all Pharaoh's counselors and the main priests with their wives.

Sacmis planned the menu with care. Male servants roasted geese, kidneys, and tender gazelle, all rich in garlic and onions to release any evil. Female servants prepared desserts of figs, dates, cakes, and pastries sweetened by honey and shaped in rings or discs.

She selected both red and white wines from their own vineyard.

Entertainment would provide relaxation and amusement. Sacmis sent messengers to engage a dwarf acrobat to humor Pharaoh before musicians and dancers would stimulate his mind. She selected candles and incense that would create drowsiness and calm.

All these preparations Sacmis planned in detail. With wine in abundance and the Pharaoh's mind distracted, Sacmis schemed; the vision's message would lose its power. She hoped.

A fter two days of rest, Badru glanced outside at the setting sun. Ra would battle hard to win tonight. Badru hoped that not only Ra, but also he himself would win the battle over the evil that threatened to consume him.

Badru turned back to Sacmis who stood beside him greeting their banquet guests. He forced a smile that did not extend past his mouth. He gulped some air to calm his insides.

A banquet provided an opportunity for all to show their favored gods on their clothes and jewelry. For the men, the normal white linen tunic became the starting point for attire. Women wore long, closely fitted dresses of rich linen weave. Both sexes added colorful collars of glass beads, flowers, berries, and leaves. Men and women shaved their heads to make their wigs more comfortable. Time-consuming hairstyles kept servants busy in preparation. Black and green paint accentuated the shape of their eyes. Fine leather sandals completed their attire.

Badru listened as wives expressed false appreciation for one another's attire, and men lustily enjoyed the wine and entertainment. Everyone consumed heartily of the food and drink.

Badru rubbed his chest. He should not have eaten. His insides churned as if he were on a boat. He had consumed more wine than he should have. He did not feel the calmness that it should bring. The wine rumbled and churned inside him. His chest tightened making breathing difficult. He took a swallow of air, but it did not go far. How should he approach Pharaoh with his vision?

Sacmis had drilled him before the banquet to appear calm, to look confident. Badru caught her eye.

She shook her head.

What was he doing? He dropped his hand from twisting the beads on his collar and grabbed his wine vessel instead. He raised it to his lips but did not drink. He could drink nothing more. He put it down again with trembling fingers. His insides flopped like a snake with its head cut off. He deliberately slowed his breathing.

Pharaoh leaned over the table. "The banquet is satisfactory. What is the occasion?"

Badru gulped, grabbing his vessel again, and took a sip of wine to soothe his dry throat. "Oh Pharaoh, may you live forever. May you be worshiped as Ra, for his goodness."

Badru glanced into Pharaoh's face. His sleepy, glazed look showed that he was hardly listening. This was good. Badru continued with more confidence. "While I served in your temple, giving offerings to the gods, I watched as the flames turned from blue to green to red without my aid. As I studied the fire, the flames grew without fuel. I fell to my knees in worship.

"As I watched, the flame spoke. I could not look at it, for it was great and powerful. The voice said, 'Beware, a betrayer to you, oh, great Pharaoh, is coming, and you must prepare for him. This betrayer seeks to take the power of Egypt with him. Beware and be ready.' I know not the betrayer. I tell you my dream, so that you may be prepared."

Pharaoh's relaxed, sleepy expression was now gone. His eyes looked colder than the Nile during the rainy season. His reddened face displayed anger. He leaned toward Badru.

Badru flinched and slumped against his cushion. His heart thumped loud enough, he thought, for the entire table to hear it. The wine was taking effect now, for he needed to run to his chamber to relieve himself, but his legs would not work.

Pharaoh sat without speaking. His neck bulged and twitched.

Badru could not take his eyes from him. He felt like the prey of a snake, about to be eaten. He tried to swallow, but his mouth was too dry. He licked his lips and forced himself to look down from Pharaoh's gaze.

Pharaoh stood and pounded his fists on the table.

The sounds ceased. All conversation had stopped to listen.

When Pharaoh finally spoke, it was with a confidence that amazed Badru. "No one has the power to take away my throne." He surveyed the room with deliberation, and stalked out.

Badru rose, as did everyone, when Pharaoh stood, and watched without a word as he left the house. A great silence remained. No one dared to suggest what the future held for any one of these great men or women.

Nitocris, Pharaoh's wife, rose, and followed leisurely. Her graceful, calm exit left Badru wondering if she even sensed the tension.

After their exit, Badru glanced at those remaining for comfort. They settled in their chairs, looking at each other for an answer.

The vizier remained standing and raised his vessel into the air, declaring, "I served as vizier not only for the great Pharaoh Merenre Nemtyemsaf II this harvest, but also for the great Pharaoh Phiops II, his father. He ruled for over eighty harvests. I served during his rule five harvests. In my youth, Thermuthis, Pharaoh's daughter, adopted a Hebrew into Pharaoh's house. This Hebrew was trained in war, taught law, and presided in judgment in the Egyptian courts. He was tutored to be the next leader.

"In warnings by the sacred scribes, they predicted that a child of Pharaoh would trample upon Egypt's government and provide the Hebrews with a hope. The scribes thought he was the man. Both Thermuthis and Pharaoh protected this man, in spite of the warnings.

"After an embarrassing battle with the Ethiopians in which the Egyptians were defeated, Pharaoh appointed this man as General of the Army, and sent him into battle at great risk to his life. This Pharaoh did to appease the counsel that continued against this man.

"The land before the Ethiopians bred serpents in vast numbers. These serpents excelled in magic, power, and stealth. They would fly through the air as they struck without warning. This land of snakes protected the Ethiopians from any secret attack.

"This impossible battleground gave the sacred Egyptian scribes pleasure, for should the nation of Egypt suffer defeat, the general would be slain and the Hebrew army would be beaten.

"But this great general of the Pharaoh provided tactical shrewdness never before seen. He filled baskets with tame *ibis*, the natural enemy of these serpents. When the army approached the breeding grounds of these snakes, he freed these birds. They devoured the snakes before the army marched one foot over the ground. Then the army marched through the land, unharmed.

"The Ethiopians were caught unaware. The Hebrew army overthrew their cities. In fact, with this leader's diligence, they reduced the Ethiopians to slaves.

"The general of the Egyptian army continued to pursue those

who escaped. He besieged the city of *Saba*, although surrounded on all sides by water and a strong wall.

"While the army rested from their march, Tharbis, the daughter of the King of Ethiopia, watched from the wall. She spotted this great general, towering over his soldiers in stature, giving direction, skill, and courage to his men. She realized the danger the city faced with this powerful man. She watched daily as his army attested to his skill. She requested marriage with him.

"He agreed, providing he gained possession of the city. They married immediately. The city was his. He praised his God and returned to Egypt.

"Not only had this general conquered the Ethiopians, but he had thwarted the Egyptian council's plan to be rid of him. He came back victorious.

"Animosity against him continued, fueled by those who felt threatened by his God. Others felt uneasy in his presence. Until one day, rumor reported he killed a supervisor for beating a Hebrew slave. He fled to the desert. He remains there, as far as anyone knows. If he is still alive, perhaps the betrayer—who knows Egypt so well—is he."

Badru could now breathe. He asked with renewed confidence and hope, "And his name?"

"He is called Moses. Even his birth showed protection by some God other than ours," the vizier concluded. "I will speak to Pharaoh concerning this man."

Badru observed all those present. He would not be blamed for the betrayal. He was safe as long as Pharaoh focused on this Moses.

The evening passed and the guests departed in couples and in groups. Badru saw to his visitors' departures with relief and almost ecstasy after the despair that he had lived through the past day. His future was secure. He would continue to guide the Pharaoh to glory and great power.

As he turned from seeing the last guests to the entryway, he glanced at Sacmis. One look at her eyes and Badru asked, "What ails you? We are saved by this betrayer in the desert. We have only to find and slay him, and our power remains. Why do you fear?"

Sacmis placed her arm in his, directing him to be seated on a bench against the wall. "If this God of his protected him at his birth and has kept him alive in spite of all of Pharaoh's wise counselors, who are we to think that we could dispose of him?"

Badru stroked her fingers. Who was this God Who protected one lone man from harm? His fears returned anew.

# CHAPTER 4

The campfire had burned to coals and the servants had settled to sleep for the night by the time Moses recounted to Aaron his experience with the Lord at the burning bush. He shared the mission, even confessing his desire for God to send someone else.

Aaron threw some fuel on the fire. "Didn't you fear the Lord's anger?"

Moses shuddered at the memory. "Zipporah wondered about my sandals. I had left them behind when I ran to tell her. I was concerned more about whether I'd live."

Aaron smiled. "But you still questioned Him?"

Moses nodded. "He asked me, 'What about Aaron? He speaks well. He's coming to meet you. I will help both of you.'"

Aaron shook his head. "So you volunteered me. I'm always the big brother rescuing you from your troubles." They both laughed. Even though they had grown up separately, Moses at the palace and Aaron at their parents' home, they had always been close.

Aaron pointed beside Moses. "Is that the staff?"

Moses nodded, rubbing it.

"May I see?" Aaron reached for it as Moses extended it across the coals. He caressed the wood. "It is nothing on its own, but in the hands of the Lord's man, with the Lord's power and the Lord's direction, we will soon see the suffering of our people vanquished."

Aaron and Moses returned together to Egypt. When they arrived, Aaron sent for the Hebrew elders to meet that evening to tell them what the Lord would do.

Shifting his thoughts to his patients, Aaron walked through his corridor to Amos's chamber. Standing in the doorway, he studied the scene. Amos's sister sat beside the bed where he slept. Aaron entered the room. Touching Amos's brow and then his neck, Aaron commented, "No heat. His fluids run strong. He's a fighter."

She nodded as she stood to watch.

Amos stirred as Aaron opened the wrapping. He struggled to sit straighter so he could watch. "How does it look?"

Aaron checked the wound. "The redness is gone. That is good. The flesh is joining together nicely." Aaron patted the other leg. "The evil won't win over you."

Amos leaned his head against the cushion and shifted as Aaron rewrapped the wound. His face beaded with sweat at the exertion. "Will I be able to work?"

Aaron finished covering the leg before answering. "Life is a fight, but you are a strong warrior."

"And if I don't want to fight?"

The girl paled and squeezed Amos's good leg.

Aaron held his gaze. "You accept what the Lord wills."

"It's hard."

"That's why it's a fight." Aaron studied both the girl and the lad a moment before continuing. "When you do, you find strength that runs deeper than the flooding Nile."

The girl rested her head on Amos's shoulder.

Amos shook his head. "My strength does not run that deep."

Aaron placed his hand on Amos's good leg. Aaron waited until

Amos looked him in the face. "You draw from God's strength. His runs as deep as you need."

S hortly after the evening meal, the elders arrived. Each of the twelve sons of Jacob had an elder chosen as their representative.

God had promised Abraham a nation from his offspring, Isaac. Isaac's son, Jacob, whose name was changed to Israel, would carry on the promise. Jacob had twelve sons, representing the tribes of Israel. Now from each of the twelve tribes, a representative would come to hear the news and spread it throughout their tribe.

Most wondered at the call for a meeting. Why would a swne call them together? All gathered on the floor around a low table set with jars of wine, figs, and dates for refreshment.

Aaron prepared to address the gathering. Would they acknowledge the Lord? "Shalom. I stand before you to tell you what the Lord has said."

Moses showed the men the signs from the burning bush. Once again, his staff turned into a snake and his hand changed to one of a leper.

The men fell on their faces and worshiped the Lord Who saw their people's suffering and Who desired to redeem them.

The night passed quickly. Most had not directed their worship to the Lord for many years. Hearts convicted, and minds convinced that the Lord had entered their midst. They resolved to tell their clans of what the Lord would do for His people.

T he morning following the elders' meeting, Aaron and Moses prepared to speak to Pharaoh. They waited in the threshold of his throne room. The sun streamed through the open doorway and filled the room with light. The height of the ceiling and the large pillars spoke of excellence. Aaron leaned closer to Moses and whispered, "Let's pray our reception will be like last night."

Moses shifted the rod to his other hand. "Pharaoh listens to all requests. He then knows how to rule his people well."

Aaron stepped closer to Moses. "Listening does not guarantee ruling well."

Moses nodded.

A guard motioned for their attention. They followed him through the doors into the throne room.

Aaron had never stood before Pharaoh. The long corridor before Pharaoh's throne stretched many *fathoms*. Large columns on either side of the corridor reached toward the sky.

Aaron blinked after viewing Pharaoh's throne. It sat on a platform at the end of the corridor. Golden stairs led to it, where Pharaoh lounged. Servants kneeled by him. Important officials stood behind him, waiting instructions.

Guards stood at the stairs before his throne. Their stoic stance made them blend with the pillars.

Aaron's sandals clicked on the polished tile. His heart beat in rhythm with the drummer who sat at the base of the stairs.

Glancing at Moses walking beside him, Aaron licked his lips. "Just like old times?"

Moses shifted the staff in his hand. He nodded toward Pharaoh. "Similar. But God's mission is far more important than any petition that I brought before the previous Pharaoh. But that doesn't stop the eagle's wings bashing inside me now."

Aaron smiled. They stopped at the base of the staircase. He looked again at the staff the Lord would use to demonstrate His authority.

He looked down at his common Egyptian white tunic and then glanced at Moses in his shepherd's garb. His white tunic glimmered beside Moses's goatskin cloak. As he turned his eyes toward Pharaoh's silks, linens, and jewels, and his gold-paneled throne, Aaron's status as a swne could not compete with Pharaoh's grandeur. Pharaoh's servants were dressed better than he.

He reminded himself of Moses's words: "This is God's mission."

They waited for Pharaoh to acknowledge them.

Pharaoh's vizier moved to stand beside Pharaoh. "If it pleases the Pharaoh and his power, this is Moses, the man from the vision that I consulted you about, and Aaron, a swne to the Hebrews."

The mighty Pharaoh Merenre Nemtyemsaf II turned for a drink from a vessel held by a servant at his side. He swallowed, lingering over the mouthful. He broke the silence with a mocking laugh. "What entertainment do you bring me today?"

Aaron stepped forward. "The Lord, God of Israel, says: 'Let My people go, so that they may hold a festival for Me in the desert.'"

Pharaoh laughed again. "Who is this Lord, that I should obey Him? I don't know this God." He paused, selected some grapes from a vessel a servant held beside him, and tossed them into his mouth. "I won't let Israel go."

Aaron saw the vizier start forward, hesitate, and then step behind Pharaoh again.

Moses spoke for the first time. "The God of the Hebrews appeared unto us. Allow us to sacrifice to Him, or He may strike us with plagues."

Pharaoh raised an eyebrow and tilted his head. His mouth tightened. "Who are you to request favor from me?" He leaned forward to stare at Moses. "Oh yes, Moses, the mighty soldier who fled afraid. And Aaron who is wise enough to treat dogs and slaves.

"Why take *my* people from *my* labor? The people have important jobs to do for me. You are trying to stop them. Be gone!"

M oses felt the eyes of all on them as they retreated from Pharaoh's presence. The distance stretching before them appeared longer than when they had approached the throne. Their steps echoed against the tile.

When they stepped from the palace into the sunshine, Aaron sighed deeply. "We didn't even show him the signs of the Lord's power."

Moses shrugged as they started walking home. "Pharaoh has

been taught from his infancy that he is god. The Lord must change their thinking to acknowledge Him as the only God."

Aaron's voice raised, "But Pharaoh makes God's people suffer."

"The Lord wants all to see Him, not just His people."

"Don't you think judgment should be soon?"

Moses stopped walking and looked at Aaron. "Don't you want mercy before judgment?"

Aaron swallowed. "But the suffering of His people…"

Moses leaned on his staff. "I don't like to see any suffer, but suffering should make us look to God. His own people must see Him. They can't because they aren't ready for Him."

Aaron started to speak but then shut his mouth.

Moses continued walking.

Aaron hastened to catch him. "Exactly what did you learn in the desert, my dear brother? You see God more clearly than I remember."

"Living without the people I love taught me what is important. Living without obeying God taught me what is essential."

Once Moses and Aaron left the presence of Pharaoh, the vizier stepped forward to speak with Pharaoh. He was hesitant to counsel Pharaoh when his mood appeared to be arrogant. The vizier studied Pharaoh, wondering how to approach him.

The previous pharaoh had allowed the Hebrews their religious festivities. If this pharaoh would not, they might rebel. Did he not realize the strength behind all those men who daily worked the stone quarry for his pyramids and temples, made bricks for his canals, plowed for his food, and trained as soldiers? These strong, powerful men were made to do Pharaoh's bidding.

They had never rebelled before, but now they had a leader they would follow. Pharaoh must not push them too far. The vizier waited without speaking. He must get rid of Moses, discreetly, or an uprising might happen. Pharaoh's dominion was threatened. How could he encourage Pharaoh to listen?

Pharaoh tapped his finger against his hairless chin. "Declare a new decree: the Hebrews must find their own straw for making bricks, it will no longer be provided for them. They must meet the same quota. They are lazy. If they have time to cry about sacrificing, they do not have enough to do. Make them work harder. I will pay no attention to lies."

The vizier reminded himself that Pharaoh was one-step below divinity and that he, as his vizier, was one-step from giving advice that could cause his own death. The vizier nodded stoically. "At your command, oh Pharaoh, greatest in power."

He executed the order. He spoke to the slave masters who oversaw the labor camps of the Hebrews. They would relay the order to the slave drivers in charge of specific projects. The Hebrew foremen in charge of each labor group would know by tomorrow. If this did not push the Hebrews into rebellion, the vizier was not sure what would. He would expect the Hebrews' response within three days.

# CHAPTER 5

Nathan, a Hebrew foreman, received Pharaoh's order. His ten-man team would now have to produce the same quota of fifty thousand bricks per day, but they would not have straw. The men wasted no movement. Now without straw could they make them?

Nathan announced the new ruling to his team without looking at them.

Ellis wiped his face and shook his head. "We have to find our own straw?"

Nathan scratched his jaw and looked at his feet, before raising his gaze to meet Ellis. "No straw will be given."

Ellis folded his arms over his bare chest. "The flood waters cover the harvested fields. The only hay to be found lies piled in Pharaoh's storage tents. I know because we put it there."

"I know."

Ellis pushed further. "Does he want weaker bricks?" If they used more mud from the Nile, the bricks would be heavier, but would crack easier. The straw strengthened the brick while making it lighter.

Nathan looked at the tents of stored straw. Guards surrounded them. Nathan sighed. "We need to work."

Michael, a member of their team, suggested, "Cattails, growing along the northern part of the Nile, might make the bricks stay together."

Nathan nodded.

The swamps stank of decay. Mud oozed between their toes, sucking their legs into its grasp with each step. Cattails sliced their callused hands and pierced their thick-skinned feet.

Nathan looked at the western horizon. The sun was setting. No one would be going home anytime soon. The quota must be met.

The moon took the sun's place in the sky as Nathan watched his crew. They worked without stopping. When they harvested enough cattails, they mixed the bricks and poured them into forms.

Their bodies swayed. Some rubbed their faces, tipping their heads back and closing their eyes. Others laid their heads on their arms as they squatted on the sand. Nathan heard rumblings beside him from hunger not yet satisfied. No one needed to remind them that they had not eaten.

Michael lifted the brick form from bricks made with cattails. The mud crumbled.

Ellis stomped in a circle. He yelled, heedless of the guard who stood with a whip in his hand, "What do we do now?"

Nathan did not silence him. He did not need to look at his circle of men to know their shoulders sagged. Nathan heard their groans. Some rubbed their eyes to look through the darkness at the crumbled mud. Others squatted to rest their legs before they fell.

"Let's go home."

He shuffled his feet to cover the distance from the brick-making location to where the slaves lived. He stumbled with his men to their adobe huts where bean stew and barley flatbread had long grown cold.

Once in the slave town, they separated to meet their own families.

Sleep was needed before the sky would lighten for another day. What would that new day bring?

Dinah was stirring the pot of stew when a noise at the doorway startled her. "Ellis, what happened? You're so late. I was worried." She stopped talking when she realized that he did not hear her and laid their pallet on the floor for him to rest.

He grunted loudly as he bent himself to the dirt floor.

She dipped her cloth into a clay basin of water to wash his feet. "Where've you been? Your feet are slashed like hemp strings."

His only response was a groan before he fell asleep.

She stirred the beans before removing them from the coals. Maybe he would awaken in the night to eat. She looked at him again and doubted he would waken at all.

Dinah retrieved a jar of rendered fat. She smeared the fat on his sore feet while he slept. What had happened?

Before the sun's light crept into their dark adobe house, Ellis gulped the wheat softened by cooking, then washed it down with a swallow of milk. He saved the rest of the milk for Dinah who carried their first child. He felt her gaze and tried to smile. How could he provide what she needed after Pharaoh's new demands? The payment for bricks yielded enough barley, wheat, and beans to make flatbread *if* they made quota.

Dinah watched him.

He tried to smile. "Good meal."

She gave him a tentative smile as she placed her hand on her swollen womb. "Toda raba."

"The midwife will be close?" he asked.

She nodded.

He struggled to his feet.

Dinah stuffed the beans from the previous night's stew into flatbread.

He took it and gave her a hug.

She looked into his face. "May the Lord bless your day."

Ellis clenched his jaw at her words. "The Lord does not bless my day nor my life. I want none of His blessing."

Dinah backed from his embrace. "I'm sorry, Ellis. I just want you to be happy."

He laughed with no humor. "Happy? God turned His back on me when I needed Him most. I turn my back on this God now." He looked into Dinah's ashen face and felt remorse for his harshness. He left without another word.

Before the sun rose, Ellis arrived where his team molded bricks. Before yesterday's decree, they would mix the straw with the Nile's mud and pour the mixture into molds. He would not start until the others from his team arrived. He watched them shuffling from the village.

His cracked feet and hands bled from the cattail slits. He rubbed his neck and rolled his head to ease the stiffness. His back was tight. His bare legs and back showed many knife-like slices from the cattails from yesterday.

Hoping yesterday's decree was just a bad dream; Ellis looked at the tents filled with straw.

Guards stood posted. An Egyptian driver appeared with a whip.

Ellis's wish was shattered. Yesterday was the dream. Today became the nightmare, but not one to be awakened from anytime soon.

Dinah walked to the Nile to fill her last jar with water. The Nile's overflowing banks spoke of the rainy season. The coolness of the early morning would not last. She shifted the jar for water on her shoulder. She would need extra water to soak Ellis's feet tonight. Those slices that she saw on his feet and hands were deep.

After she married him, his tender features had changed. He

often looked past her rather than at her. His hard expression made her retreat and feel rejected. When she commented about God, he stiffened and ignored her. She felt her marriage was a mistake. She loved Ellis, but when he was home, she felt her insides tighten, and she tried not to anger him. She did not know what to say that would please him.

She shifted the jar from one shoulder to the other, being careful not to spill any water. Today, she trudged slowly from the Nile. Her side gave a sharp twinge. She stopped, placing her hand protectively on her babe. Perhaps today, little one. She was ready to hold him in her arms. The twinge slowed, as she massaged her side. She resumed her walking, bringing the water inside the house where it would stay cool.

She took three handfuls of barley from the vessel by the hearth. The amount would be enough, if she stretched it, to make four flatbreads. If only she could make something special for Ellis, maybe he would eat more—and be happy. He worked so hard.

She crushed the grain beneath a molded rock in the hollow of a second rock until coarse flour formed. She gathered it into a wide-mouthed clay bowl, added a pinch of salt, a dipperful of water and a few finger mounds of rendered fat. She must stretch the fat to last until Ellis could barter for more. She renewed her kneading, flattening four round discs and placing them close to the hearth. She would heat them later. Her hands were busy, but her mind lingered on Ellis.

Cleaning the pot from breakfast, she put onions, garlic, dried beans, and some herbs that she had gathered during the harvest season. She covered them with water and placed the pot close to the heat by the hearth. It would cook slowly for dinner.

Dinah finished her work quickly so she could go to Salome's. Salome mentored and encouraged her.

They had harvested reeds from the Nile's edge yesterday. Today they would make baskets. She needed the baskets for the grain that Ellis brought home from his labor. She gathered the reeds piled in the corner and hurried to Salome's. Maybe she would have answers about Ellis.

Nathan wiped the sweat from his forehead with the back of his arm. The team had scrounged the riverside for growth. They had already harvested and stored the straw in tents. No new straw had grown more than a few inches during this rainy season, and was not dried enough for use.

After spending most of the morning searching, Nathan called his team to him. "We can't keep looking. Let's make the bricks without the straw."

The men nodded without a word.

Nathan usually had only two men carrying the mud and two the water. Without the straw, more men would carry the mud. "Ellis, you and Michael help the others haul mud."

Other teams from the gravel pit, located in the stone quarry, hauled pebbles.

Thoughts of the stone quarry made Nathan shake his head. If his men did not meet their quota, they would be sent to the stone quarry where slaves hauled room-sized boulders for Pharaoh's pyramids. Slaves working the stone quarry did not last. They died daily, working in the heat of the desert as Egyptian drivers watched. Nathan could not allow his men to be sent there.

They must make the bricks. They mixed the mud, water, and rock chips, poured the mixture into molds, and jiggled air bubbles from the mixture. Michael would remove the forms after several hours.

Since Nathan was the only one who could read and write, he wrote Pharaoh's name on each brick. The bricks would bake in the sun for three days on a bed of sand to prevent sticking to the ground. Then they would stack them. They repeated the process to make 50,000 bricks every day.

Today the bricks fell apart until they found the right consistency without the straw.

Nathan sipped from the warm water in the water trough. He wiped his face with his arm. Have mercy, oh Lord.

The sun heated the air without remorse. Sand concentrated the heat and returned it on weary feet. Bodies glistened from the sweat of hard labor. The sun stole their strength and depleted their reserves.

The men worked, for they feared the ever-ready whip. They had families that would die without their source of grain. Egyptian overseers' whips lashed all day.

Nathan's team shadowed him, preventing the overseer's discipline, but by late afternoon, their weariness caused them to lag. They left Nathan alone.

The overseer found him. "You didn't meet your quota yesterday or today."

Nathan said nothing.

The silence made the overseer smile. He coiled the lines of his whip as he stood waiting for an answer. He heaved the whip over his head, striking Nathan repeatedly. "Where's your God now?"

E llis's baskets were loaded with mud and balanced on his shoulders. He stretched his neck, adjusting his load when he saw Nathan on the ground. The overseer stood over him, using his whip. Nathan did not flinch.

Anger flooded through Ellis at the sight. He dropped his baskets and ran toward Nathan. When he reached him, the Egyptian stepped back, turned from his task, and stalked away. Ellis dropped to his knees. "Nathan?"

Nathan lay face down with his mouth open in the sand. Ellis turned his head gently to the side. Another team member approached.

Ellis held his head up to breathe, brushing sand out of his mouth. "Get water!"

When the water came, Ellis sloshed it over Nathan's face. "Call the others. We're taking him home."

No group ever left their work early. The other members' eyes widened. "There's half the day to work."

"Hurry!" Ellis rolled Nathan to a sitting position, so the sand would not stick to his bleeding back.

Ellis poured more water on Nathan's face. Nathan licked the water, and then dropped his head back onto Ellis's arm. The team gathered. "Link arms. We'll lift him." Ellis pointed at four to support him.

Nathan groaned.

Ellis felt the eyes of the overseers on his back as he walked away. The overseers would beat them later. One good beating could cripple or kill a man. Ellis was ready to grab that whip and lash any Egyptian who stopped him. Let them come.

The day had grown hot early. Dinah's walk to Salome's drained her. She shifted the reeds under her arm as she paused to catch her breath. She must talk with Salome about Ellis. Was she just an ignorant bride of fifteen or was this how marriage should be? Why did Ellis not talk to her?

When she reached the doorway, she allowed her eyes to grow accustomed to the darkness inside.

"Dinah, come in, Salome called from the corner of the room.

Dinah put her reeds in a stack by the door and hurried over to hug her. "Shalom."

Salome held Dinah at arm's length and studied her face, "What's the matter?"

"Something's happened, but Ellis won't tell me."

"He's probably trying to protect you."

"But I'm not a child. I'm his wife."

Salome adjusted the tattered sheet over her two napping children. "Men process differently. You talk through problems then you have an answer. Men must have an answer before they talk."

Dinah's eyes filled with tears. "By the time he has the answer, he's found a new problem and still won't talk with me. I am losing him. I fear to talk to him."

Salome moved to the pile of reeds against the wall. "Why do you fear him?"

Dinah gathered her reeds and followed Salome outside. "His face shows anger, needing no reason to pour it out.

Salome pushed a few of her reeds into an earthen vessel filled with water. They would soak the reeds to make them pliable for weaving. She leaned over Dinah's shoulder. "This reed is too brittle. Try this one, it's soaked enough." She handed Dinah another reed, holding onto it until Dinah looked into her face. "It is not like you to be afraid of people. Why is he angry with you?"

Dinah sniffled. "This morning, he told me he didn't want God to bless his day... I just want him happy."

Salome hugged her. "Dinah, he sounds angry at God not you. As his suffering increases, he fears for your safety. He can't protect you and becomes frustrated."

Dinah pulled away from Salome's embrace. "Does God hear our cries?"

"I trust His love when I can't see through the pain."

"If He loves us, why do we suffer?"

Salome handed her a reed from the earthen vessel of water. "Do you look for Him when you don't feel pain?"

Dinah thought for a moment and shook her head.

Salome nodded. "When everything around me is a whirling sand storm, I focus on Him and find rest."

Dinah folded up the reeds from the base of the basket that she was forming. "I don't even know where to look for Him. He hides from me."

Salome dipped more reeds into the water. "Search for Him with all your heart. He won't stay hidden."

"I've nothing to give Him." Dinah rubbed her front as she leaned back against the wall. "I could use a bit of food for this baby who eats all day."

Salome laughed. "I love you, Dinah. You don't make me guess what you're thinking. The flatbread by the hearth may still be soft. Your baby reminds you of your needs. When you hold your babe in your arms, he will remind you of your need for God."

Ellis reached his house, directing the men to lay Nathan on the cloak that he threw on the floor. "Toda raba. Does anyone know where the Hebrew swne lives?"

Most shook their heads and looked down at their feet or around the house. None responded.

"I know you all have families, but this is for Nathan..." Ellis's voice petered out.

They had left work before making their quota. None knew what penalty they faced. Nor would they risk their lives going to the Egyptian section of town in a slave's loincloth looking for the swne. They shook their heads.

Ellis sighed. "Could someone tell his wife?"

Several agreed with a nod and left like beetles running from the sun.

If Nathan were not so wounded, Ellis would have laughed. He understood their fear. His heartbeat still raced. He took a deep breath and began dabbing cool water on the lashes on Nathan's back.

"I'll go."

Ellis jumped at the voice. He had assumed that he was alone. Expecting an overseer, he turned to the doorway.

"I'll go," Michael repeated.

Ellis calmed his heart. "To the swne?"

Michael nodded.

"Toda raba. May the Lord be with you," Ellis said. Why had he added the blessing? He no longer believed that God even cared. He shook his head. Why did Nathan trust a God Who allowed this?

Ellis looked at Nathan's wounds. Nathan's breathing was shallow.

Nathan had told him of Abraham, their ancestor, who was called a friend of God. Nathan knew this God as his Friend, telling Ellis that he could know Him, too. Who wanted a friend that would treat His faithful like this?

Nathan's eyes struggled to open. He tried to speak.

Ellis quickly touched his lips with water. "Don't talk.

Just rest."

Nathan swallowed with great effort.

Ellis heard a step inside the doorway. He turned defensively to see Salome enter.

She fell to her knees beside her husband. "Nathan!" She touched his hand.

Nathan's eyes struggled to open. "May the Lord's people..."

"See Him." Salome finished for him their prayer from the night before when Nathan shared the new decree. She saw the whip marks and gasped, "May the Lord help us."

Ellis watched Dinah stumble inside with Jabin, Salome's baby, in her arms, and Etania, Salome's child, by her side.

Looking to where Ellis sat, Dinah inhaled sharply. "What happened?"

Ellis glanced at the doorway. "Michael went for the Hebrew swne, if he will come."

"He must come quickly." Salome patted Nathan's arm. "The Lord will help."

A sandaled footstep outside the door brought Ellis to his feet. No slave would wear sandals. He grabbed the poker from the cooking fire and crouched ready to defend Nathan.

A man entered, dressed in Egyptian clothing, although his beard and head covering showed he was Hebrew. He carried two baskets. "No need for that, my friend. I am Aaron. I come to help."

Ellis put the poker back and allowed the swne to kneel at Nathan's side.

Aaron asked, "Has he opened his eyes?"

"He took a small drink, then went back to sleep," Ellis answered.

Aaron removed several jars of dried herbs from his basket. "Honey aids healing. Mine has special herbs." The honey sealed the wound and prevented the fluids from leaving.

Ellis watched Aaron coat the wounds. Nathan groaned without

waking. Ellis held his breath, waiting for Aaron's verdict.

The swne addressed Ellis. "Why was he beaten?"

Ellis glanced at Dinah and lowered his voice. "Pharaoh gives no straw but demands the same number of bricks to be made."

"When did this begin?"

"Yesterday afternoon. We tried cattails in place of straw, but..." Ellis looked at his hands and feet.

"I'll leave salve for you. What about the other teams? Their foremen?"

Ellis's voice rose in anger. "We took Nathan home. The other teams left their foremen until the end of the day."

"It was good that you didn't." Aaron lowered his voice, glancing at Salome. "Your man will make it. His heart beats strong."

Nathan's eyes opened and rested on Salome. He groaned but tried to smile.

She extended her hand to rest in his callused one.

He breathed deeply and closed his eyes again. "The Lord will change hearts, my Salome."

Her eyes filled with tears. "He will indeed."

Aaron dribbled some drops of tonic into Nathan's mouth. "This will help with pain. How many other foremen were..."

Ellis glanced at Dinah, who was busy with the baby. "Ten for sure." He jerked his head, trying not to say more.

Aaron shook his head. "Lord, have mercy as we obey You." He faced Ellis. "I'll leave this honey for all wounds. Apply several times throughout the day. Give him drink as often as he will take it. The wine will help with pain, but drop these into his mouth every meal time." He gave his vial to Salome.

Aaron emptied the second basket beside the hearth: bundles of figs, raisins, dates, leg of a lamb. Ellis's eyes widened and he could not look away.

Dinah watched with open mouth. "Meat! It's like a festival and we are to be blessed. The Lord answered beyond what I could dream." She met Ellis's eyes and shut her mouth. Hebrew custom did not permit women to speak in the presence of men.

Ellis attempted a smile. He watched her cheeks flame red as she lowered her head and busied herself with the baby. Dinah deserved better. If only he could provide for her and the coming babe. They lived on beans, wheat, and barley. The amount he provided enabled only survival. And if their quota was not met...

Aaron turned to Michael. "Would you show me the others?"

He nodded, silently looking to Nathan.

Aaron placed his hand on Michael's shoulder. "He'll live."

Michael gestured to his foreman. "Nathan showed me the way to peace."

Aaron nodded to the man on the floor. "He'll make it." He followed Michael to treat the others who needed his herbs and his prayers.

D inah cleaned the common bowl with sand from outside the doorway. Her family and Salome's had finished eating.

Nathan's groans of pain had subdued conversation.

Salome stayed by Nathan's side, holding his hand or chasing flies from his back. She held Jabin close to her. Etania clung to her as they watched Nathan.

Ellis rose. "Dinah, I'll be back."

She arched her eyebrows but did not ask where he was going.

He gave her a rough hug and left without a look back. He squared his shoulders, held his head high, and strode with purpose.

Dinah watched him leave. He looked angry enough to kill someone. Would he?

Salome gave Dinah an understanding look. "Tell the Lord."

Dinah nodded with eyes full of worry. "God must be appeased by your family's sacrifice to give calmness like this. I want to rest in a God like this."

Salome nodded; her eyes were full of tears. "Rest comes in letting Him control. Tell Him all your thoughts, but don't try to control what He does."

Once the sun began its journey across the sky for another day, Ellis gathered the supervisors of the brick-making work force.

They walked with a mission toward Pharaoh's palace. These men represented not only their own lives and their teams, but also their families. Some hesitated, fearful. They studied Ellis in the lead, shoulders thrust back, muscles toned and firm with only a slave's loincloth concealing them. Ellis's confidence gave them courage.

Ellis stopped to allow the men to reach him. Most struggled to walk, but he would not humble them by offering aid. No team made their quota. All were beaten. The swne had been busy throughout the night.

Ellis had not told Nathan where he was going. If Nathan knew, he would tell Ellis about his God's ways. If this was God's ways, Ellis wanted no part of them.

This looked more like Pharaoh's ways. He acted like a spoiled child. Pharaoh was not Ellis's god. Ellis could strangle this Pharaoh for his treatment of him and his people. Furrowing his brow deeper, he turned to walk again. He clenched his hands at his sides. He must curb his tongue if he wished the favor of Pharaoh.

His life held no pleasure. Dinah's face came to mind and was almost enough to make him smile. She was the only sunshine in his hard life, remaining cheerful despite their hardships.

She had been fourteen when they married, bubbling with life's joys. Why had she lost that? Perhaps the babe tired her. He knew she did not eat enough.

Pharaoh stole from everyone and lived a life of ease, authority, and god-like existence. What kind of a God would allow a man like him to rule over any people?

What of the Lord's "chosen people," as Nathan would tell him? Chosen for what? To make bricks for some spoiled grown-up child? Ellis would rather have no god, than a God who allowed that.

The men reached the palace entrance. Clustered around Ellis, they waited permission to see Pharaoh.

Previous pharaohs had allowed any subject of his kingdom seeking his deity's wisdom and favor to enter his presence. This Pharaoh was no different.

When they entered, nothing Ellis imagined could have prepared him for what he saw. The palace pillars displayed strength as they reached toward the sky in columns wider than his hut. The marble floor felt cool beneath his callused, bleeding feet.

The guards at the entrance, although not holding whips, made Ellis glare his hatred.

Pharaoh appeared small before this grandeur. His throne sat a long way from the entrance, raised on a golden platform. Ellis looked to the men with him. Would they be able to walk the distance without stumbling and falling? He slowed his pace so the others could stay with him.

Ellis looked with contempt at Pharaoh. A normal slave should feel intimidated by the wealth, the architecture, the protection of his soldiers. Ellis did not. He felt hatred.

Before they reached the stairs of the throne, Pharaoh stopped them. "That's far enough. The stench of your bodies reaches me. Why do these dogs come before me in my house?"

Ellis stepped forward and spoke, choosing his words. "Oh, great Pharaoh, why have you treated your servants this way? You give us no straw, yet told us, 'Make bricks!' Your servants are beaten, but the fault is with your own people."

There was a silence, pregnant with contempt.

Pharaoh leisurely took some figs and ate them. He chewed them slowly. "Lazy. That is why you say, 'Let's sacrifice to the Lord.' Now get to work. You will not be given any straw, yet you will produce your full quota of bricks."

Ellis bit his tongue until he tasted blood. He looked to the others. What did Pharaoh mean, sacrifice to the Lord? They had asked for nothing. Their brick quota was impossible. How could these men continue?

With heavy hearts, they limped and staggered to their work. The sun was now overhead. The quota must be made.

R eturning to their brick area, Ellis wondered what Pharaoh had meant by "sacrifice to the Lord." When Ellis saw Moses and Aaron waiting for them at the Nile, he recalled the elders' report after their meeting with Moses. He had asked them to worship. Moses had caused this added suffering.

Ellis strode to stand beside Moses and spat at him. "May your God judge you! You made Pharaoh treat us like dogs. His officials whip us until we're barely alive." He did not wait for an answer. He stomped over to his yoke, where he had dropped it yesterday, and trudged to the riverbank to haul mud. His anger did not cool during the heat of that day.

M oses spoke not a word to the man who spit at him. He watched the man stalk away. His eyes followed him until he could see him no longer. How could God's people suffer so? Where was God in this man's struggle for daily survival?

Moses looked at the other men who had resumed their work. Their shoulders bowed forward in defeat and hopelessness. This people, who knew only to make the next brick, could not believe his message of deliverance. He swallowed several times, trying to breathe. He could not speak. The weight of God's suffering people overwhelmed him.

God must prepare His people to leave. His people did not know Him. They must seek Him.

Moses watched the workers through tear-filled eyes.

He turned to Aaron and nodded. Without speaking, they retraced their steps to Aaron's house. Moses fell on his knees by his bed, and poured out his heart to his God. "Oh Lord, why have You punished Your people? I speak in Your name and Your people hurt more. When will Your people seek You?"

He silenced his questions to wait.

The stillness was full.

When he began, the sun had shown high overhead, but now it lay on the horizon. As Moses tarried, he listened.

The Lord spoke, "You will see what I will do to Pharaoh. By My mighty hand, I will bring My people out of his country."

Moses nodded. He knew of the Lord's mighty Hand, but Pharaoh did not.

"I am the Lord. I will make known My name to you. I hear the Israelites' anguish. I will judge Egypt with mighty acts. I will make you My own people. I will be your God. You will know that I AM the Lord your God."

"I am your servant, Lord. I will obey." But in his heart, Moses wondered how a people crushed under the heavy hand of bondage would hear his message.

He did not have long to wait.

After telling Aaron of his prayer and the Lord's message, Moses returned with Aaron to the brickyard. The sun had long since set, but the men still worked. When Moses shouted for their attention, only a few half-heartedly listened. Most glanced at the overseers, and kept working

Ellis returned from the river with a load of mud. He yelled to Moses, "Are you going to meet our quota?" He paused and laughed bitterly. "Then we won't listen to you. Tell the elders we don't want your help. You have brought nothing but suffering to us and to our families. Leave us alone!

Moses looked at the men, their shoulders stooped over loads of burden. He sighed. The message from the Lord had come, but the men were too discouraged to hear it.

Moses took his heavy heart to his bedchamber where he asked the Lord, "If the Israelites won't listen to me, why would Pharaoh listen?"

The Lord answered, "Pharaoh won't listen until all of Egypt acknowledges that I am the Lord."

# CHAPTER 6

When the Hebrew slaves came before Pharaoh with their request, the vizier stood behind him. The vizier cared nothing for the marks of the beatings on their backs, except that they were grotesque and ugly. The Hebrews were dogs anyway. What concerned him, because it affected him, was how their leader, the one with hatred in his eyes, looked not only at Pharaoh but at him, as well.

The vizier did not fear him personally. He should have one of the Egyptian overseers humble him with a beating. That is what he needed.

What concerned him was the hatred, hatred for everything about Pharaoh. Hatred motivated. This man could unify the Hebrews to cause an uprising. This man concerned him.

The vizier lived hatred. He often contemplated the unfairness of his life. He depended not on all these gods, for worshiping them weakened a man. He was not weak. He desired power and strength, especially Pharaoh's.

Pharaoh's uncontrolled demands forced everyone to fear for their lives. He toyed with people and then discarded them when the fun was over. He was doing that with the Hebrews. The vizier saw him do that with Moses and Aaron.

The vizier saw no problem with that, except with this situation. He tapped his finger on his hairless chin in contemplation. He saw a big problem. The Hebrews now had a leader they would follow and now had a cause to fight.

He ordered the records of the Pharaoh Phiops II (Pepi), the previous pharaoh, brought to his room. He searched the papyrus sheets until he found the period that he wanted to know about. He read the records chronicled there.

Pharaoh Pepi noticed the Israelites' numbers and controlled them. He feared if war erupted, they would join their enemies and overthrow Egypt. So Pharaoh Pepi forced slave masters over them. He built the cities of Pithom and Rameses through their work force. Even with this oppression, the Hebrews' population increased. So Pharaoh ruled more ruthlessly. He forced them to make bricks and mortar. When flooding was over, he took their produce while they worked his fields.

In spite of all this, their population continued to increase. Finally, Pharaoh Pepi called Shiphrah and Puah, the midwives to the Hebrews. "Kill all boys at birth."

Pharaoh issued the command secretly. He waited for the population to decline. His informants reported, "The midwives feared God and didn't obey; they let the boys live."

Pharaoh summoned the midwives again. "Why have you let the boys live?"

Shiphrah bowed before his feet. "Hebrew women aren't like Egyptian women. They give birth before we arrive."

Pharaoh Pepi shook and jabbed a finger in their faces. "I want every Hebrew boy thrown into the Nile!

The women left his presence and obeyed.

The vizier took a drink from his vessel. Pharaoh Pepi would have been twenty seasons old, just like the present Pharaoh. Pharaoh Pepi had considered the future for his kingdom. The current Pharaoh Merenre saw only himself. He did not recognize the danger of Moses being the Hebrews' leader—again. He saw no threat to his throne.

The vizier paced his chamber. Even though he hated the Pharaoh, he did not wish Pharaoh's power grabbed by another. The vizier turned back to his reading. Pharaoh Pepi had a daughter, Thermuthis. She would then have been seven seasons old.

The vizier scowled. He looked out his window at the Nile River. Its snake-like ramblings gave beauty to the land around it. The vizier saw neither the beauty nor the god-like status that the people gave to the Nile.

He thought about this pharaoh's daughter. She reminded him of his mother. All women wanted to control men.

He picked up the papyrus sheet to continue reading. The Pharaoh had been about thirteen seasons when he fathered Thermuthis, the custom of the times.

Thermuthis went bathing at the Nile with her attendants. This was before Pharaoh Pepi made the Hebrews construct indoor bathing vessels. She heard crying in the river and found in the reeds a basket containing a Hebrew baby boy. Seeking to keep the baby, she carried him toward the palace. A Hebrew maiden approached her, suggesting a Hebrew nursemaid. Thermuthis returned to the palace with the baby. She beguiled her way into her father's heart, and the dog of a Hebrew ended up in the palace.

The vizier shook his head in disgust. That is what happened when women controlled the hearts of men. Thermuthis had jeopardized the nation's security with Moses's presence.

Her nagging reminded the vizier of his mother's badgering, making any son kill his mother. He had done just that but escaped justice. The present pharaoh's arrogance kept him from thinking anyone could threaten his throne. The vizier counseled without threat of justice, while the pharaoh imagined his own deity.

Princess Thermuthis raised Moses in the palace. He learned architecture, law, war, and agriculture. She groomed him to be the next Pharaoh.

The vizier remembered the power struggles between some of the officers and this Moses. The vizier's father complained much about him. The vizier may have been young, but he remembered his father being furious about decisions in high places.

He was troubled that Moses had been born—against all odds and against Pharaoh Pepi's command and lived in the palace, and excelled in everything taught by the pharaoh's own instructors and scribes. He remembered the general story, which he had retold at the banquet at Badru's.

Where in the records could he find why Moses would now return? Did he seek pharaoh's power? Maybe Badru could find him in the temple records. The vizier must find answers about this Moses.

The vizier suddenly stopped his reading. Moses had this presence that enabled him to escape danger, to avoid death, to rise as a leader. Maybe the vizier could get this presence for himself, or maybe this presence would not allow Moses harm. The vizier must find answers.

B adru stepped into his house after a day at the temple. A servant informed him of a visitor.

Badru tugged at his tunic. "Who is it?"

The servant whispered with discretion, "The vizier waits in the garden."

Badru swallowed the lump in his throat that grew whenever memories of his vision in the temple replayed in his mind. The nightmares of colored flames, the voice, and the message still haunted him. He shivered.

The vizier was a man of evil. Badru laughed nervously. He dealt with good gods and bad gods all the time, but they did not sour his innards like this vizier who wore an evil ka. He straightened his shoulders and walked into his garden.

He found the vizier before the fountain. "You have come." Badru motioned toward the tray held by a servant for the vizier to take a drink. After sipping from his vessel, he wiped his sweaty palm on his tunic.

Badru could feel himself scrutinized by the vizier. He sipped again from his drink, trying to appear confident.

"Tell me, Badru, what do you know of the Hebrew God?"

"Not many people ask about their God." Badru did not think the vizier cared for any god. "Their God is a jealous God. They are allowed only one. They combine all of ours into one. "I haven't given much thought about what they believe. I suppose we could ask a Hebrew scribe." He filled the empty spaces of silence with chatter.

"You know Adlai? He is a scribe for Pharaoh, but very knowledgeable about the Hebrews. Well, he is a Hebrew," he added lamely.

The vizier stared at Badru without saying anything.

Badru rubbed the back of his neck, biting his lips to keep from saying too much.

The vizier looked at Badru in disgust.

That made Badru more nervous. If the vizier continued to stare, Badru felt sure that he would tell the man all he had ever done wrong. The vizier would remember and use anything against him.

Why had he exposed himself to this man by telling his vision?

Finally, the vizier nodded. "Where might I find this Hebrew scribe?"

"My servant could take you to his house right now." Badru summoned a servant.

Just when he thought that the vizier would leave, the vizier asked another question. "Have any more visions lately?"

Badru did not trust his voice. He avoided eye contact, looking instead at the walkway. Should he tell of the vision that recurred nightly without fail? He saw again the flame growing larger and larger, seeking to consume him. Each night it threatened to touch him. He always woke before it did. Badru shook his head, his forehead beaded with sweat. He paused. For the first time during the conversation, he just shook his head. He struggled to voice his denial.

"Really, Badru, no more visions?" the vizier pressed.

Badru nodded more forcefully, again not trusting his voice.

His response prompted a lighthearted laugh from the vizier.

"What information do your visions tell you about Egypt's future?"

Badru squeaked, "No information, I mean, no more visions." Then he shut his lips tightly to keep himself from speaking further.

The vizier nodded.

Badru tried to direct the subject away from himself. "Thank you for sharing at the banquet the true betrayer, Moses. We can all be cautious of him now."

The vizier smiled again.

Badru dreaded the vizier's next words. Would the vizier use this information against him?

"Yes, Moses. Do you know why he returns to Egypt?"

Once again, Badru wished he had kept his mouth shut. He shook his head and tried to still the shaking of his limbs. He needed another drink, but his jar was empty. He did not want to get more lest the vizier stay longer. He wiped his forehead with his sleeve. "It's a hot evening, isn't it?" He tried distracting the vizier as he walked toward his gate.

The vizier did not move.

Badru stopped and turned. He must not appear rude. After all, the vizier held much power, but he wanted the man to leave. He probed into things that made Badru nervous. "My servant will show you to the house of Adlai." Badru left without waiting for a response, calling over his shoulder, "May you hear only good things." He did not wait to be thanked for his hospitality, but fled to his chamber.


The vizier followed Badru's servant to the house of the Hebrew scribe. He had received no valuable information from Badru, other than confirmation of the incompetence of both the chief high priest and the pharaoh who allowed his existence. How could he have thought that the priest would know any information? Badru was an absolute fool and a weasel in action.

Perhaps this scribe would provide him with the information that he needed.

The servant requested admittance at a house where the richer Hebrews lived. Badru had said he was a Hebrew scribe. Why would Pharaoh need a Hebrew to do the work that an Egyptian could do?

After an introduction to the gatekeeper, the vizier was ushered to a garden to await his host. He contrasted this garden with Egyptians' gardens, not so much by the type of exotic plants growing, but by the absence of statues and shrines to gods. He did not see the gods of the water, sun, nor light. Everywhere in Egyptian houses, gods struggled with each other for power. This absence of any form of god was disarming.

"Welcome. You have come, Vizier. How nice of you to visit." The Hebrew scribe said as if he meant it.

The vizier looked at him closely. This scribe, in Egyptian garb and Hebrew beard, showed confidence. He would bear watching. He might give some information. He smiled and responded, "In peace. Scribe—"

"Adlai. The name is Adlai. Go on."

"Yes, Adlai." He hated when someone corrected him. "I wondered if you would tell me about your God."

Adlai's face brightened. "Certainly. What do you wish to know?"

"All that you want to tell me."

Adlai led him to a bench in the garden beside a fountain. He gazed toward the splashing water. "All about my God. Let me see. Our God made everything that we see. Our people came from Abraham. He obeyed God and went to a land promised to him."

The vizier interrupted, "The Hebrews have their own land?"

Adlai nodded. "The story gets better." He resumed speaking, "Joseph foretold of our exodus, requesting his bones to be taken when we leave."

"Wait!" the vizier interrupted. "Who is this Joseph that has his bones here in Egypt? And when will they be removed?"

"When we leave," the scribe said calmly.

"How do you know that you'll be leaving?" the vizier narrowed his eyes, wrinkling his brow. What was their plan?

"Before Joseph died, he predicted that God would help us leave. Joseph made his sons swear an oath to carry his bones with them.

"Who is this Joseph? I've never heard of him."

"Oh yes, you have," Adlai responded. "You Egyptians called him *Imhotep*." He paused to let the vizier realize the significance of that person.

The vizier stood and paced. "Your Joseph is the Great Architect Imhotep, the vizier, the treasurer to the great Pharaoh Zoser?"

"The one and only."

"How did he get here from Abraham's land?"

"Joseph's brothers sold him into slavery. Merchants brought him to Egypt."

The vizier interrupted, "He was a slave? How did he become so powerful?"

"He interpreted the dreams of Pharaoh Zoser, which promised plenty for seven harvests and extreme drought for seven harvests. He stored the grain for the world during the time of plenty for the coming famine."

This was information that the vizier could use. "But how did all the Hebrews come?"

"When the famine came, Joseph's family moved to Goshen, where they pastured their flocks.

"Imhotep, or Joseph, masterminded the building of the first pyramid, the step pyramid. Initially it stored the grain needed to feed the world for those seven hungry harvests. Later it was fashioned as Pharaoh's tomb." Adlai paused. "Imhotep, your god of medicine and architecture, is the same man that we know in the lineage of our tribes Manasseh and Ephraim. They are his sons."

Adlai turned to the fountain where a servant had placed a platter of fruit, cheese, and wine. "Care for some, Vizier?" He offered as he took a jar to drink.

The vizier took a jar without thinking. "This explains why the Hebrews were here. But how did you know you will leave again?"

Adlai shrugged. "We are strangers here. We do not belong. Our God is not your god. Our God must take pre-eminence. He is jealous for His rightful place not only in our lives but also with our people. Surely, you know that we are not treated like the chosen people that God has called from among the world, here in Egypt?"

"When?" The vizier had to know their plans. He had gained much by coming here. "When will you leave?"

"When God tells us," Adlai said with confidence. "We wait His word."

"What kind of an answer is that?" The vizier exploded and then stopped himself. He needed to remain calm to get their plan.

Adlai sipped before stating, "Allow me to finish my story of my people. Maybe then you will understand more of the God that you seek."

"By all means." The vizier clenched his jaws, trying to appear calm. He gulped from his vessel and grabbed a bunch of grapes that he stuffed into his mouth. Distractedly, he sat again and chewed.

"I told you about Joseph. Moses's parents—"

At the name, the vizier stood and stared at the scribe, who continued.

"Moses's parents, not fearing pharaoh's decree, hid him three months after he was born. Moses chose to suffer with God's people rather than be known as the son of the pharaoh's daughter.

"Why do you say that he chose to suffer with God's people?"

"Another way to say it is that he remembered his God. When he became of age to counsel Pharaoh Phiops II, he helped employ many Hebrews in high positions of government. They had a perspective that would not only help the Hebrews, but would assist Pharaoh because they knew the true God. He helped my father become a scribe. That is why I was able to become one."

The vizier nodded. A common practice to employ those who would support you. "Who was your father?"

"Korah. He began the training the Hebrews that enabled us to know our history and to record our language."

The vizier sipped from his drink. "I remember him." He had been in the background yet influential. Now his son Adlai held his position.

"What now?" The vizier would get the secrets of these people and then control them. Moses fled Egypt because he had chosen the people of this God. The fact that he was back in Egypt must also mean that his God directed him. Why? Was Egypt's work force the power that the betrayer would take? Was Moses that betrayer? He had to be. How could he stop Moses when his God directed all of this?

Adlai smiled. "We wait for our God. The suffering of God's people will end soon. Our God will show Himself, not just as the Provider during times of famine, and Sustainer during many times of oppression, but now He will show His power as Deliverer from Egypt, so His people can go home where they belong. You asked about our God. Does that help?" He rose and began walking to the doorway.

The vizier followed. He needed to think. He neglected to take leave of his host as he left.

This God of the Hebrews was greater than he imagined. He made the vizier feel little and needy, and out of control. He must plan about this new God. If this God was real, He was supreme. How could the vizier be like Him? How could he get His power?

This Hebrew God was nothing like the Egyptian gods that a person could worship when he wanted and forget when he did not. This God held too much control. He demanded your all, all the time. That was more than the vizier would give.

The vizier slept little during the night, and the disturbing questions from his conversation with Adlai did not diminish with the rising of the sun.

If this God decided to take His people, would Egypt be able to fight back?

Today, the vizier must speak with the General of the Army,

Chike. He would know the state of Egypt's power, should this God attack.

The vizier must be in control. He would direct the pharaoh toward making wise decisions regarding this betrayer.

Instead of going to the general's house, he walked to the outskirts of the Egyptian town where the troops practiced. To the east lay the desert where their soldiers trained for strength, skills, and stamina.

Pharaoh Phiops II had built a powerful army. Egypt controlled the nomadic irritants who sought to control the Nile River. Pharaoh Pepi pushed those peoples beyond the deserts that surrounded Egypt.

The vizier thought that this present pharaoh maintained the army by default rather with any foresight. Pharaoh cared not what his army did. The army practiced but not for any campaign.

The vizier did not know how the soldiers trained, but he thought he had better learn for the welfare of Egypt's future. He came to the wall that separated the town from the desert. He could see the soldiers separated into groups. Their uniform was a short kilt. Their bodies looked toughened by the army drills. He observed Egyptian officers controlling each group. He found General Chike who strode between the groups giving directives.

General Chike finished his dictates and turned, showing pleasure at the vizier's presence. "Greetings, Vizier."

"In peace, General Chike. How do you train your men?"

"Training begins early, before the sun beats strong on the desert, and before the pink of the clouds can be seen in the eastern horizon. Wrestling and lifting sand bags consume time before a light break of archery and knife throwing. That completes the morning training, before the heat of the sun requires light refreshment. In the afternoon, we complete the workout with free fighting and stick fighting. Sometimes, if there are enough Egyptians, we include charioteer maneuvering."

"So only the Egyptians of proper status are charioteers?" the vizier interjected.

"Of course. They stable their own horses at their houses. They train in the evening after they've completed their other occupations."

"Are most of the footmen, archers, and spearmen Hebrews, then?" the vizier asked. If they had no other occupation, they must be slaves.

"Yes, all are Hebrews," he said with a nod of his head. "Have you heard how they defeated the Ethiopians during the time when Moses was General of the Army?"

"Indeed, I have. Was that when the Hebrews became such a great part of the army?"

"I think that started it. They would have followed Moses anywhere. He had the presence of their God, they say."

The vizier hesitated and then asked, "If the Hebrew people decided to fight against Egypt, could our people withstand it?"

"If the Hebrew people wanted Egypt today, they would have nothing to stop them," Chike replied, then shrugged. "But Moses isn't here, and they have no leader. Most of them have no concept of who their God is. We can be safe from that threat."

The vizier remained silent, thinking.

The general started walking toward another group, yelling the instruction to begin another drill. His supervisor echoed the command around the circle of trainees.

The vizier watched the general. "Moses is here."

General Chike stopped mid-stride. "He couldn't be. He disappeared about forty seasons ago. That would make him...eighty seasons now. Where? Did you see him?"

"He requested the pharaoh let the Hebrews sacrifice to their God."

"He better let them go," the general responded, quickly looking at the vizier.

The vizier nodded, noting that Chike understood the danger. "Well, the mighty pharaoh oppressed the people more instead. They petitioned Pharaoh for better treatment, but he denied them. They left angry."

The vizier studied the man in front of him. Chike let out a long breath. His face was very troubled, but he said nothing.

Chike raised his head after several moments. "What do you wish me to do?"

The vizier smiled. This man knew Egypt's peril. "Why don't you rest; don't work the Hebrews for a while. Perhaps bring the foremen—they are Egyptians right?"

When he saw the answering nod, he continued. "Perhaps the Egyptian foremen could entice some Egyptian men into contests of their strength and skill. Build an Egyptian army to be ready for the Hebrews and their God." The vizier smiled again, for this plan should work. It required nothing for Pharaoh to approve, but would give Egypt the army she would need in the near future.

Chike smiled. "It has been a long time since I've rested. I will enjoy my wife, and see to my house."

"Good." The vizier felt in control. His plan—if they had enough time before Moses and his God tried to take control—would work. He walked toward the palace with a light step. Egypt could do it, if they had the time.

The stars had not left the sky when Dinah heard footsteps outside their doorway. She knew they were not from a Hebrew, because the noise was the shuffling of leather sandals. No slave owned sandals. She nudged Ellis awake.

The unknown man entered the house, grabbing Ellis by the hair, and threw him out the door. "The vizier sends his regards." He laughed.

Dinah's heart raced as she crept to the doorway. She saw the man coil his whip into a circle. She held herself standing by the doorframe, and willed herself not to look with every lash she heard. She jolted with every grunt Ellis made. Her baby responded to her pain with added movement.

The overseer hissed. "That will teach you to make quota. That will teach you not to leave work early." He drew a deep breath. "That will remind you to be thankful for what Pharaoh gives you." He dusted his hands before sauntering down the street.

Dinah ran to Ellis.

He groaned, pushing himself up from the ground. He spit out the dirt in his mouth. "I must get to work." He raised his body to a sitting position.

Dinah ran for a dipper of water. She held it while he drank. She brushed her hand across his forehead, pushing his hair from his face. His eyes showed an intensity that caused her to pull her hand back in alarm.

She gasped at his expression.

His face showed no pain. His lips were pulled back, in a sneer of rage.

She whimpered, "Ellis, let me cool your back with the salve from the swne."

He staggered to his feet. "No, Dinah!" he shouted.

She withdrew, placing a protective hand on her belly. She stepped from him, biting her lip to keep from crying. Who had this man become?

"Dinah, I have to get to the brickyard. I can't let them think they have won. Don't you see?"

Dinah did see. She saw that his hatred consumed him. She nodded, keeping her eyes downward. When she heard him rise, she watched as he walked down the street. He thrust his shoulders back in spite of the pain she knew he felt. How could a heart filled with such hate ever have shown her tenderness? Had she ever truly known her husband?

Her pain intensified. She crawled from the street into her house and rested against the wall. The pain came with rhythm and intensity, easing enough to allow her to catch her breath. Her time had come. She delivered their firstborn son on the day that she lost her husband to his hate.

She cradled her son to her breast and wished to know this God Who controlled all.

# CHAPTER 7

B efore the day was half over, Chike came home.

Amunet ran to him. "What's wrong?" She threw her arms around his neck.

"Can't a man come home to see his wife without a reason?" Chike laughed as he encircled her waist, lifting her to give her a kiss.

"Many a man does, but not you. What's wrong with the army?" Amunet persisted, leaning back in his arms to study his face.

"I had an interesting visit with the vizier today. He requests that I train more Egyptians for the army."

"Are you finally given permission to develop the chariots? That would be wonderful!"

"No, not the chariots. I must train more footmen and archers."

"Will Egyptians be consigned like slaves to bear arms? Who would dare attack Egypt, the leading power of the world? Would they march through the desert, where the Hebrews guard our entrance? What foreign country threatens us?"

"It's for another time to solve the kingdom's problems." He embraced her. "I came home to see you."

"I've something to show you." Amunet grabbed his hand and led him through the hall to her chamber. "Close your eyes."

"What have you done now?" Chike laughed as she positioned him at the entrance of her door.

"Open your eyes and look down," she commanded, when she was satisfied with where he stood.

Chike opened his eyes. "It's Sekhet. You mummified her."

"Now she will always protect me while I sleep."

"When I am not here to protect you, she will." Chike stooped to touch the top of the cat's head.

"Don't speak of not being here. Do you know something that I don't? Is your army going on campaign? Oh Chike, tell me it's not."

"Do not fear. This pharaoh believes his kingdom will last forever. I go nowhere. We practice for nothing." Chike shook his head. "I'll always be here to protect you."

"You better be. I cannot live without you." She placed her hand on his as he stroked the cat.

He took her hand and kissed it.

"Let me show you something else." She took his hand and led him inside her chamber where she had a table prepared. *Sacmis*, the goddess who protected pregnancies and births, sat with incense holders and gifts arranged around her. "Sacmis will be appeased. She'll give us an heir."

"You are with child?" Chike's eyes glowed and he squeezed her hand protectively.

"Not yet. Having you home will lead to success, will it not? And having the shrine will guarantee it."

He took her in his arms. "You know an heir would please me, but it's you that gives me the most pleasure."

She nestled in his arms. "You being home should guarantee an heir. One thing would make me happy…"

"What?" He smelled her wig. "Is this mint?"

"I tried mint soap, do you like it?"

"It rejuvenates me from the sun's rays."

"Chike, you are distracted. Are you listening to me?" Amunet pushed away from him.

"Of course." He held her tighter. "What one more thing would make you happy?"

She waited until he looked into her face. "Since my Sekhet died, I've missed her. Do you think that I could get another cat?"

Chike laughed. "Amunet, you are my Kitten. You may get a litter if that would make you happy."

Amunet tipped her head back to look directly into his eyes. "You make me happy."

He looked into her face. "But a cat would make you happier."

She pecked his lips quickly with a kiss. "Yes."

He squeezed her tighter. "Then get another cat."

Amunet paused before speaking again, "There is another thing."

"You didn't get yourself a lion, did you? You know I have seen too many turn on their owners. They are still wild beasts." Chike held her at arm's length, studying her expression.

"No, nothing like that." Amunet paused to make sure he was listening. "I sent Reut to the Hebrew silversmith to create an amulet that will guarantee an heir for you."

"Kitten, any amulet needed for the gods gives me pleasure. But you do not need jewelry to enhance your beauty."

"I want an heir for you, Chike."

"You will have an heir for me. I can wait. It'll come in Sacmis's good time."

"It has been so many years. The women whisper of my failure." Her voice grew small and trembled. Her body wilted in defeat.

He squeezed her tightly against himself. "They are just old women who talk of nothing. Do not listen to them."

"Do you think we could?"

"I know so."

She allowed him to console her, and wondered how soon the heir would come.

Ptah, after making another statue for pharaoh's temple, revisited Aaron. Mack greeted him and ushered him toward the room where Amos slept.

Ptah stopped before entering the room. He hesitantly whispered, "I've come to speak to Aaron, not see my servant."

Mack nodded and showed him to the garden.

Aaron joined him a short time later. "Ptah, hello, you have come."

"In peace. I come to share my good news. I've found another apprentice for my sculpturing. I'll no longer need my servant to return."

Aaron looked at the man, forcefully swallowing a retort. "What success you have with your craft and skill. You must feel accomplished." He began to escort him toward the gate.

"I'll sell this servant to the stone quarry. He won't bring a good price with his handicap, but maybe he can haul water for those who work." Ptah sighed, shrugging.

Aaron inhaled a deep breath, willing his words to appease. "Perhaps, if you allow me time, I might find a craftsman willing to accept Amos as an apprentice."

Ptah brightened at the thought. "Would you? That would bring me more money. I would be grateful." He bowed as he started to leave, and then turned back. "I cannot wait too long. Each day he does not work is money that I do not receive."

Aaron nodded. "I understand. I will make it my priority."

"I thank you."

Aaron pushed the gate shut behind Ptah. He wondered where he could find a place for Amos that would not require two legs. The stone quarry would kill him. It killed men with two legs.

Aaron knew he could not eliminate all the suffering of his people, but he would do what he could. He would not allow Amos to work in the stone quarry after all he had already suffered. Where would the Lord place him?

Aaron checked on Amos every day. "You're growing stronger. No evil ka threatens you."

Amos shifted on his cushions. "I'm not in a cloud all the time anymore. My head clears and I can speak."

"How many times do you take the tonic?"

When Amos hesitated, his sister answered. "It varies. When its power needs replenished, I give him more, but not enough to make him always sleep. I want to talk with him sometimes." She laughed.

Amos had accepted his stump, much to the credit of his sister's prayers and reminders of the Lord's ways. She stayed by his side constantly, and changed the dressings covering the stump without flinching.

Aaron nodded. He had grown accustomed to her presence. She would make a fine assistant for his grandson Phinehas, also a swne. When he thought of introducing her to him, Aaron realized he did not even know her name. Almost a full moon phase had passed since her arrival; he could not ask her now.

Aaron went to ask Mack. He found him pulverizing some herbs for a tonic. Mack paused in his work. "What do you wish?"

"You can tell?" Aaron laughed. He found himself whispering, even though they were alone in the room. "What is the name of Amos's sister?"

Mack laughed as well. "She's too young for you, Aaron. But she'd make a good assistant."

"That's what I was thinking for Phinehas."

"Oh." Mack's smile disappeared and his voice became flat. "Her name is Hannah."

"What's wrong? Is the thought of Phinehas and her not good?"

"Phinehas is not... Hannah is very... Hebrew."

Aaron laughed again. "That she is. And so is my grandson."

"In lineage, but not in thinking. Phinehas consults too much with the magicians and gods of the palace in order to appease his Egyptian patients. Maybe he doesn't actually believe their works, but... he uses them. That would make all the difference to

Hannah. She knows the Friend of Abraham. They are too different."

Aaron had counseled Phinehas against only treating people who had money. Aaron did not like to think what superstitions Phinehas added to his treatments to make him acceptable to the Egyptians, but he knew that Phinehas did. These additions would not be acceptable to Hannah. He sighed. "You're right."

Not many servants would instruct their masters this way, but their unusual friendship had grown through suffering. Mack had helped Aaron with his wife's treatments. Some evil had attacked Elisheba. Her body had shriveled to almost nothing.

Aaron whispered as she lay in his arms, "I wish to take away your suffering."

Elisheba placed her hand against Aaron's beard, her face leaning on his. She spoke with difficulty. "Don't wish for absence of suffering. That's what made me seek the Friend of Abraham."

"What good is being a swne, if I can't help you with your pain?" Aaron's voice cracked as he tried to speak.

"You don't heal, Aaron. This is not in your hands. The Lord heals. You point people to know Him. I have found Him. I'm ready to meet Him." She stopped talking to catch her breath. The conversation had taxed her. She closed her eyes but held a smile on her lips. She spoke once more without opening her eyes. "He's worthy of our friendship."

Aaron held her, watching the peace shine through her expression as her life slipped from her. The smile on her face never left.

Mack found Aaron some time later, holding her as the tears slipped quietly down his bearded face. Elisheba had completed her journey to meet her Friend.

Aaron and Mack had suffered through much together. Now Mack anticipated what Aaron needed for a patient before he asked. He often substituted for him when Aaron was absent. The Lord blessed their ministry together. The magicians and priests wondered at what great magic Aaron performed to achieve such success. Aaron attributed any healing to the Lord where all praise belonged.

Almost a cycle and a half of the moon had passed since Moses's arrival. Now he and Aaron waited outside the Pharaoh's court again. When summoned, they would show Pharaoh the strength of the Lord.

Pharaoh permitted them into his presence. He lounged apathetically. "So, Moses, what do you show me today?"

The vizier stood behind him, breathing deeply but saying nothing.

Aaron threw his staff down.

It turned into a snake.

Aaron and Moses stepped back as the snake began ascending the steps toward Pharaoh's throne.

Pharaoh leaned forward in his throne and watched its ascent. He waved his hand to a servant. "Call the magicians." To Moses and Aaron, he said, "They will show their power to your God."

The magicians came eagerly, wishing to show their strength. They cast down their staves, and they too became snakes.

The floor moved with the motion of all the snakes slithering and sliding on the smooth, glassy tile. Their tongues tested the air for their next victim.

Pharaoh gloated over his power. "The gods of mine work their magic for me. How is your God any different? Why should I listen to you?"

As he spoke, Aaron's snake turned from climbing the stairs and attacked the magicians' snakes. They battled. All eyes watched as Aaron's snake mastered and devoured each snake. The snake became huge from eating all others.

The magicians trembled, backing away from the snake. Their eyes widened. Sweat beaded their foreheads. The silence in the room was broken as they began to chant, "His power is great. His power is great." The priests and magicians cowered, dropping to their knees, bowing their heads, giving homage.

Aaron caught hold of the engorged snake's tail.

The magicians crawled further away.

Moses watched their reaction. He had watched how they held their "staves" merely pinching the heads of snakes. Squeezing a snake's head would briefly paralyze it, causing it to appear stiff like a staff.

Aaron's snake became a wooden staff in his hand once again.

The magicians' eyes widened and their mouths circled in surprise.

Moses smiled. They had expected his snake to curl back onto Aaron's arm and strangle him.

All looked to Pharaoh for his response.

His face showed no emotion. His hardened features revealed nothing.

The magicians meekly rose from their knees, trembling. Would Pharaoh kill them for bowing to another god before his very face?

When Pharaoh said nothing, the look in his eyes told Moses he would not listen. Moses and Aaron said not another word but walked the same long walk back to the outside world.

M oses fell on his knees in his chamber and beseeched the Lord for His people.

The Lord told Moses, "Pharaoh's heart yields not. Go to Pharaoh in the morning. Wait by the bank of the Nile. I will tell you what to say. He will know that I am the Lord."

Moses rose to tell Aaron of the visit planned for the morning. They knelt together to praise the God Who would relieve the suffering of their people.

# CHAPTER 8

Every morning the pharaoh and the chief high priest met at the Nile's edge to wait, to watch if the sun would indeed rise or whether the great serpent that dominated the darkness would strike its fatal blow. Every morning that the sun rose, the serpent was defeated. This gave them confidence that *Nun* would fill the Nile's banks during the flooding season. Then Nun receded and the growing season followed. Seeding would come. Afterward, the harvesting season would bring the food upon which all life in Egypt depended.

The Egyptians paid homage to Nun; fore without the Nile, Egypt would be nothing. The god Nun brought forth the flooding of the Nile annually. Too much from Nun and they could neither seed nor harvest their provisions. Too little from Nun and there would not be enough food for the coming year.

They were now in the flooding season. The Nile covered all the lowlands, bringing the rich soil from the south to its banks. The waters teemed with life. Fishermen would soon embark in boats to capture what Nun had brought to them. They would give thanks and sacrifice to Nun. They needed no temple; the presence of the Nile and its life-giving flow would suffice.

Chief High Priest Badru prepared his chant. The vizier stood behind him and watched.

Aaron and Moses walked into their service of worship. They approached Pharaoh, not before his throne where his power lay, but before the Nile, where Egypt's life depended upon its resources.

Badru stopped lighting the incense and stared. How could mere man dare enter Nun's worship? Pharaoh was part deity and Badru was the instrument to bring the deity of Pharaoh to the deity of Nun. However, these two Hebrews would corrupt the offering. They would anger Nun so that his banks would not produce food. No one had ever interrupted this worship.

Without a greeting, Moses said, "The God of the Hebrews sent me. Let His people go, so that they may worship Him. When He is finished, you will know that He is the Lord.

Moses nodded to Aaron.

Aaron stretched the rod over the Nile River, turning a complete circle. Under his staff, the clear waters changed to blood, like a ripple that grew.

Pharaoh summoned his magicians and sorcerers. They chanted and preformed their secret arts. They changed a tributary to blood as it met the Nile.

"Your God only mimics what my gods can do. Your entertainment is disrupting my worship." Pharaoh walked away.

When Pharaoh entered his palace, he passed a fountain. The calming water would spray his face and hands to clean his body from the city's dirt. He bent to refresh himself, but his fountain poured blood. He backed away, gagging from the smell. Shouting for a servant, he ordered his feet and face washed. "Cleanse me from the city's dirt!" He wiped his hands on his white tunic.

A servant entered the room but responded quietly from a distance. "My lord, there is no water."

"Find some in any jar!" Pharaoh screamed.

"There is no water anywhere." The servant cringed in fear as he replied.

Pharaoh's neck muscles strained against his skin. His voice pitched higher, shouting for his chief architects. They constructed the temples and pyramids. They designed his tomb for when he would lie with the gods and control those who lived after him.

"Begin construction on more canals." He turned to his manservant. "What are you waiting for, bring me wine!

All hastened to do his bidding.

This Moses and Aaron would not control him. He would bow his knee to no God.

A munet woke after enjoying the night with Chike. This morning, she would ensure conceiving an heir with a long bath with salts and fragrances. She called for her maidservant.

Reut appeared, dressed in the simple long tunic of a maidservant, with a tray of oat bars, pomegranates, and juice.

"I wish to bathe."

Reut did not answer her.

"Just get my things ready for me. I especially want those fragrances you purchased from the merchant yesterday."

Reut hesitated, then blurted out, "My lady, there is no water."

Amunet rose from her bed. "What are you talking about?"

"The Nile has turned to blood."

"The cares of the kingdom don't concern me now... Just bring the water from our reservoir to the tub in my chamber here. I will bathe in here."

"But my lady, no water is found anywhere. All water was turned to blood. Check your drinking vase."

Amunet picked up her vase by the side of her bed. Her nose wrinkled as she swirled the thickened liquid. Blood. She brought the vase to the table with both hands. She stood staring but not seeing. What God had challenged their god Nun? Why did Nun not fight back?

"Chike! Amunet rushed into his chamber.

He stirred but did not waken.

"Chike!" She grabbed him and shook him.

He opened his eyes to look at her. "What troubles you?"

"The Nile is blood. Look! She handed him the vase by his bed. He lifted it to his lips.

"Don't drink it!"

Chike swirled the contents in the vase, smelled it and returned it to his table. He stood and hugged Amunet. "The evening was nice, my Kitten." He spoke into her hair, and then sighed. "Duty calls."

Spoiling a nation's water source was grounds for war. How did a country strike war on a God?"

A munet searched the entire house for water. There was none. The loss of water would touch every part of her life.

Amunet assigned servants to clean all blood from the vessels throughout the house. Servants scrubbed the stained vessels with reed rushes and sand before the blood spoiled the containers.

She sent other servants to find drinking and cooking water. They returned without any. Amunet's frustrations grew.

Many servants normally laundered the white tunics. They remained white at a cost of several servants washing, wringing, and drying the clothes by the Nile. They would do none now.

The day progressed, increasing Amunet's frustrations. She walked the garden, sipping wine and seeking calmness.

When she reached the bench by the fountain, she glanced at the swirling ripples of liquid. Her fountain spit blood. After the day of unsolved problems, she could not see another one. Her scream split the air.

Reut came running. "What is it?" She stared at the blood pouring from the urn into the fountain of blood. She gulped as she turned away. Her hand held her nose. The strong smell splashed from the fountain's basin and permeated the garden air.

The god Nun was not pleased. What had Egypt done to make him angry? What could Amunet do to please him?

Pharaoh sat in his chamber, staring ahead but seeing nothing, except the Nile changed to blood.

Blood was good. Pharaoh assured himself. Did they not worship the fluids of the gods because they brought fertility, production, and blessings?

The gods produced bodily fluids just like humans. Anything from a divine body that touched the ground brought productivity. When blood dripped from *Horus's* nose, pine trees sprouted. When *Shu* and *Tefnut* wept, their tears brought resin. When Ra sobbed, his tears dropped to the ground, changed into bees, and brought forth flowers, enabling the production of wax. Ra grew tired and sweat fell to the ground, which sprouted and allowed flax to grow, yielding cloth.

The Nile changing to blood was a good thing. Pharaoh was still in power. This would bring Egypt even greater production of their harvest. Blood would not defeat him. He was in charge. He was god.

The vizier attended to all the needs of the palace while Pharaoh remained in his chamber. Servants reported from all tributaries, canals, and streams flowing into the Nile River that everything was undrinkable. Without water, the Egyptians would not need the Hebrews to make war. Pharaoh's own people would rise up against him.

The vizier called for Chike. "Use the army to dig wells for drinkable water." He stopped production on all the temples, pyramids, and other non-essential structures, to find available water for the people.

He called the magicians.

They stood before him, shaking.

"Turn the blood back into water," he demanded.

They looked for a representative. None stepped forward.

The vizier grabbed one by his tunic. "Can't you turn the blood back into water?"

The magician shook his head, unable to speak. Beads of sweat formed on his upper lip.

"What good is your magic if you cannot undo it?" The vizier let him go and shook his fists. "Leave! Figure out how to get water. Report back to me, or I will search for you." The vizier watched them run from his presence. If he believed they could turn the blood into water, he would make them. Their great spells were useless. Their chants did not trick him. Their magic was without power.

Before the sun reached its zenith, those providing Pharaoh and all of Egypt with fish poured into the palace. "All the fish in the Nile are dead. What should we do?"

The vizier did not hesitate to act on behalf of the pharaoh, whom he had not seen all morning. "Can any be salvaged, at least for the slaves?" Without fish, their staple during the Nile's overflow, what would they eat?

The fishermen shrugged their shoulders. No one had an answer.

Following the fishermen's report, the gardeners and farmers of Pharaoh's nurseries, orchards, and courtyards flooded into the palace. "The waterways that irrigate all Pharaoh's gardens are clogged by the dead fish and the thickness of the blood."

The vizier sighed deeply. He may want the power of pharaoh, but this was beyond his control. He would request Pharaoh's help.

When he entered the pharaoh's chamber, he found Pharaoh worshiping before a shrine to Nun with offerings of grain, figs, and drink. The vizier had never interrupted the pharaoh's worship before, but the nation was in a crisis. "Oh, great Pharaoh." He concealed his disgust from his tone. "Your nation needs water or they will rise up against you."

"What can I do?"

"Did you ask Moses to request his God's help?"

"Wouldn't that admit His control?"

The vizier nodded. The people cared not who was in control.

They just wanted water. Desperation led people to do anything. No one controlled when a mob ruled. They would destroy whomever they thought should be helping them. The vizier kept his thoughts of the future and of his pharaoh to himself.

Chike commanded his men to dig canals, working with the slaves.

News reached him that the Nile crocodiles were moving toward Egypt in large numbers and attacking people. "Why are the people even at the bloody water?" he asked his messenger.

"The people set up shrines along the river to appease Nun."

Chike muttered, "We must protect the people from their own gods."

The crocodiles were dangerous on any day. People went to the river in groups to watch for them. Safety came with numbers.

The Nile crocodile could be ten *cubits* long, weighing fifteen *talents*. It attacked, killed, and stored its prey under submerged tree roots until the flesh rotted. Then it would feast.

Its eyes and nostrils lay on top of its head as it rested in the water. With no visible warning, it attacked, allowing no time for resistance. Its jaws sank into its prey. It killed instantly.

Now it had numbers.

Although skilled with bow and arrow, knife throwing, and stick fighting, Chike's men knew the Nile crocodiles did not die from these weapons. The soldiers could not puncture the crocodile's thick skin with anything unless they hit one location no bigger than a large grape between its eyes. Even shooting that location with an arrow would not necessarily kill the crocodile.

Chike's men must be close and at hand. If they shot and merely injured it, a crocodile's fury would be worse than a lion defending her cub.

The army watched the river for the crocodiles' increasing numbers. The stench of blood made their eyes water and their lungs hurt. Their low boats made them easy prey for the beasts that attacked without warning.

A scream of terror echoed over the river of blood followed by a splash. Chike turned toward the sound, but the thickness of the river made everything hard to see, the waves harder to detect. The soldier was there one moment, the next instant he was gone. He was no more.

Chike looked to one of his assistants in his flatboat. He wondered if his own eyes reflected the same intense fear that he saw in his subordinate.

What kind of God had they stirred up? How could they appease Him?

Chike reported to the palace before going home.

The vizier stood a distance from him with his arms crossed and his hand covering his nose.

"One man killed, no crocodiles killed and their numbers are increasing. I posted sentries to keep the people from worshiping at the Nile. The crocodiles are not just staying in the river; they are swimming into the canals and tributaries."

Chike left the palace and walked home. His steps dragged. His leather sandals were blood-logged from sloshing in the river.

The day was worse than any battle; in battle, he could hope for victory. His eyes burned from the sun reflecting off the blood river. He tipped his head back and closed his eyes. The image of his captured soldier and the scream replayed in his mind. He could do nothing. He rubbed his face and eyes. The man had been a good soldier.

Chike reeked of blood. He had fallen from his boat, trying for a kill. When he fell, his men surrounded him with their boats, beating the river with their oars to keep the crocodiles away long enough for him to scramble back onto the boat. His men had saved his life.

After sloshing around in the river all day, he wanted a bath. A moan escaped his lips when he remembered there was no water. He walked into his house.

"Chike." Amunet hurried to approach him. Before she hugged

him, she stopped, backed up, and put her hand to her nose. "Oh, Chike, how awful! What can I do to help you?"

He looked at her from head to toe, and then looked down at his feet where a puddle had formed from his dipping tunic. "Absolutely nothing." He walked toward his chamber where he changed his tunic and sandals and splashed scented oil to mask the odor of the bloody river. How could he fight against this God and win?

P eople gathered at the steps of the palace. The vizier could hear their petitions from within the walls. He stepped outside to keep them from entering.

Merchants and artisans gathered. "We need water!"

The vizier raised his arms to quiet the people. What could he say that would bring answers to these people?

They grew quiet, expecting a miracle.

The vizier liked the power of control. When he had silenced the crowd, he stood hoping for an answer.

The people tired of waiting. A woman stumbled to the bottom of the stairs. "My child grows weak from hunger. I cannot feed him."

The vizier looked at the limp infant in her arms. When would these people learn to solve their own problems? "Drink wine and refresh yourself. Your son will revive."

The woman looked into his eyes with hope. "Will Pharaoh provide wine for all who have none?"

The vizier faced her, even though he had no answer. Wine was for those of his class. He had no answer for her.

"How will we grow Pharaoh's food?" an overseer shouted from the middle of the crowd.

The vizier did not grow food. It appeared at his table. "Use the blood just like the water."

The overseer nodded.

The vizier had a burst of pride at his plausible answer.

The overseer stopped nodding and objected, "We could use the blood, if the fish weren't stuck in the waterways."

The vizier shook his head and clenched his fists. What did they expect him to do, solve all their problems?

Ptah stepped forward. "My daughter went for water, but she did not return. What will Pharaoh do for our sacrifice to Nun?"

A murmur ran through the crowd.

The vizier could see the people's desperation. He heard their cries for help. He cared nothing for the people, but to avoid mob rule he must offer help. He licked his dry lips and wished for a drink. He turned to re-enter the palace.

A voice from the back of the crowd stopped him. The crowd parted to allow the speaker before the vizier. He fell on the steps at the vizier's feet. "Vizier, my daughter stood outside our dwelling. The overflowing Nile that runs through the streets brought a creature so big that it snatched her before I could see it. She is gone. Gone." The man's voice broke.

The vizier swallowed. "The Hebrew leader, Moses, has brought this upon us. Find him and we will have water."

Murmurs of agreement circulated.

"But will he bring back my daughter?"

The question silenced the crowd.

The vizier did not have an answer. "It is Moses who hurts our people. It is Moses you must ask." This time the vizier did turn and re-enter the palace, ignoring the cries of the people.

The slaves could not make bricks without water. They could not make canals without bricks. The slaves could not work without water.

The overseers beat them, but it could do nothing to motivate them.

Without water, the desert sun melted their skin like fat off meat over a fire. They could do no more. The overseers did not report to Pharaoh. Although some of the overseers enjoyed inflicting pain, they did not want to stand in the heat with nothing to drink. They left to go home.

The slaves looked at one another and began to disperse.

Nathan trudged home with Ellis. Nathan's wounds had healed enough to protect his back from flies. His eyes sparkled.

Ellis looked at his friend. "What are you thinking? We'll have to work more tomorrow when we do have water."

Nathan laughed. "The Lord is getting everyone's attention. Everyone will know who He is. What a powerful God we serve, Ellis. He chose us. Doesn't that excite you?"

"If this is God's good work, I don't want to be around when this God becomes angry."

Dinah spent an entire day trying to soothe Japhet. How could her own baby frustrate her so much? She paced, holding him and patting his back.

His incessant crying made her angry. Was it wrong for a mother to dislike her own child?

When Salome visited in the afternoon, Japhet still cried.

Salome patted Dinah's hand. "He's hungry. You are faint and do not make the milk that he needs. If drinking blood were not so repulsive, I'd tell you…"

Dinah shook her head. "I cannot do that."

"Then he will be fussy." Salome turned to Jabin. "Just like mine."

Chief Priest Badru shivered. His face flushed. He clutched his hands over his torso. He had started his chant that morning at the Nile, burning his incense to worship Nun at the river's edge. Then Moses shifted all attention to his God. Badru had watched Pharaoh's face turn from contempt and irritation to stone.

Pharaoh had called for his magicians and sorcerers, while he, Pharaoh's own chief priest stood by, as if he knew nothing of the magic spells and chants that could perform the same feat. Why did Pharaoh not ask him? He could turn water to blood.

He watched them chant. Their spells were mere pittance in

comparison to the Hebrew God changing all the water in Egypt, even water in jars. Badru knew that not all the magicians in Egypt could do that. Now the vizier demanded he turn the blood to water. No amount of magic could bring back the water.

Badru spent the day reading his magician scrolls, searching for a chant or ritual that might change the blood back into water. This would be his chance to show Pharaoh his importance. It was right that Pharaoh should ask him, not all the magicians, what spells to do.

He had searched all the old records. Papyrus sheets lay scattered all over his table. His bloodshot eyes watered from reading the small writing in the dark room where all the chants, potions, and spells were stored.

He laid his head on his arms on the table for a short time to rest his eyes and mind from all that he had read. He could quote any spell for anything, but not for turning the Nile back into water.

The sun was setting. The redlined western horizon only mirrored what Badru saw when he looked out the east window to the Nile. He could report nothing to Pharaoh. Should he tell Pharaoh and risk his anger, or just not report his lack of findings? It would be safer to appease Nun for whatever they had done. What would Nun want that he had not already given him? Should he appease Moses's God?

Moses only asked that the people be allowed to worship. Could Pharaoh not let them do that? Was Moses's deity stronger than Nun? Did He not prove that by destroying Nun's productivity? What would it take to please the Hebrew God?

Badru's pondering brought no answers; his thoughts brought only defeat. He fell to his knees, scattering his parchments, and cried.

A s the sun set, the golden jackals roamed in packs. The Egyptians heard their excited barks. Other nocturnal animals came boldly during the night, smelling the blood. Swamp and sand cats, foxes, and wolves came. Even from the desert, cheetahs, leopards, and lions advanced. Their roars of invasion, of conquest, of triumph split the night's quiet.

*Jackal* was the god of death. Jackal feasted well that night while the Egyptian people lay in their chambers seeking peace and getting none.

I nstead of the evening breezes bringing cooling temperatures, the night was sticky with humidity. Pharaoh sought relief on the roof of his palace.

The vizier had interrupted his worship, and informed him of all the problems because of the blood, as if Pharaoh had made the blood. What was he supposed to do?

He lifted his vase, empty now of wine, and threw it across the courtyard. It hit the brick wall and splintered into shards. He looked for something else to throw and found the bowl that held his grapes. The bowl shattered like the vase. Pharaoh walked to the wall, slicing his feet on the shards as he went. He defied the pain and looked to the east where the bloody Nile flowed. He looked again at the blood dripping from his feet. He was still in control. He would defy this God who turned water to blood.

A servant hovered by the stairway.

"Don't just stand there. Clean this mess up!" Pharaoh yelled, walking past him to stalk down the stairs to his chamber.

He heard the roaring of lions, yipping of jackals, and the fighting of great animals. His head split with the pain of it all. After stalking his garden, walking his throne room, tossing in bed, and venting his anger at anyone who brought him news, Pharaoh finally decided to call Moses and Aaron in the morning. He could wait. He controlled the time. He returned to his chamber where rest did not come.

B efore the sun chased the stars away, he summoned Moses and Aaron to his throne.

When Moses and Aaron reached the palace, Pharaoh saw them immediately.

Before they reached the stairs to his throne, Pharaoh yelled, "Take the blood away!"

M oses beseeched the Lord to change the blood back into water.

The Lord did.

No one could measure the blood's destruction.

The Egyptian people began to know the insufficiency of the gods they served.

# CHAPTER 9

Seven days passed after the Lord struck the Nile. Then the Lord told Moses, "Tell Pharaoh, 'Let My people go, so that they may worship Me. If you refuse, I will plague your country with frogs.'"

Moses and Aaron again sought Pharaoh at the Nile River as the sun arose. They ignored the smell of decaying fish floating in the water. They stepped through the shimmering blades of rye that sparkled in the rising sun. They walked to Pharaoh, and told him the Lord's message.

Pharaoh ignored their words and listened to Badru reciting his chant.

Moses stretched his staff over the streams, canals, and ponds.

Pharaoh looked at his feet. Frogs covered them. Some jumped, some walked, all moved away from the water. His eyes traced the moving carpet from his feet toward Egypt. No blades of green grass were visible. The frogs overtook everything.

"Call my magicians. They will show whose power you mock."
Pharaoh waved to a servant.

The magicians worked their magic. More frogs arose on the land.

"My gods are no different than your God, Moses. Be gone from my presence!" Pharaoh commanded.

Moses and Aaron left. They could hear their steps as they squished over the land covered with frogs.

Chief High Priest Badru turned to Pharaoh. "Shall I construct a shrine to *Heqet*?" She was goddess of childbirth, creator of life and fertility. Her frog-head symbolized the fruitfulness and new life brought by the frog.

When Pharaoh answered with a nod, Badru lit incense to worship the frogs. The smell covered the stench of decaying fish. Badru's chants escalated to gyrations to please the god.

Pharaoh did not need to appease any more gods. He, too, was divinity. They must please him. This worship was tiresome. Besides, the dead fish smelled and reminded him of the food that Egypt did not have. Pharaoh left before the chief high priest finished.

The frogs arrived at his palace before him. He called for food. As the servant presented his meal, a frog jumped from a chair onto his plate. He brushed it off. As he reached for his wine glass, a frog landed in it, splashing wine in his face. He threw the cup across the table, causing more frogs to scatter. He was no longer hungry. He called for a vessel of wine. Holding his hand over the top, he brought it to his lips.

A frog jumped onto his hand just as the vessel reached his mouth.

He held his breath as he drank deeply until the wine was gone. He shoved frogs off his table, off his dish, off his headdress.

He must be in control. He stood, swiping another from his lap. "Get these frogs away from me!" he yelled. The servants crunched and squashed their way to do his bidding. This frog-god Heqet was an irritant. Why did Egypt worship it?

S everal evening breezes had blown the odor of blood from the Nile away. The crocodiles were still a danger but their numbers were diminishing. Chike's guard duty stopped. He was able to go home.

The rainy season brought cool evenings. Chike stood behind Amunet as they looked out their balcony at the Nile. Amunet shivered as the breezes began.

Chike placed a blue cloak around Amunet's shoulders.

"What is this?" Amunet felt the rich weave.

"A gift for my queen."

"You treat me like a queen." Amunet snuggled inside the thickness of the cloak. "It reminds me of your protection." She turned in his arms to look into his face. "You are my king and protect me well."

Chike rested his hands around her shoulders. "I will be here to protect you, always."

Now he was again able to sleep beside Amunet. The night was short. He awoke early.

What had wakened him from his sleep? Listening, he felt rather than heard movement surrounding him. As he listened, he sensed something jump on his uncovered hand, leg, face. He jerked, knocking whatever it was to the floor. He leaned on his elbow, fully awake now, to see a carpet of frogs covering the floor, leaping to his bed, even on his sleeping wife.

He could only guess that Pharaoh had again refused to let the Hebrew people worship. Did Pharaoh not see that this God of the Hebrews made fun of his gods? Where could they go for reprieve? Could they leave the presence of this God?

A piercing scream interrupted his thoughts. Amunet was awake. The frogs had found her. She jumped to her feet, flailing her arms and wiping her body to remove their slimy residue and the feel of their spongy feet.

Chike laughed heartily.

His laughter incited further yelling from Amunet. "Help me, Chike! I'm covered with these things! Don't just lie there laughing at me!"

"Oh, my Kitten, you look lovely garbed in gods. The deity becomes you."

"Should you make fun of our gods, Chike? Won't they take vengeance upon us?"

"Haven't they already? It is good to laugh after all these serious things. We'll picnic in the desert, while Pharaoh fights with the Hebrew God. Prepare the meal and let's leave Egypt for the afternoon." He attempted to embrace her as she flung frogs across the room.

D uring the day, Adlai taught Hebrew history and Hebrew to young, rich Hebrews who would lead worship in the days to come. Some Egyptians, though entrenched in the gods of Egypt, also came to listen.

When he reached home, Carmel, his wife, met him at the door. "You're home early. Were you not able to teach?"

"We had a good discussion about worshiping the Creator instead of created things. The students could see how annoying the created could be." He laughed.

"Tamara has been showing me all day frogs she wants to keep. I finally told her that when the Lord takes them away, they better all be gone." Carmel hesitated. "They will be, won't they?"

Adlai laughed again as he hugged her. "God will leave some at the river, but when God removes them, they will be gone."

"Good. My head spins from seeing all this movement. One jumps and causes five to jump, which causes..."

"The Lord controls the water and all that live in it. That's hard for the Egyptians to accept."

"That's hard for me to accept," Carmel added. "Speaking of Egyptians, Chike and Amunet are here."

"Did Reut come?"

"Of course."

"Good. We must prepare to leave."

"Leave?" Carmel's voice caught.

"To Abraham's land. Tell Reut."

Carmel nodded with furrowed brow.

Adlai had first met Carmel, when eating at Chike's home. She was Amunet's maidservant. After subsequent meetings, Adlai bartered for her freedom, pledging that their first daughter would serve Amunet instead. Chike had consented. The situation was unusual, but so was their friendship. Once their first daughter, Reut, reached her fifth harvest, she was given to Amunet for service.

Adlai changed from his teacher's robe to his white tunic. "Ready for our guests?"

"They wait in the garden." Carmel followed him there.


"You have welcomed us in our need." Chike greeted Adlai with an embrace.

"What an honor you bring to my house," Adlai responded. "Forgive me, my fountain stays clogged by last week's miracle from God. I miss the coolness of its spray."

Chike shook the frogs off his feet. "Today's frogs sent us to the desert for part of the day."

"Did you visit the pyramids?"

Chike shook his head. "The outer foyers of the temples. We left too quickly to bring offerings for the gods."

After scraping the frogs off a bench, Adlai and Chike settled under a fig tree. "What kind of security do the pharaohs' tombs have?"

"Why are you interested?" Chike asked with a laugh. "Have you plans to rob a pharaoh of his afterlife?"

"I hope not to rob, but to request."

"Request what?"

"Imhotep was Abraham's descendant. He requested burial in the land the Lord gave His people. I wish to take his bones with us when we leave for our land."

"Should I report you to the pharaoh?"

Adlai laughed. "It's not the riches of the tomb, but only the bones of my people's ancestor. A request of a leader second only to Pharaoh should not be ignored. Shouldn't we fulfill his request? Wouldn't Pharaoh Zoser do what his faithful servant asked, if he could?"

Chike deliberated aloud. "Imhotep's bones lie in the step pyramid with the pharaoh that he served. Our people worship and pay homage to past pharaohs. I cannot stop you from worshiping. You do realize stealing from the tombs is punishable by death? If Pharaoh questioned my watch, both my sentry and I could be executed."

"But you'd be honoring a dead leader's request."

"Imhotep could pardon me in my afterlife... When your people leave, if Pharaoh wills, I can reassign the guard at the tombs. That is all that I will do."

"If Pharaoh wills." Adlai nodded slightly. "That is all that I request."

"Why do you speak of your people leaving?"

"The Lord calls my people out of Egypt." Adlai shrugged.

"What plans do you have?" Chike recalled the conversation with the vizier.

Adlai shook his head. "We wait on God. I can only tell you that the time when we will leave is near."

"You know," Chike expressed in half-jest. "You could help me keep my job if you don't take all my soldiers."

Adlai laughed. "Can you stop the hand of the Lord when He moves for His people?"

Chike did not laugh with Adlai. He pressed his lips together in a slight grimace. He remained quiet and reflective for the remainder of the evening.

Within six hours of the frog infiltration, Aaron was treating patients fighting evil, heat, and pain. The evil removed fluids from their bodies, leaving no strength. Aaron's medical mind blamed the frogs. Most inflicted recovered without treatment, but Aaron eased their discomfort and encouraged them to drink. The extremely young and old were most attacked by the evil. His heart told him these people were paying for Pharaoh's contention with the Lord for control. How much more would the people experience before Pharaoh acknowledged God?

B y the afternoon, Pharaoh summoned Moses and Aaron.
Pharaoh stood by his throne. His mocking banter was gone. He appeared ill and did not stand still as the frogs moved at his feet.

Before Moses reached the stairs, Pharaoh stopped him. "Pray to your Lord. Take away the frogs. I will let your people offer sacrifice."

"Oh Pharaoh, when would you like the frogs gone—except for those in the Nile?"

"Tomorrow."

Moses shook his head, realizing that Pharaoh would grasp his power until it killed him. What would happen to Egypt if Pharaoh would not acknowledge God?

"It will be as you say. May you know there is no one like the Lord our God. The frogs will leave tomorrow," Moses said.

He turned to go, but not before catching the look of incredulous surprise on the vizier's face as he stood behind Pharaoh. Moses swallowed a chuckle. By his expression, the vizier could have just swallowed a frog. Moses guessed that the pharaoh's decision to wait until tomorrow was not to the vizier's liking.

Moses and Aaron left the palace. Their steps resounded through the throne room as they crunched over the sea of frogs. They walked as if they did not see the frogs, for they did not. They saw only the sufferings of their people and the sacrifice that would take place soon.

M oses walked the streets where the Hebrews lived. "Relent, oh Lord. How long will it be? Have compassion on Your servants. May we find satisfaction with Your care. Give Your people gladness as many days as You have afflicted us. May Your deeds be shown to Your servants, Your splendor to their children."

His feet plodded through the streets as his words reached God's ears. He strode long into the night, listening to the people as they settled to a restless sleep. May they hear God's voice.

The face of Zipporah came to his mind. Moses was grateful that God kept her from coming to Egypt with him. She would not have suffered frogs on her babies without a fight. He chuckled at the thought, then sobered.

May she desire Your control soon. He covered his head with his hood as the night's cool air seeped into his bones.

Returning to his chamber, he dropped to his knees to cry to the Lord to remove the frogs.

The Lord did what Moses asked. As quickly as the frogs had appeared, they died as if some unseen hand had touched them taking away their life. Their bodies covered houses, courtyards, and fields. The people piled them in heaps. The heat rotted them. The land stank.

When Pharaoh saw relief from the frogs, he hardened his heart.

Phinehas, Aaron's grandson and one of the Egyptian's swnes, reported to Pharaoh. "Your people are weary of the dead frogs in their houses. Some fall prey to evil in their heads, bellies, and bodies. If it pleases Pharaoh, may I request aid to remove all the frogs from Egypt's lands and houses? This will rid the land of the evil that smites their bodies."

Once again, the building of Pharaoh's great temples and pyramids stopped. Instead, his workforce carried cartloads of frog remains out of the city and dumped them in the desert.

The jackals, wolves, and buzzards feasted themselves full.

The sickness brought by the frogs struck some, not all, but enough to cause the people to think of this God of the

Hebrews and wonder why He was different from all their gods. One area of life did not confine His power. He touched all life. None of their gods could both destroy and give life. They considered these things as they watched their god carted out of the city.

T he heat and sun worked quickly on the frogs' bodies returning them back to the earth. The men stepped on the softened, smashed bodies as they slipped, slid, and shoveled. Nathan's team was among those assigned to frog removal. They had scraped frogs off the dirt roads in the Egyptian part of town since sunrise. The tiles that ran down the middle of the street allowed many frogs to collect and stick. Servants from every house dumped more frogs on the road or in passing carts. Other slaves wheeled carts through the streets and piled frogs in the desert.

The mindless job allowed Ellis time to think. Dinah had given birth to a fine man-child. Having another mouth to feed stirred Ellis's need to provide and protect. With his bondage, he felt utter helplessness.

When Ellis held his son in his callused hands, he gazed at the little body. Life was so frail. He shook his head and always quickly gave the boy back to Dinah. It frightened him to hold such a fragile thing in his hand. Would his son's life be grabbed from him, as his father's life had been?

Destruction was what he saw here—not just the frogs and the dead fish but the destruction of his life. Who was he but a slave, someone to do another's bidding? What could he give his son? He toiled for another's gain. Anger burned inside of Ellis, for what he did not have, for what he longed for... for freedom.

Nathan startled him from his thoughts with a clasp on his shoulder where the whip had not touched. "Hey, Ellis, stop for a drink with me."

Ellis straightened from scraping and followed Nathan to the vessel of water.

Nathan moved the cloth that covered his nose and mouth as he drank from a dipper.

Ellis commented, "Such a mess. Makes brick-making seem like a festival day."

"Didn't you enjoy those fried frog legs last night? My Salome can take even a plague and make it enjoyable."

Ellis agreed. Whatever happened to Nathan and Salome, they accepted it from the hand of God for their good. "I couldn't have eaten another." Ellis touched his stomach. "I don't know how many I ate. I was full. Can't remember when I was that full."

Nathan said, "The Lord seeks the attention of His people."

"Pharaoh told Moses to take the frogs away a day later than he could have. Wouldn't you have said immediately?"

Nathan nodded. "We all want control as long as we can grasp it. It is easy to judge Pharaoh; he has the highest power. Power brings the temptation to think that he is in control. He is not, Ellis, and neither are you. The Lord creates, destroys, and makes new. He desires not your control, but your heart. That includes the anger that burns within you. Give it to the Lord. He can give you the freedom that you seek."

Ellis looked at the dipper in his hand. He was not thirsty anymore. "This God hasn't given you freedom."

Ellis wanted freedom. Could he give God control after what He had done to his father? Could he trust this God?

He threw the dipper into the vessel. It clanked, chipping off a piece of the rim. Would he really be free if he gave God control?

# CHAPTER 10

The frogs returned to the Nile. The people continued to worship the gods that they made. However, the Lord had not forgotten the suffering of His people nor His request for His people to worship Him. He commanded Moses to appear unto Pharaoh again.

Badru stood beside Pharaoh and the vizier at the Nile as the sun rose over the horizon. He shifted his feet as his sandals sloshed and stuck in the muck. When he struggled to lift his foot, he glanced at the puddle of mud his foot formed. Although he was relieved that the frogs were gone, he wished the smashed sprouted rye would spring back to life to absorb the mud. He had thought that a moon's cycle would take away the effects of the frogs, but it did not. Holding his breath to avoid smelling the decaying matter, he quickly lit the incense held on poles stuck in the ground. He inhaled the scent of the myrrh.

When he heard Pharaoh's exasperated sigh, he followed Pharaoh's gaze to see Moses and Aaron approaching. Badru cringed as they came near. What would they bring? The guards parted to allow their approach. Moses stood once again before Pharaoh.

"The God of the Hebrews has sent me. You have failed in letting His people sacrifice, just as the Lord predicted. The Lord commanded that I strike the ground." He stretched out his staff and hit the dirt before him.

Before Badru's eyes, a swarm of black specks rose from the place where Moses touched the ground. A cloud concentrated before the men for a brief moment, as if testing the air to find where to go. Then it drifted over the people. The black specks descended upon him. He flung his arms, protecting his face, but they covered him.

The specks prickled his flesh and urged him to scratch. He looked to Pharaoh.

Pharaoh hesitated only a moment before he called his magicians.

Badru stepped in front of Pharaoh. Any movement he made magnified his desire to scratch. He put his hands into fists at his sides and willed himself not to scratch. He dreaded the words he knew would come from Pharaoh's mouth.

"Show this God of Moses what our gods can do."

Badru swallowed with difficulty. He knew of no spell to make lice.

He considered the other magicians. They bowed their heads; none looked him in the eye. He shook his head at their lack of help. He cleared his throat and raised his head to see Pharaoh's expression of expectation.

He groaned inwardly. Glancing at the horizon, he wondered how fast he could run from Pharaoh's wrath, but instead, he kneeled on the ground before him. The repugnant smell of decay filled his nostrils while his knees sank deeper in the oozing mud. His white tunic absorbed the mud, as a hollowed reed would suck up water. He coughed to regain fresh air.

"Oh mighty Pharaoh. We give you our lives." He stopped Wrong choice of words. "We give you our works that called blood and snakes and frogs, but to bring lice from dust can only come from the finger of God."

The other magicians also dropped to their knees before Pharaoh. They murmured their agreement with Badru's words.

Badru mustered his courage to raise his head.

Pharaoh stared at him. His face masked any emotion.

Badru sat back on his knees and rubbed his prickling arms. Fear of Pharaoh's response helped him ignore the itching.

Was their power crumbling? Where was *Geb*, the god of the earth, in charge of the underworld? Why would he not help his very magicians, the instruments of his worship, to produce lice like this other God?

From what source did this God get His power? If Badru did not even know from where the power came, how could he appease this God?

Badru watched Pharaoh stalk toward his palace without another word. Badru struggled to his feet and hurried to the temple where he could be one with his ka and the ka of the gods. He would search again for the answers.

When he reached the entrance of the temple, he scratched the itches that covered his body. He could not enter. He was unclean. He scratched more in frustration.

The answers must wait until the Hebrews' God decided to remove the lice. Then Badru would purify himself and enter the temple. His life would once again be ordered and in his control.

When he arrived home, Sacmis met him at the door. "Did Moses see Pharaoh again?" She scratched at her arms. "Why don't you show his God the power of Egypt?" Her eyes narrowed as if Badru had personally caused her to have lice.

"This is the finger of Moses's God."

"His *finger*?" she screamed. "This God's *finger* controls all Egypt, telling us to scratch, making frogs jump in my food and cover my bed, taking away my water and giving me blood? This

God's *finger* has more power than all the gods of Egypt do? Can't you cast a spell and take away His power?"

Badru looked at her, openmouthed. Sacmis had always supported his power and his position. What had caused her to turn against him?

Before he could wonder further, she continued. "I ate with the priests' wives yesterday. Do you know what they suggest? Perhaps your power has dried up and another magician would show Egypt's power to this Hebrew God. They even thought that we should move to the craftsmen section of town, where we could better support a lower lifestyle." She huffed and paced the entryway.

No magician knew how to make lice fall on people or livestock. If Badru did not make the incense and perform the sacrifices, who would? He had looked into her eyes and had seen sparks. She believed the women. He would not dissuade her.

If this were just the finger of God, of what would His entire power be capable?

Badru did not want to know.

N o one could question Amunet's status as a good wife any longer, because of a lack of an heir. Dark circles had once formed under her eyes as she lost weight worrying about an offspring for Chike. Having Chike home had helped. She fingered the statue on her necklace. Sacmis was appeased. Their heir would come by the end of the year.

When she had told Chike, he had twirled her in the air as if she were a feather. His laughter still filled her mind. She smiled.

Her smile vanished. Now her entire body itched without relief. Amunet threw her wig onto a bench. Shoving her kitten off, she flopped on the bed. She itched everywhere. Besides the heat of the day, her body producing the baby magnified her misery.

Reut approached her. "I have olive oil. Shall I shave your head? I'll massage you with the oil. It may help the itching."

What was wrong with the gods? Why were they not protecting her? Had they lost their power before this Hebrew God?

D inah visited Salome's house. "Can you spare more fat? Every time Moses speaks to Pharaoh, we find that we need something else." She sighed as she shifted Japhet in her arms.

"Here, use this. Nathan will ask the swne for more ointment for his back. It helps on the children." Salome rubbed her arms. "I'd take them to the Nile to sit in the water all day but Nathan warned that the crocodiles are still too many."

Dinah rubbed some of the offered fat over Japhet. It soothed him and he stopped his whimpering. "When I got water this morning, some women told me that their herds are losing hair. The animals rub against trees and stand in watering troughs for relief. Some run to the Nile. The herdsmen struggle to keep them back."

"How do the men work?" Salome wet the bottom of her tunic and patted Jabin with it.

"Ellis seems so controlled by his anger, that he notices nothing else. With each plague, he gets angrier. Just when I think that he could not, he surprises me. I grow weary of trying to make him happy. He does not want to be happy. It's as if he wants to feel miserable. I don't even want him around."

T he vizier sent messengers to all the governors of the provinces. Reports returned. All the people and livestock were plagued with lice. First productivity had stopped because there was no water, then the frogs descended, and now the itching. At the thought, the vizier tried not to scratch. The more he told himself that he would not scratch, the stronger the desire grew.

Throwing his wig on a chair, he paced the floor and scratched his head. The relief was short lived. Once he started scratching, his entire body tickled and stung. He rubbed his torso and dug into his flesh.

What he needed was a hot bath with oil. Commanding his servants, he watched impatiently as they hauled vessel after vessel of steaming water. He stifled a chuckle as he submerged himself into the water, dunking his head to free his scalp of the annoying biters. Shaking his head, as he came out of the water, he smiled. Simple pleasures. No itches. He could conquer this God of Moses. Maybe he would stay in here until Moses commanded the removal of the lice.

Since Moses had first appeared before him, Pharaoh had not consulted the vizier for anything. The vizier had studied Pharaoh's face when Moses appeared the last time. Although he worked hard to mask any emotion, the vizier had seen through the shield of Pharaoh's resolve. His frustration and anger were evident.

Pharaoh ignored the vizier's reasons. He would not be ignored. Moses hindered his plan to seize power.

The water cooled. The itching returned. As he scratched, he schemed. This itching could drive a man to kill his own wife, if he had one. Or maybe kill the pharaoh, if he could.

From the darkened shadows of the house, Zipporah listened eagerly to her father's visitor. Her father had sent for her when the merchant arrived. She had hurried from her house with several servants and her boys.

The merchant leaned back on the cushions, making himself comfortable. "The Nile River turned to blood everywhere, even the waters in jars and wells. The stench lingered for days. No fresh water could be found for man or animal."

"What happened to the people without water?" Zipporah asked from the darkened corner. She knew she should not speak, but she had to know what had become of Moses.

The merchant paused and glanced at her, dipping his flatbread in the common bowl and chewing a bit to continue the suspense. "Pharaoh didn't do anything for them. He retired to his chamber.

The people rose against him. A mob threatened violence until they heard of the crocodiles that threatened their own families."

Zipporah gasped. Her mother Naima squeezed her hand as she sat beside her.

Spurred by her response, the merchant elaborated, "Crocodiles gathered to eat the dead fish floating in the Nile. Reports circulated of people grabbed as they worshiped at the river's edge. Those crocodiles didn't stay at the river either. I saw them swimming down streets in the craftsmen village where water from the Nile overflowed. The army couldn't hold back their numbers." He looked again to the corner. He swallowed his drink and shook the vessel.

Naima rose to fill his cup.

"Oh the people watched during the day for the crocodiles, but by nighttime every animal from the desert arrived. The scent of blood was in the air and they wanted a part of the feast. The animals filled the nights with roaring and fighting. Even though I wanted to leave, I couldn't then. Animals stalked the rivers."

"What did the people do without water?" Jethro asked.

"This God returned the water to the people. Then He made frogs rise from the river, more than the stars in the sky." The merchant chuckled. "Talk about stench—when they died, everyone was looking to leave Egypt."

Jethro asked, "What do you hear of Moses?"

Zipporah sighed in relief. Bless her father for asking.

The merchant chuckled again. "Who do you think started all these things in Egypt? Everyone blames Moses. In fact, when Moses first went before Pharaoh, asking to worship their God, Pharaoh forced his slaves to build bricks without giving them straw. Everyone hates Moses."

Zipporah covered her mouth with her hand, preventing a sob.

The merchant continued. "Moses won't take the blame. When confronted, he claims that his God told him to do it. Many people are ready to kill him. Others find hope in these trials. They say their God will save them.

"Their God seems powerful enough. Can't see why the

Pharaoh won't let them worship their own God. That's all Moses is asking. Many Egyptians are losing their faith in Pharaoh."

Zipporah sighed. She had not considered that Moses's own people would threaten him. Who knew what his God would do next?

She was glad he had obeyed. Had he not done enough? She grew tired of waiting for him. The sheep and goats wore her out, even with the help of some of her father's servants. The neighboring shepherds fought with her over water, something Moses always did for her. Should Moses not take care of his family first?

What little food she had tried to eat collected in a ball in her insides. She swallowed water to settle it. How did the Egyptians survive without water? She cringed. What kind of God would take away a people's water? Surely not the Friend of Abraham.

The memories of the night before Moses left came to her mind. That was not a friend she wanted—someone who was willing to kill her son.

She scraped the bowl with sand, cleaning it after dinner.

Gershom hovered near her. "What does a crocodile look like, Mama?"

"I've never seen one."

The merchant stretched his neck to look at Gershom. "It lies like a log on the river. Its eyes and nose holes are all you see. It glides without ripples or waves. Its jaws are..." He looked down at Gershom's legs that stretched beneath his tunic. "Its jaws reach from your feet to your head."

He laughed at Gershom's widened eyes. "And its jaws are lined with teeth that clamp on its prey like a donkey when he's stubborn and won't let a bit in its mouth. But these jaws kill instantly without any struggle."

Zipporah shook her head, wishing the merchant would stop. What dreams Gershom would have tonight!

Jethro interrupted the merchant. "What products from Egypt did you bring us?"

Zipporah looked with gratitude at her father. She shushed Gershom from his questions and hurried him to lie down on his pallet. She would return to her house in the morning. She was grateful for news of Moses. He was alive. At what cost would he stay alive?

She stroked Gershom's hair from his forehead. How could she quiet his mind from visions of creatures with jaws filled with teeth, devouring people? She shook her head. What imagination this merchant had. Was any of his story true?

She settled beside her sons. Gershom nestled against her. She stroked his back as he calmed for sleep. Eliezer grunted in his sleep on her other side. She felt alone. Her sons' touches only made the hole Moses left bigger. She wished the Lord had never come. No people deserved this much attention.

M ack reached for more herbs to add to the jar of oil. He crushed them in his fist before dropping them into the vessel of oil that would soothe the itching. In his haste to seal the jar, he splashed some of the contents down the front of his tunic. He wished to immerse himself in some before he scratched himself raw.

Hurrying out the doorway to give the jar to a family, he bumped into Aaron.

"What's your hurry, Mack?" Aaron grabbed him by the shoulder to catch him before he stumbled.

"All the children's flesh is raw from scratching. They whimper and hurt. If the Lord has come to help His people, He's not doing a good job."

Aaron released his grip from Mack's shoulders. "Do we know what is good, Mack? Isn't the Lord by definition 'good'?"

Mack dropped his gaze. "But the little ones suffer so. Is that good?"

Aaron shook his head. "I hurt for them. Don't you think the Lord hurts more?"

"If He does, why doesn't He do something?" Mack spoke harshly, spitting out his words.

Aaron nodded, his hand resting on Mack's forearm. "At what

point does a child become the adult, wiser than his parent? At what point do we become wiser than our Creator?"

Mack shook his head. "What wisdom is there in suffering?"

"Will anyone seek God, if he doesn't know he needs God? Pain drives us to God or away from Him. We need Him, Mack. Pain makes us seek Him more than anything else."

Mack scratched, his shoulders hunched. "It is so hard."

Aaron gave a gentle squeeze to Mack's forearm. "The Evil One wants us to focus on the scratching, and lose sight of the bigger battle. The Lord will take us to our land. Don't lose sight of the land because of the bugs under your skin."

A aron watched Amos's recovery. His leg healed. Amos adjusted well to the loss. He no longer apprenticed with Ptah but sewed canvas sails for Egypt's ships.

The lad's mental state pleased Aaron. No evil had overtaken his ka. The Lord was good.

As Aaron checked on Amos's wound, he thought of Hannah. He had wondered how to help those suffering with the lice in the servants' quarters. She could help.

He sought Hakeen, her father. They conversed of Amos's healing. Finally, Aaron scratched his arms with deliberation.

"What is it that you seek?" Hakeen prompted.

"I request your daughter's aid in distributing oil to those in the servants' village."

Hakeen paused. "Is God seeking to bring deliverance to His people?"

Aaron nodded. "Although Moses states that deliverance must come from within first."

Hakeen considered briefly, and then nodded. "God healed my heart by Hannah's presence after my wife's death. She will point others to see God's healing, too. I give my consent."

Pharaoh scratched himself until he bled. He paced restlessly. His thoughts turned to his wife Nitocris. Perhaps a visit from her would appease him tonight.

Nitocris entered his chamber in response to his summons. She smelled of olive oil and flowers.

He motioned her forward. "Oh, Nitocris, you alone bring a smile to my face. You have the noblest, loveliest, fairest complexion of anyone."

"Merenre, you look miserable. Why haven't you soaked in oil to kill off the evil?" She smoothed back his wig to examine his scalp.

He pushed his wig off his head. "Am I really the god that I should be?"

She laughed. She stroked his arms, making his itches tingle, yet feel better by her touch. Her soft skin cooled his arms, hot from scratching. "What bothers you more, the bugs or Moses?"

He raised her chin with his finger to look into her face. "What should I do with this Moses?"

She snuggled closer to him. "What do you wish to do with him?"

"I wish to sacrifice him to our gods, to control the power of his God. I want my own skin free from itches."

She laughed playfully. "You want nothing short of being *Khepri*. He brings newness to everything. Perhaps you need to dedicate a special sacrifice to him. What of Geb? Don't you fear if you don't appease him, your life after this one will be hopeless?"

"I *control* the life after this one, and I *will* control the life here and now. No one, not even this Hebrew God, has the right to treat me like this!"

He pushed away from her and paced the room. "What good are my magicians if they don't stop this God? Do you know what those worthless magicians told me when the lice came?" He did not wait for her to answer. "They said—with respect that only I should be given—'This is the finger of God!' What do they know? Geb and Khepri aren't in power. If Geb can't control the dust at his feet, how can he protect me when I die?"

He paused in his pacing to grab her by the shoulders. "And my vizier tells me Moses is the betrayer from the vision." Pharaoh laughed hollowly. "Will a shepherd from Midian dethrone me? Ha! Perhaps after he removes the lice, I will sacrifice Moses to the gods. He must be shown that I am in control!"

Nitocris's face paled as she backed away from his reach.

He threw his hands up in frustration. "Do you know what my vizier told me today? He told me that my people are losing faith in my deity. How could that be? My people adore me. They worship me. They seek to appease me just as they do Ra."

"Merenre," Nitocris whispered, stepping forward, lightly touching his arms. "You're a spoiled child wanting it all now. You still hold the power of the gods. You must show the people that you are in control even when your magicians cannot do what this Hebrew God does. You must keep it all."

He hugged her. "Nitocris, you always know what to say. You bring calmness. Yes, I must keep it all." He looked down at her fair complexion and gentle eyes, finding the worship he searched. The problems were not so bad when she was with him. He would enjoy Nitocris for the night. He was, in fact, deity.

Pharaoh called for Moses in the morning to release the Egyptian country, both people and animals, from the plague of lice.

Moses stood before his throne. "The Lord will take them away."

The people sighed in relief and wondered what the Hebrew God would do next. They did not have long to wait.

# CHAPTER 11

When Pharaoh saw Moses coming to the Nile, he prepared to demonstrate his control and power. He would offer Moses as a sacrifice before his gods. He nodded to his guards who would seize Moses at his command.

Moses pushed past the guards and stood before Pharaoh. He gave Pharaoh no time to dictate. He asked no permission to speak. He stood straight and tall. "Let God's people worship Him. If you do not, He will send flies. Egypt's houses will be full of flies, but in the land of Goshen, where His people live, there will be none. You will know that the Lord is here. He has set apart His people from your people. The flies will come tomorrow." Moses did not wait for a response. He turned and walked away.

Pharaoh listened, speechless that someone dared speak to him without consent, not waiting for his command. He looked at his subjects. His guards had allowed this man into his presence. They looked at the ground and did not acknowledge his gaze. Would any defend his honor?

He had spoken to Nitocris of the god Khepri, god of creation and rebirth. This Hebrew God would now create flies. He dared to attack Khepri. Did this God know his thoughts and hear his words?

E llis glanced toward the Egyptian town. He stretched his neck and rubbed his back. His eyes widened. "Look at that! What is it?"

Michael glanced where he pointed. "That black cloud? It's hovering over the Egyptian town. It can't be rain during the dry season. And that doesn't look like a rain cloud."

Ellis shook his head as he rubbed his back. His scabs itched as he healed from his beating. "Listen. It's like a swarm of... something."

What had God sent?


A munet was sick, the blessing of carrying a child. Two cycles of the moon had passed since she found that she would finally give Chike an heir. Her body ached with the changes that allowed the baby to grow.

Going to her window to distract herself from the discomfort, she heard buzzing. As she watched, a black mass descended on the street. The noise increased, sounding like the drumming of an attacking army. She searched beyond the city streets for invaders. Where was Chike? Was he safe? What was coming to their country? "Reut! Come quickly!"

Reut hustled into the room.

As Amunet watched, the sun grew dark. Ra fought against the darkness, but failed. The black cloud swarmed. It roared. It descended, covering the houses.

When Amunet could see the cloud closer, she cried in horror, "They are gadflies! Let's cover ourselves with a blanket on the bed!"

The swarm descended upon the room.

Amunet and Reut hid under the sheet.

The flies crept under it and found their skin. They bit their flesh, leaving welts.

Amunet and Reut could not escape. They screamed, clutching each other.

The vizier had watched Moses confront Pharaoh again. Pharaoh had boasted to the vizier that he would restrain Moses, prohibit him from seeking his God. The vizier had listened and waited. Not only had Pharaoh not restrained Moses, but Moses had promised flies. Every time Moses came, Egypt depended upon him to rid them of the next plague. The vizier's bitter smile had concealed his cursing under his breath.

Now, flies crawled over his bathtub, where he had submerged himself for relief. They fell over the side as those behind them pushed forward. They walked on the backs of others. They searched for his body. They found it. They bit and found it to their liking. They devoured his flesh as if taking vengeance on him for getting them wet. They bit.

He swatted. He ducked his head under the water. He grabbed a vial of oil and dumped it in the water.

They swarmed the oil.

He fought them as he stumbled out of the water, grabbing his tunic and wrapping it around himself, squashing many as he dressed.

Moses said that the flies would not be present in the land of Goshen. He would go there. He ran from his house amidst the swarm around his body.

He looked to his barn for his horse and chariot. Where was his barn? The swarm was as thick as the Nile when it had been blood. He ran to his barn. Through the wall, he heard his horses. He followed the wall to where the door was bolted shut. Pushing the bolt open, he hesitated. He considered his prize horse; it had once saved his life. The vizier could not help him now. Covering his face, he left his horse and ran to Goshen.

He darted through the streets, unable to see where he was going. Trapped in sand storms unable to see his hand in front of his face was better than this. Sand may bite into his skin, but it never stayed to devour him. His steps grew weak, causing him to stumble. He rested against a house along the way, catching his breath and trying to see which way to go. When he stopped, the flies landed faster and bit harder. He pushed off the wall to renew his efforts. He shook his head at the thought. He was fighting his way *to* Goshen, the land of slaves. He rubbed his arms, shaded his eyes, and plunged toward Goshen. He saw the black fly-cloud thin and lighten around him as he stepped into the Jewish craftsmen section of town.

He looked behind him: the black cloud remained. He looked in disbelief in front of him: nothing. An invisible wall separated the Hebrews from the Egyptians. Not a fly did he find on his flesh. Moses's God had done what He said He would do. He protected His people.

The vizier brushed at his arm, still feeling the flies. Leaning against a Hebrew craftsman's store, he rested. He looked at his arms covered with bloody welts. Breathing deeply, he had escaped this plague for now.

Who was this God Who had selected this helpless people? Where did He get his power? The vizier shook his head to clear his thoughts. If this God helped these dogs, He must be a lowly God that did not deserve the recognition of any nation as great as Egypt.


Pharaoh pondered. Had he angered Khepri? Why did he continue to appease the gods when they did nothing to help him against Moses?

Nun controlled the Nile and its flooding. Egypt's produce depended upon it. Yet Moses's God had attacked Nun and won.

The frog represented Heqet, god of life. This God mocked Heqet.

Geb, god of earth, controlled all that came from the earth. Moses's God challenged Geb by bringing lice from the ground.

Khepri, god of resurrection, controlled the movement of the

sun. The Hebrew God created lice from sand, covering the sun's power. He defied Khepri.

Moses's God overpowered even the god of magic, *Thoth*. Pharaoh's own magicians could not mimic the Hebrew God's power.

How did this God overpower all Egypt's gods? From where did His power come?

He summoned Moses.

When Moses and Aaron arrived, not a fly bothered them. They walked with an invisible shield protecting them, and stood before Pharaoh on the stairs of his throne.

Pharaoh glanced behind him for his vizier before speaking. Where was he? "Go, sacrifice to your God here in the land."

Moses answered him, "That would not be right. The sacrifices we offer the Lord our God would be detestable to the Egyptians. If we offer sacrifices, won't you stone us? We must take a three-day journey into the desert to worship."

"I will let you go, but not very far. Now pray for me." Pharaoh swatted at the flies, and fanned a palm leaf around him. The movement brought no relief nor did it slow the swarm.

"I will pray and the flies will leave," Moses paused and stared at Pharaoh. "Be sure not to deceive us again by forbidding the Lord's worship."


Badru had attended Pharaoh, summoning Moses to remove the flies. He had heard the request of Moses and the dictates of Pharaoh. No one ever dared to question the Pharaoh, let alone say no to him. Yet Moses still lived. His God must have special powers to protect His man from Pharaoh's wrath.

Badru watched Moses. What spells would he cast? How would he take away all those flies? Maybe Badru could add the chant to his book of spells. When Moses and Aaron had left Pharaoh, Badru hastened from the palace behind them. He followed them, surprised when they did not enter the Hebrew district, but instead returned to Aaron's house.

When they entered, he almost followed them inside without a word. Perhaps he could listen from the outside of a window. No, he would lose his chance.

He called a greeting.

Aaron's eyes widened as he saw Badru at the doorway. "Welcome. You have come."

"In peace." Badru did not know what to say now. Looking down at his feet, he mumbled, "I've come to watch you appease your God and make your request to Him."

Aaron chuckled and motioned for Badru to follow Moses to his chamber, where they removed their sandals, knelt on the floor, and prayed to the Lord to remove the flies from the Egyptian land.

Badru followed, hastily removing his sandals and kneeling too. Aaron and Moses blessed the Lord. They thanked Him for what He had done and what He was going to do. They worshiped Him.

Badru listened as Moses prayed. "Lord, you have been our dwelling place throughout all generations. Before the mountains were born, You brought forth the earth and the world; from everlasting to everlasting You are God..."

Badru watched with open eyes as they prayed. They did not chant. They did not burn incense. They did not appease their God with food, gold, or gems. They brought nothing in their hands. Sometimes they raised their hands toward heaven. As they prayed, he heard silence outside in the streets.

He rose from his knees and ran to the window. The flies were gone. No swarm. Not a single fly. Nothing. Like they had never been. He rubbed his hands over his arms. After the lice had dug into his arms, the flies had feasted on the exposed blood. Welts covered his body. The tormentors were gone! Badru felt like praising their God.

Badru wondered at the words Moses had spoken to Pharaoh. He said their sacrifice would be detestable to the Egyptians. How did they sacrifice? Hebrews emphasized sheep, which Egyptians detested—but how did they do it? What magic did they perform before their God?

Aaron and Moses still prayed. "We are consumed by Your

anger and terrified by Your indignation. You have set our iniquities before You."

Badru felt naked without his leopard skins that he wore before his gods. The skins allowed him to feel at one with the gods. Before Moses's God, he felt exposed. He must leave. He looked to Aaron and Moses. Their eyes remained closed. They would not see him leave.

Badru hurried to his house where he could think about what he had seen.

This God was different. Badru did not understand Him nor know Him, but He was different. Badru had lost his courage to ask for their God's power. He did not share it.


A dlai continued to teach the Hebrew scholars, even though the Egyptian lads had not arrived.

"Why are we spared?" they asked.

Adlai explained, "Our God is separating His people so we may know Him. He treats us differently, but He also expects us to act differently because of it. We are to look to Him."

They nodded but did not comprehend.


A dlai returned home after teaching.

Carmel met him at the door. "Adlai, shouldn't we ask Chike if Reut can come home while God sends the plagues?"

Adlai thought before answering, "Can't God protect her where she is?"

Carmel wrung her hands. "Wouldn't she be safer with us?"

Adlai put his arms around Carmel. "Safe is not always best. I want to protect them, but I also want them to be where God wants them to be. Maybe Reut will show Chike and Amunet that the Friend of Abraham can be their God. Life shows us that we are only safe with Him."

Carmel did not respond.

Adlai led her through the house and into the garden. "When

we had no water, did you worry about whether my tunic was spotless and white?"

She laughed and shook her head. "There were more important things to worry about."

He nodded and squeezed her hand gently. "When we have troubles, it shows us what is important, but it also directs us to look to Who is important."

"So you'll put your daughter in danger to make her acknowledge God?"

Adlai laughed. "There's no danger when we are where God has put us. And the Friend of Abraham has put Reut right where she needs to be."

"Does she know God enough?"

"Do we? The Friend of Abraham wishes us to know Him. We must trust Him to do what is best, even when it hurts."

"But does Reut know God enough to be strong?"

"Can you be strong without being tested? She's my little girl, too, Carmel. The Friend of Abraham is bringing His people to know Him. We must change our thinking; we must trust His ways. Yes, it hurts, but I must trust Him."

# CHAPTER 12

Salome and Dinah finished hauling the water for their families' needs. The morning had been comfortable, but they knew those mild temperatures would not last. They wrapped their babies around them with cloth so their hands would be free to work. Etania, Salome's daughter, bounced at their side, swinging one of the baskets they had made several weeks ago.

Salome directed their steps to a tributary of the Nile where the flood waters had receded. "Nathan thought the crocodiles might be fewer down here."

*Lotus* sprouted where the waters had been. Dinah and Salome dug out the tender bulbs. The tubers were the sweetest when the stalks were not too tall.

"I can't wait to add these to stews," Dinah commented, as she shoved her stick into the mud around the base of the stalks.

"It'll thicken them and fill the hunger," Salome added. They worked in silence for a while. Etania flung mud in the puddles. She stamped in one and giggled as the mud covered her tunic.

Salome heard her laugh and sighed. "Etania."

Etania smiled and tilted her head at her mother, her eyes twinkling.

Dinah glanced at her and laughed. "Etania, you could be a tadpole with all the mud that covers you."

Etania squiggled and jumped higher.

Salome shook her head and laughed.

In the exchange, they did not notice a man approach behind them. Dinah jumped when she heard his deep voice, "A tadpole turned frog."

Salome turned. "Shalom."

He held a staff in his hand. He bent and grabbed several stalks and yanked hard to pull the tubers from the mud without digging.

"That seems easier," Dinah commented. She tried to yank the tubers and fell back on her knees with a grunt. "Well, if I were strong enough, it would be easier."

The man broke off the stalks and placed the tubers in her basket.

"Toda raba." Dinah sat back from kneeling in the swampy mud. Her arms were muddy up to her elbows. Japhet lay asleep against her back in the cloth wrapped around her. She went back to using her stick.

Again the man leaned over. "Here, use this." He handed her his staff as he continued to pull with his hands.

She took it. She dug deeper around the tubers and pried them without difficulty. "Your staff is very helpful."

"That it is. It has proven to me how faithful our God is."

Dinah leaned on her arm. It felt good to take a break from bending over. "How has it done that?"

"When I was a shepherd in the desert, it killed many snakes and protected my sheep from animals that would steal them. When I left the desert, although I left my sheep, I found another kind of sheep. They needed my staff's protection in a different way."

"You are Moses?" Dinah laughed. "Your staff turned the river to blood, the frogs came at your command—I should thank you. The frog legs filled my husband's belly better than any flatbread that I ever made."

Moses laughed. "You have seen the Lord's protection in spite of the plagues then?"

Salome nodded as she came closer to talk. "We look to worship our God soon."

Moses agreed, "Sometimes I wonder if the Lord's people know Him. It's easy to see the suffering but not see our God."

Salome answered, "But He is turning hearts to acknowledge Him."

Moses pulled another tuber. "That is good to hear."

While they were speaking, Japhet began to cry. Dinah untied him from her back. She held him so he could see around him.

"A little one," Moses said softly. He smiled, making faces at Japhet.

Japhet responded with smiles of his own.

Moses reached toward him with both hands. "May I?"

The request surprised Dinah but she handed Japhet to him.

Moses took him in his arms and crushed him to his chest. He sighed. "Smells like a baby. I do miss that smell."

Salome asked, "You have children?"

"Two. Four seasons old and now ten cycles of the moon."

Dinah's mouth fell open. "They're young."

Moses smiled and shrugged. "They are missed. But I will obey God." He handed the baby back to Dinah.

His voice broke. "Toda raba." Moses turned and walked away.


Dinah served the stew to Ellis that night. The sun had long since set. He lounged on the floor as she handed him his bowl and the flatbread. He smelled the stew before eating. "You've been busy today. Is it already the season for lotus?"

"You will not guess who helped us dig." She waited with expectant pause.

"Did you go with Salome?"

As she spoke, she kept her head down but watched Ellis's reaction. "Yes, but Moses helped. I used his staff. He helped fill our baskets."

"Moses! Because of him we make bricks without straw." He stood, his food forgotten.

Dinah cowered. "Ellis, he doesn't want us to suffer. He was gentle."

"How so? Did he touch you?" He looked her over as if inspecting for marks.

Dinah hesitated. "He held Japhet, but—"

"You let him hold my baby!" He towered over her.

She bowed her head to her chest, making herself small.

"Look at me when I speak to you!"

Dinah lifted her head but her voice was low. "He misses his family."

Ellis continued to stare at her. "He should return to his family."

"Wasn't he told by the Lord to lead us to worship?"

"Has he?"

Dinah, although not wanting to risk his anger, could not stop herself. "Have we worshiped?"

He swallowed several times, glaring at her through cold eyes. "You stay away from him. He's caused nothing but grief for me and my family."

"Your family was helped by him today."

"I work sixteen hours every day because he wants to intercede for us. How much help is that?"

"Ellis, you work hard. But how is that Moses's fault? His God will save us."

Ellis grabbed her by her arms and lifted her off the ground. He looked directly into her eyes. His eyes reflected the heat of his next words.

She wilted in his grasp and could not look into his eyes.

He spoke through clenched teeth. "Look at me."

Dinah raised her eyes to look at his face.

His beard quivered as he tried to control his voice.

She shivered as she looked into his eyes. She saw the hate that he held. Her eyes filled with tears.

He spoke deeply and slowly. "Stay away from Moses. I do not want my son touched by that man."

She nodded.

He stared at her as if to view the impact of his words. When he seemed satisfied that she would obey, he let go of her arms.

Her feet touched the ground again. She rubbed her stinging arms.

He left the house, even though the moon was high and the sun would soon rise for another day.

She cradled Japhet to her breast for nourishment but also for her own calm. She took several breaths. She talked to the Friend of Abraham. Who was this man that she had married? Where was the tender man who once cared for her?


D inah and Salome returned to the Nile's waters to harvest the leaves of the lily. A sickle would be the easiest way, but having none, the women brought their knives. They would dry the leaves in the sun on their roofs and pound them into flour for loaves. This would stretch their food and fill bellies.

They stacked the leaves out of the muddy swamp. Other women worked around them, doing the same.

Dinah pushed back a stray hair from her face. "How does Nathan heal from the beating?"

Salome paused to get a breath. "The swne has been generous with the healing salve. His wounds are closed. He only complains of itching where he can't reach. Does Ellis allow you to put the salve on his back?"

Dinah hesitated. "It's almost like he wants the pain to last as long as he can. He holds onto it like it is a blessing, reminding him of what he should hate. I..." Dinah shook her head and sawed at a stubborn stalk with her dull blade. "I fear to be around him... I look into his face and see danger." She shuddered. "He is not the man I married. He used to be tender and gentle with me. I fear..." She did not finish.

Salome had stopped cutting to look into her friend's face. Salome gathered her in her arms.

"What have I done to cause his anger against me?"

Salome squeezed her tightly. "He fights against God. He takes it out on anyone in his way. Nathan and I must pray harder for both of you."

P haraoh watched Moses approach. He would silence this shepherd from the desert. He would give no ear to his God.

Out of the corner of his eye, Pharaoh studied his people. They watched Moses's entrance with fear.

Pharaoh did not receive that much respect anymore.

Moses reached the stairs. He did not wait for acknowledgment. "Let God's people go. If you refuse again, the hand of the Lord will smite your livestock in the field—your horses, donkeys, camels, cattle, and goats. But Israel's livestock, He will protect. No animal belonging to the Israelites will die. Tomorrow, this will happen." He turned and walked away.

Pharaoh stood open-mouthed. What had happened to his plans of capture and victory? Now he depended on Moses and his God again. What could he do now?

A s Moses left the palace, he walked past preparations for the following day's festivities. The people would celebrate the strength and fertility of Egypt. They would praise their Pharaoh for his wealth and provisions.

Aaron studied Moses's face, his eyebrows creased. "You aren't coming home?"

Moses shook his head. "I'll see you at home." He walked past the town to the pastures of the Hebrews. He watched the antics of the lambs as they leaped and played.

He leaned on his staff. *This Pharaoh does not recognize You, God. These people know You not. How long will it take all to know You? It's been many moons since I've left my family. Is*

Zipporah turning to You? Will Pharaoh concede to You when I ask him tomorrow?

He received no answers, but he knew he would continue to do what God told him to do.


B adru left the palace. He must prepare for the festivities of tomorrow. He hurried to the temple. Behind the temple, where the pasture grew thick, the bull representing Pharaoh's deity grazed. The word of the Lord said that all livestock would die. Badru scurried through the temple to reassure himself. This bull was special, picked by Pharaoh himself one harvest ago. Badru gazed upon it now as it chewed its cud. The sleek black coat shone from extra grain and rich grass. It would represent Pharaoh as deity. Tomorrow they would kill the bull. Pharaoh would eat it. He would partake of the deity's essence. He would become *Apis*.

Badru would ignore the words of this God. His god would prevail. All would be well.

He shivered with excitement. This is what he loved about his office. He united one deity with another. He controlled their success. He whistled.

The bull raised its head and faced him as it stood in the shade of a fig tree.

"You will show Pharaoh tomorrow, with your broad shoulders and hefty body, that my power to appease the gods still holds strong."

It sauntered to the fence where Badru held the pan of extra offerings given at the temple that day in preparation for tomorrow.

The bull nuzzled the pan from Badru's hand. It finished the gain.

Badru laughed. Tomorrow it will walk through the entire Egyptian city toward the palace. Its strength would bless the city with its fertility to its people, its harvest, and its land. The people will see what care it has received for this entire year under my diligent care. I will slaughter and prepare it for Pharaoh. By its mummification, it will sanctify the future burial of Pharaoh.

Badru nodded. The festivities would elevate him as guardian of the gods, instrument of their deity. The city would appreciate him. He turned from watching the bull to enter the temple, whistling.

The sun rose and with it, Ra. Ra had once more defeated the powers of darkness. Badru shortened worship at the Nile to prepare the bull for its walk through the streets of Egypt. All was ready.

Pharaoh prepared himself for the ceremony. His white tunic provided the foundation for his costume. A servant presented him with his collar of jewels honoring Apis. It reflected the sun's light and shone with wealth.

Pharaoh paced his chamber, waiting to make his appearance on the stairs of his palace. He could hear the crowds lining the street waiting for the ceremony. His subjects lined up in front of houses waiting the blessing, ready to honor him as Egypt's strength and source of prosperity.

He thought of Nitocris. She would share this moment of greatness with him. She would stand beside him. Her fair skin would show his people the beauty Egypt created.

A messenger arrived. "The bull, oh mighty Pharaoh, is coming."

A servant lifted the crown of horns and placed it on Pharaoh's head. His head bowed under the weight. The horns pointed toward the heavens, symbolizing his strength and the strength of his people and land. He glanced around the chamber. He licked his lips. The moment had arrived.

He walked from his chamber down the hall to the entrance. He stood at the open door, looking down the street for the bull. Badru had assured him at Ra's worship that the bull lived and was well this morning.

Nitocris stepped to his side, dressed in fine linen of white with a collar containing amulets.

He reached for her hand and smiled. They began walking toward the doorway.

She took his hand and returned the smile with confidence. "Merenre, the fertility of Egypt has rested upon us. We are with child. You will have an heir."

He stopped mid-stride and looked at her. Her face glowed with happiness. He wished to embrace her but the bull approached. "You have blessed my day. My power is secure."

Together they stepped through the doorway and into the sunshine. The sun reflected off their jeweled collars. He continued to hold Nitocris's hand.

They walked as one down the stairs of the palace toward the bull.

Nitocris hesitated at his side.

He drew her beside him, squeezed her hand, and let go.

She would remain here as he continued the walk to meet the bull.

The people hailed his presence, chanting, "Oh migh-ty Pharaoh. Migh-ty Phar-aoh." The chant began low, but as more people joined, it became deafening.

Pharaoh watched for the bull at the end of the street. It strode with power. As the bull came closer, Pharaoh saw its enormous size. Its marked head of white confirmed the gods' selection. Pharaoh took a deep breath. This would be a feast worthy of all gods.

The time had come for Pharaoh to meet it in the street.

He walked, his head held high. The horns on his crown raised in victory toward the sky.

The bull saw him and began to trot toward him.

Pharaoh's hands rubbed his tunic. He ceased to hear the chanting of the people. He saw only the bull.

Badru ran beside the bull, panting and puffing, holding a rope that was taut but did nothing. Other priests fell behind the bull as it picked up speed.

Pharaoh's heart raced as the bull charged at top speed. He stepped back.

He saw Badru stumble and release the rope. Nothing held the bull from its charge.

Pharaoh's sandals stayed rooted to the ground. He licked his lips like sand from his dry mouth.

The bull kept coming. It was only fathoms away now.

The priests continued their futile run to catch it.

"May the gods have mercy on me."

The bull lowered his head.

The people stopped their chant.

Nitocris screamed, "Throw your crown!"

The crown represented Pharaoh's power.

Pharaoh threw the crown at the beast that was barreling upon him.

Immediately it slowed, approaching the crown with distrust and curiosity. It circled the horns on the crown, snorting and blowing as it pawed the ground.

Pharaoh breathed deeply. He gave a wobbly smile at Nitocris.

The priests approached and circled the bull.

The bull snorted and blew through its nose as it trampled the crown in the dust of the street.

Badru grabbed the rope dragging on the ground and stood as far from the bull as the rope would allow.

The bull raised his big head to look into Pharaoh's eyes. He took several steps toward Pharaoh, stopping before him.

Pharaoh could feel its breath on his face as it snorted. He could not move his feet. He lowered his eyes from the bull's stare. It snorted once more.

Pharaoh saw its eyes roll back into its head. Its knees buckled under its great weight and it crumpled in a heap at Pharaoh's feet.

Pharaoh stared, waiting for it to stand, but it never would.

Pharaoh took great gulps of air. He covered his chest with his hand as it heaved. First my crown, now the bull. What does that mean for my power? What does that mean for Egypt?

The people stood in stunned silence. Pharaoh backed away from the bull, trying to distance himself from the animal. He backed into the stairs and fell, sitting on them.

There would be no feasting today.

The people left in hushed tones. What did this mean for their great land Egypt and their great god Pharaoh?

Badru stood beside the fallen bull. He dropped the motionless rope.

The priests shook their heads and left.

Pharaoh sat alone with the dead bull. What did this mean? His stomach growled. The heat from the sun rose over his head, and beat on his uncrowned head. Where was the power of Egypt?

The vizier started watching the ceremony with boredom. Every year it was the same thing. His interest perked when the bull started charging. He even smiled. This was one way to allow him power. Nitocris screamed next to his ear for the pharaoh to throw down his crown. He felt disappointed. But when the bull died... The vizier nodded his head, almost chuckling. What entertainment.

He waited for the pharaoh until all left. Then he left.

As he entered the palace, Chike was waiting.

"Word from Pharaoh's stables. The army's horses have died. The stable servants claimed an unknown sickness. I went to see for myself. None survived."

Egypt's wealth rested in these resources. Without horses, they were equal to any other country. They could not attack other countries that interfered with Egypt's commerce or boundaries. This God was leaving them defenseless against attack.

As Chike spoke, another commander approached the vizier. "Sir, I just received word from Pharaoh's pastures for his camels. An unknown evil spread quickly and killed them all."

As he finished speaking, another approached the vizier. "Sir, I am from Pharaoh's merchant section of town. We trade and sell the wealth of Egypt's goods, bringing back whatever Pharaoh desires from far lands. I received word from Pharaoh's pastures for the donkeys. An evil spirit entered them. None survived."

Without camels and donkeys, commerce with other countries

would stop. Egypt would depend exclusively upon what they could grow and produce. The variety of foods, the precious stones mined from the desert, the exotic plants for their gardens, the lions and cheetahs that the pharaoh used for pets would cease entering Egypt's borders. This God stole all of Egypt's potential wealth from neighboring countries.

The words were not out of the man's mouth, before another stepped forward. "Vizier, I am Pharaoh's servant in charge of Pharaoh's meat for his table. These include the oxen used to plant, water, and harvest his gardens. An unknown sickness smote—."

The vizier raised his voice. "Don't tell me. They're all dead."

Without the oxen, construction of the temples and tombs would stop, again.

A month had passed since the flies had swarmed. The Nile had receded. The season for seeding and plowing had come. Without oxen, they could not plant the barley and flax.

Without cattle, what would they eat? The vizier could not fathom a meal without meat. This God hit them where they ate.

What power did Pharaoh and Egypt have left?

The vizier turned to his servant. "Investigate the Israelites' pastures, stables, and lands. Check their livestock. Report to me immediately."

The vizier left the palace. He had thoughts of one thing. He walked down the now empty streets to his own barn. He paused before the door, listening for the soothing nicker and the restless movement of horses chewing. He heard nothing. His heartbeat quickened in rising anticipation.

He unlatched the door and stood in the doorway, allowing his eyes to grow accustomed to the dark interior. The silence alarmed him. He covered the distance to the stall where he kept his horse. He pulled the bolt of the stall's door. The door squeaked open. He blinked, denying what he saw. His horse lay dead on the straw-littered floor.

This God had killed his prize horse.

He fell on his knees. Grabbing the mane between his fingers, he pulled up the horse's head. "My Ramses, you cannot be dead." The vizier, who cared not for the suffering of God's people, wept.

What God would dare touch the only thing that he valued? He did not know how long he stayed on the floor of his barn. His tears ceased, but in their place came a resolution that he would make this God pay. With that purpose, he walked to his house.

The vizier took a drink offered from a servant.

Ra lowered on the horizon and would soon fight the darkness for its power to shine another day.

A servant reported that a messenger had arrived.

The vizier shook his head and looked to the doorway. He returned to his emotionless mask. This God would pay. He would pay dearly. The vizier had to plan.

He turned his anger on the messenger that reported. "What do you want?"

The servant bowed, trembling. "I return to bring you news of the Hebrews' cattle."

"Why has it taken so long?"

"Pharaoh's horses were not available to use, Vizier, we had to go on foot."

The vizier nodded. Of course. All the horses were dead.

The informant, fearing another rebuke, whispered. "Not one died in Goshen."

This God possessed power over everything. His power was not for sale, bought by appeasement, bribes, promises, or stealth. He possessed it alone. He did not share it. How could the vizier get this power? How could he make this God pay?

# CHAPTER 13

After hearing the reports given to the vizier, Chike returned home. If Egypt had no army, he had no position.

Charioteers were Egyptians. They maneuvered horses, at speeds unequaled by the rest of the world. None compared to their training, skill, or weapons. That was before.

Now, without horses, how could they fight? When attacked, the charioteers arrived first, allowing the footmen time to get into position. Could they protect Egypt now?

Amunet found him in the garden, staring into the fountain. "You're home early, my love."

He broke his gaze from the water. "Ah, Kitten, you make me almost forget the troubles of the kingdom."

"Almost," she laughed. "Not with all these welts and scratch marks that are slow to heal or this big belly."

"Our son grows and makes you glow. Your presence makes me forget my troubles."

"But you continue to scowl. What's wrong?"

"Come. Sit with me." Chike embraced her. "Just the destruction of my entire charioteer division."

"No, Chike, not all your work! What happened? Was it more of the Hebrew God? Couldn't Pharaoh just let them worship?"

"Pharaoh is a proud man. He can't let go what belongs to him."

"Do the Hebrews really belong to him?"

"He thinks they do, so they do." Chike sighed. "But let's think of something more encouraging, while I'm here with you."

She leaned against him, and ran her hands over her roughened skin. "How can we be encouraged, when our nation is falling apart? This God holds our lives in His hands. What more can this God do to Egypt?"

E llis ran to catch up with Nathan as he was walking to work. "Have you heard? All the Egyptian livestock died! But not one of ours died."

"The Lord is getting our attention."

"He's taking revenge on how we've been treated all these years," Ellis triumphed.

"Ellis, these people suffer."

"They care nothing of our suffering. They treat us as if we were dogs."

"Why do you hate so?"

Ellis raised his voice. "Do you know what I hate? I hate that I cannot provide for my family. I work sixteen-hour days for what? Four flatbreads and watered-down soup. Don't you want more for your family?"

"You talk about caring for your family, but they live in fear of your presence."

Ellis stopped walking. His mouth hung open. "Why would you say that?"

Nathan softened his voice. "You frighten Dinah. When you are angry, you are harsh. You're angry most of the time."

Ellis swallowed and took a breath. "She's told you that?"

"She's told Salome."

Ellis swallowed several times. "I'm not angry with her."

"When you live with hate, it touches those you love." Nathan started walking again.

"I can't be like you, Nathan. When people beat you, you pray for them and bless God. That is not me."

"Do you think that's me? Peace comes from God. He calms me so I can trust Him when all around is a whirling sandstorm ready to gouge my sight."

"I don't understand."

"If you could trust Someone Who wouldn't move regardless of what went on around you, and if you knew that Someone loved you more than anything, wouldn't you trust Him?"

Ellis kicked the dirt. "If that someone made this evil, I could never trust Him to show me good."

"Would you rather make Dinah respect you or have her respect you willingly?"

"What kind of question is that? I want her respect given freely."

Nathan grabbed Ellis's arm and stopped him. "God didn't make evil. God is good. He allowed evil so you would choose Him over evil. If you *had* to worship Him, what kind of worship is that?"

Ellis opened his mouth to respond, but then shut it. He wanted to keep his anger. Would he lose his family if he did?

B adru walked to his house with his head bowed. After returning to the stairs where Pharaoh still sat after everyone left, he had led Pharaoh to his chamber and helped him into his bed.

Now as Badru walked, he reviewed the events of the past few days. Moses had said that his God would kill all their livestock. He had done what He said He would do. This God attacked Egypt's gods every time. Not only did he attack Apis and Pharaoh, but Hathor who protected and regenerated. By attacking Egypt's livestock, this God threatened their very existence.

Badru reached his home. He sat on a small bench by the doorway while a servant washed his feet.

Sacmis met him there. "The Hebrew God has killed our cattle. What am I to eat for dinner?"

Badru stared without seeing her.

Her voice rose in pitch and a whine crept into her tone. "Are you listening to me? Badru! I can't have fish—you didn't protect the fish with your power over Nun. What kind of priest are you?"

Badru stood to walk past her.

She blocked his way, "Answer me! What can I have for dinner?"

Badru pinched his lips together. He scratched the back of his neck, feeling the bumps left from scratching at the lice. The reminder only irritated him more. He enunciated his words as he spoke, trying to withhold his frustration. "Sacmis, can't you fix something with cheese and vegetables? I noticed that the fruit trees are blooming, surely something is growing in that great garden of yours?"

"I don't want vegetables. I want meat. What happened to the feasting that would take place for Pharaoh?"

"Sacmis," Badru began inching around her as he spoke. "The stars do not speak to me anymore. This God has His finger on my spells and they do not work."

If he had struck her, he would not have received a stronger response. "Your power is slipping. You must work harder to get it back. What will our son do, if he cannot be a priest? You are destroying my life and my son's future. You must show this God that you have power."

Had Sacmis forgotten her quest for dinner? She now had a new target.

Badru slipped by her and hurried through the hall.

"Badru, stop! You must keep your power. What will people think of me if you cannot control our gods?"

Badru ran to his chamber and slammed the door before she reached him.

She pounded her fists on his door. Her voice sounded far away. "Badru, answer me."

He ignored her. Walking to the window, he stared at the

pastures, finally turning green from the Nile's flooding. Their richness would feed no cattle. His labor for the bull was for nothing. He would receive no recognition. Did Pharaoh need him, if he could not talk to the gods?

When the new day broke forth and Ra again proved victorious over the darkness of the night, the vizier waited outside Pharaoh's chamber for him to rise. He reported the news to Pharaoh. Once he told of all the destruction, he fell silent and waited.

The vizier studied Pharaoh's furrowed countenance. He sat with his head resting in his hands. Finally lifting his head, he spoke through clenched teeth. "I want the Hebrews' livestock confiscated. They will be mine."

The vizier nodded, saying nothing.

The Hebrews had no horses worthy of a chariot. The Hebrew merchants kept only a few camels, nothing of what Pharaoh would need for his trade and imports. Much of what the Hebrew merchants used were donkeys. Pharaoh had already taken the quality donkeys. Highwaymen would not even steal what they still owned as an asset.

The Hebrew merchants made better deals with other countries for common goods. They bought their wares cheaply and held on to them through the deserts while the larger Egyptian caravans often fell victim to thieves and bandits. If Pharaoh took their donkeys, he would endanger his own people's provisions.

The Hebrews' oxen already plowed, seeded, and harvested Pharaoh's own food. They did not have enough oxen to plow all the fields of Egypt.

The Hebrews lived in Goshen because of their detestable goats and sheep.

The vizier thought about the Pharaoh with disgust. His lust for control made him irrational. He was obsessed with winning. How could he win against this Hebrew God? He cast his own people to their death by these thoughtless reactions.

The vizier decided he would take horses for the army from the provinces of Ethiopia that Egypt controlled. He would bring camels from the south where their indentured countries paid taxes. He would buy donkeys from the Hittites who had the best. He would order a barge of cattle from the southlands. Their cattle were fit for a king's table.

He hurried. Plowing and seeding time was now. All this he would do without consulting Pharaoh.

He must find the right diplomats to acquire these necessities. He could not have the weaknesses of Egypt shouted to the world before building her reserves and restoring her army. He would ensure secrecy and secure quality purchases with Egypt's gems. He could buy anyone with the right price. These diplomats must purchase quickly and quietly. He would reclaim Egypt's wealth and control.

He remembered Adlai's information of the Hebrews leaving. Recruiting lazy Egyptians would not solve the army's deficit. He would require Ethiopian slaves, used to protect Egypt's conquered lands, to march here. He sent a messenger to bring them.

Time was pressing. The vizier could feel it. This God was bringing something to a climax. Egypt must be ready to retaliate. So far, this God had not fought fair. How did one fight a God who attacked with insects and disease?

The vizier had not forgotten his quest to see this God pay. He must meet the requirements of the kingdom. He must rebuild Egypt's strength. Then he would pursue his vengeance.

# CHAPTER 14

Two full cycles of the moon passed before Pharaoh again saw Moses approach his throne. He sighed deeply. What now? Could he stop Moses's God from acting? He watched Moses and Aaron as they stood before him.

Without a word, Moses flung something into the air. Black specks floated over Pharaoh and his people. He looked at the flakes on his arm. They were ashes. Instantly, festering boils broke out on his body.

Pharaoh lifted his head and glared at Moses. He refused to look at his skin again in the presence of Moses and Aaron. He could feel the boils on his flesh—hot, tingling, tender.

He looked at his chief high priest. Badru's body was also covered with boils.

He turned to look at his vizier, standing behind him. His crossed arms over his chest and spread feet resembled a statue, showing no emotion. Pharaoh looked into his eyes. They reflected the pain that his posture hid.

Pharaoh faced Moses and Aaron. He pointed a finger at them. "Leave!"

Moses and Aaron left without asking to worship. They left

without any boils on themselves, and without healing the boils they had caused.

Pharaoh did not finish court. He left for his chamber, calling for his swne.

When the swne came, he advised applying hot towels or soaking in a tub before rubbing honey over the openings. He did not stay to treat Pharaoh.

Pharaoh turned his back on his swne's retreating form. Couldn't he stay and treat his deity, before his own flesh?

Pharaoh ordered hot water. His servants came but did not stay. Pharaoh felt the disrespect. He soaked in the water until it grew cool. He dreaded putting on his tunic. The tenderness penetrated deep under his skin. When the boils opened, they seeped clear, white liquid, releasing the evil. Indeed, evil was present.

He summoned Nitocris to his chamber. She always made him feel good. She would minister to him gently, reassuring him of his power and his deity.

When she appeared in his doorway, he stood and motioned for her entrance.

As she approached, he saw her face was disfigured by the oozing, seeping boils on her once fair and beautiful skin.

He was startled by a look in her eyes that he had never seen before, at least not intended for him. Her eyes revealed hatred.

He whispered, "Nitocris."

She stepped forward to stand almost touching him.

He lifted his arms to touch her, but dropped them as he saw her shudder.

She vomited at his feet, wiping her mouth with her hand. She spit the next words that he would remember for a long time. "Your firstborn makes me sick. Your hardness of heart makes me ugly. Don't call me to come to you again." She turned and stalked from his chamber.

"Wait. Nitocris..."

But even if she heard, she kept walking.

He looked at his feet. Perhaps another hot, soaking bath would soothe him. "Servant!"

One approached with faltering steps.

"More hot water."

He returned to his bath, but could not remove the emptiness inside him nor forget the look on Nitocris's face when she rejected him.


The vizier had stood at attention while Moses and Aaron stayed in Pharaoh's presence. Once they left, he did, too.

"Vizier," a servant called, following him on the street. "I'm from the five barges that just arrived with your cattle."

"How long have you been waiting here?" the vizier asked.

"A few moments."

"When you left the barge, how did the animals look?"

"We bought only the best, sir."

"Yes, but how did they look?"

The servant bowed his head and lowered his voice. "They are covered with boils."

"Just as I thought." The vizier began walking.

"What should I do with them?" the servant questioned.

"Unload them. I'll check your work later." The vizier spoke without turning around or stopping his steps toward his house. He wished only to reach his chamber and stop the burning of his flesh.


Badru again followed Moses and Aaron to Aaron's home. He did not want be humiliated by showing his boils. But perhaps they would heal him by their God's power? Then he could worship their God. What kind of temple should he build for a God like this?

He listened as they talked of their God's goodness. How could this God have goodness? Badru could not bring himself to interrupt their praise to beg for healing.

The Hebrew God attacked more of their gods. *Isis* was the goddess of medicine and peace. Where was she now?

Imhotep was patron of wisdom and medicine. Why did he not help?

*Sekhmet* was the deity preventing epidemics.

What was the power of this God that overran all other deities? Without the gods, what was left of Egypt? What remained for him?

Badru's courage faltered, once he reached Aaron's house. He turned away disappointed.

He could not enter the temple; he was unclean. How was he to appease any god if the Hebrew God kept him from worship?

He arrived home and called for a hot soak.

Sacmis found him after he had bathed. Her body, too, was covered with boils. "Don't you have any spells that can make these boils disappear? Look how ugly this makes me!"

He remained silent.

"Don't you have any power with the gods anymore? Shouldn't you be worshiping the gods somewhere? Make up a spell. Do something!"

"I've searched the spell books. There is nothing that can control this Hebrew God. I've even watched Moses and Aaron to gain wisdom about their God. He shares His power with no one. What more can I do?"

"You cower to this God instead of controlling Him. You allow Him to destroy our gods. Your power is gone. What power will be left for our son? What power do I have?" She paused to catch her breath. "Your position gave me power. Now I am

ruined. They whisper behind my back. They pity me. If I could, I would leave you."

He listened in silence. He could not escape to the temple. His power could not even control Sacmis. Bowing his head, he closed his eyes and ignored her.

Chike returned from the palace. He had watched Pharaoh refuse Moses again. Moses had already asked four times to allow his people to worship. Chike saw no reason for Pharaoh's continued stubbornness except his desire for control. He understood that need to control. That was why he made a good general. But he did not demand from his men, what he did not give himself. Pharaoh sacrificed his own people. Was Pharaoh the god that he had thought?

He knew if the Hebrews left to worship they would not return, but what would be left of Egypt if they were not allowed to go?

Taking care of his soldiers crossed his mind. What could he do? The boils did not affect them. He could not help his other soldiers and charioteers any more than he could help himself. Despair came over him. What was his life without the army?

He was miserable. His strong physique was marred by tender, seeping sores. Looking at them made him nauseous. He brushed his arms. The dripping sores left his fingers sticky. He wiped them off on his tunic.

He sought his chamber before Amunet could see him. He did not want to appear less of a man in front of her. He curled in a ball on his bed as he had when he was sick as a child.

He tried to sleep but found that even that he did not control.


When the sun rose over the horizon the next morning, no Egyptian overseer appeared to demand bricks. Only slaves appeared at the work site. As they waited, a horse-pulled wagon approached the gathering. The horse was driven by a Hebrew house servant. In the bed of the wagon lay an overseer.

The servant stopped the wagon before the slaves and turned his attention to the man in the wagon.

Ellis recognized the man as the one who had grabbed him from his house and whipped him. He watched him attempt to raise himself.

The overseer winced as he pulled himself to sit. He gripped the wagon sides to brace himself. He squeezed his eyes shut when he reached a sitting position, and expelled a grunt. "No brick-making today." He panted before continuing. "Go to the Egyptian officials to haul water." He leaned back and grimaced. He spent his energy.

The driver of the wagon motioned the slaves to follow. He directed them to various houses.

Ellis brought water into the house of the vizier through the servant entrance. He entered the kitchen. The room was steamy and hot. Wiping his forehead with his arm, he looked for the source of the heat. A fire roared where he would pour the water into big brass pots to heat. The fire was big enough to roast an entire goat.

After pouring the water into the pots, he looked around the room where onions, garlic, rosemary and other spices hung from eaves. He heard a moan from the corner of the room. Searching the darkened area, he saw a servant lying on a pallet.

Ellis went to him with a dipper of water. "Take a drink." He braced the man against him in spite of the man's flinching when his flesh touched Ellis's.

The man sipped until the dipper was empty. "In peace. You must be a Hebrew."

Ellis nodded, although the man had shut his eyes again.

In spite of the apparent pain the man experienced, he spoke, sweat gleaming on his face. "Your God must cherish you. Only the Hebrews were spared this evil." His lips whitened and he drew still. "I wish to know this God."

Ellis did not know what to say. He lowered the man gently onto the pallet and hurried to bring another dipper of water. "Here. Take another drink."

The man panted through lips covered in boils. "I want to know this God," he repeated.

What could Ellis tell him? What had Nathan said? Ellis searched the room as if it held the answers. He finally recalled Nathan's words. "The Friend of Abraham, our ancestor, wants your trust." He gulped deeply of the hot air in the room as he hoped that was the right thing to say.

Ellis studied the man. He lay so still that Ellis was not even sure if he breathed. He lowered his head to feel the man's breathing against his cheek.

The man smiled in spite of the additional pain the words cost him. "Trust Him."

Ellis watched him. His face reflected a hard life in the sun. Lines etched in the flesh around his eyes and mouth, allowing the boils' seepage to pool in the valleys of his face. He continued to smile. His body grew still.

Ellis arose from kneeling and retrieved the heated water. Lifting the water to his shoulder, he left the kitchen without a backward glance. Death won where he had tried to help. He did not know if his words had been right.

The memory of death pushed him to hurry from the room and down the hallway. He followed the sound of cursing and screaming to the bedchamber of the vizier.

Ellis shifted the water to his other shoulder before reaching the doorway. His whip wounds still itched. He stilled his quaking insides by taking deep breaths.

Ellis saw the vizier lying on the bed naked. He pictured the vizier's curled lip, his cold, hard eyes when Ellis had petitioned Pharaoh for straw and less suffering.

Now Ellis could not recognize the vizier's face. Boils erupted around his eyes.

The vizier arched his back. The sores between his legs were raw. He cursed his gods loudly.

Ellis watched Aaron apply honey to the open sores. "Friend of Abraham, relieve the suffering of this man so that he may recognize You."

Ellis stretched his back. He could still feel the sores from the whip sent by the vizier. Why did Aaron help the man who caused the Hebrews so much pain?

"Help me or I die!" the vizier screamed.

Ellis shuddered at the memory of the man in the kitchen. He shook his head at the temptation to feel sorry for the vizier's pain. He scratched his back where the edges of the wounds itched and stared at the open sores of the vizier.

The death of the man in the kitchen brought back painful

memories of when he was six seasons old. They flooded his mind as he stared out the window without seeing anything.

"Father, let me carry the basket." Ellis had begged, wanting to feel important. His father had just received his weekly supply of barley.

His father handed him the basket. "You got it?"

"Yes, Father." To lose it would mean no food for their family for the week. His father stood over him, guiding him with a hand on his shoulder as they moved through the crowded street.

A ruler rode by on his horse, whipping those in his way.

Ellis was jostled by people as he tried to stay close to his father. He could not find his father as others crowded around him. He panicked. Bumped from behind, he tripped over someone and landed on the dirt street. His family's barley spilled, and he watched as feet ground it into the dirt road. Frantically trying to gather the grain, he yelled, "Father!"

The crowds suddenly parted. He could breathe again. As he scooped up the fallen kernels, someone fell on him. His breath gushed from him. His nose was pressed into the dirt road. He was choked by the dust.

"Be still, my son," he heard whispered in his ear by the man who lay on him.

Ellis felt joy. It was his father. He was not lost in the crowd. His happiness turned to horror when he felt the impact of a whip through his father's body. The lashes did not hit Ellis but with each one he heard his father's grunt and felt the twitching of his back and shoulders.

A voice commanded. "Get out of my way, you lazy dog."

Ellis feared that his father would obey. If his father moved, Ellis would be whipped. His father stayed. The whipping continued. Ellis covered his head with his arms. His father's grunting lessened. Ellis could no longer feel his father's breath in his face. The whip stopped. He heard the Egyptian continue down the road, leaving only horse droppings to remind others of his passage.

Ellis remained under his father, afraid to move. The crowd

filled in the gap left by the Egyptian. Ellis was kicked as the crowd stumbled around his father. Was his father resting before getting up? His body felt heavy on him. Ellis had trouble breathing. "Father. You are heavy."

A man finally stooped to move his father to the side of the road. As he lifted him, he exclaimed. "What have we here?"

A woman helped Ellis to his feet.

Ellis reached to get the crushed basket and the fallen grain. "Our family needs the food."

The woman grabbed his face and hid it in her tunic. "You do not want to see, little one."

Ellis fought to turn around. He hit her with both fists. "I must get our grain for our family." He broke loose and turned his head. Then he saw. His father's back held no skin. The insides lay open. Ellis stared. He shook his head and screamed, "No!" This back could not be his father's. He fell to his knees by his father's head and grabbed his face in his hands. He cradled it in his arms. "Wake up, Father. Don't be so still!"

The man, attempting to move his father's body, protected the two as the crowd moved around them.

In the days and years to follow, Ellis continued to see. He saw what Egypt had done to his father and he remembered. The seed of hatred planted in his young child's heart had only grown to bear fruit. He would not forget.

Now Ellis shook his head. His sightless staring allowed him to see deeper things. Holding the man in the kitchen as he died was like re-living his father's death. The wound of when he was six seasons old had not healed, because he would not let it.

Recognizing the voice of the vizier as the official on the horse so long ago, Ellis had felt again the death of his father. Ellis thought seeing the open sores on the vizier would make him satisfied. Vengeance would be complete. But it was not. He felt empty. His hate left a hole that could not be filled.

Hannah helped Aaron treat the Egyptians. She applied honey to the open sores of the Egyptian woman.

"What's her name?" she asked.

A young Hebrew servant stood wringing her hands beside her mistress. "Amunet."

Amunet's baby swelled her middle, and the heat appeared to sap her of energy. She moaned, wiping her head, then lay still.

Glancing at Reut to make sure she understood, Hannah explained, "Cover each boil with this honey heated with herbs. The honey keeps the evil away and brings healing."

Hannah placed her cool palm lightly on Amunet's fevered forehead. "May the Lord watch over you and your baby until He delivers you." What more could she tell a people who did not know the Lord?

She walked quickly to the next house assigned by Aaron. She knew the craftsmen section of town well, but Aaron's description of the house did not prepare her for her feelings when she saw it. She knew this house. Hannah stopped. She did not want to enter it. She shook her head and wondered why Aaron had given her this house. He must be mistaken. She would help anyone else but not them.

Ptah, the sculptor, lived here. How could she help this man after he dismissed her brother following his accident? She dragged her feet to the door. Hoping no one would answer, she knocked softly.

A child came to the door. She was not covered with boils as badly as some. She led Hannah to a room where Ptah's wife lay moaning. Hannah looked at her suffering and remembered her own mother as she died. She wished someone had helped her mother. She thrust her shoulders back and resigned herself to her duty.

She instructed the girl, "Put water over the fire. Bring honey and a clean cloth."

Hannah knelt by the woman whose suffering only accentuated the lines on her furrowed brow. She felt like a traitor to her brother by helping the family that hurt him. When she thought about Amos and his hardship, anger bubbled up. She wiped the sores with hard strokes.

The woman whimpered and arched in pain, calling to her gods to save her.

Hannah paused to wipe more gently. Her father's words returned to her. "We must show all that the Friend of Abraham can be everyone's friend." She blushed at the memory.

Hannah had asked her father, "How do you continue to work for a man who maimed your son?"

"Hannah, bitterness and anger will consume you. No one else will notice until there is nothing left on the inside."

"But how do you not let it bother you?"

He held her hand in his large one and stayed silent for a long time.

She thought he would not answer.

Finally, he spoke, "When your mother died, I wanted to die, too. I was angry at the Lord for letting her die." His voice cracked. He paused as he swallowed several times. He raised his eyes to look into hers. His were filled with tears. "I can still hear your mother's voice, 'Love the Lord with all your heart, with all your mind, with all your ka. Do not let the Evil One win. He will take your strength. Let the Lord be your strength.'

"When the Evil One slips into my mind to make me doubt the Lord's goodness, I recount His goodness until I can hear the Evil One's voice no more. After a long time, the Evil One stopped pestering me. The Lord fights. I just obey."

Hannah sighed. It was for her to obey, as well. She counted ways the Lord was good as she put hot cloths on Ptah's wife. She hoped that if she obeyed, the anger inside her would not consume her.

Phinehas sighed and wiped his forehead with his cloak. Some of the boils had drained, but others showed signs that the evil stayed within. He must open them to release the evil.

A woman had come to help the family. She put honey on the

open wounds. "This will make the evil leave and you will be able to rest."

The patient started to fret, but the woman spoke again, "You must be proud of your little one. She has warmed towels and kept the fire going since I told her how much the warmth will help you."

Ptah's wife opened her eyes. They rested on her daughter at her feet. "She's a good help."

"She cares for you."

The woman appeared too taxed to speak again.

The maiden turned to the seated girl. "Place some onions, garlic, and salt in a pot covered with water. You can make a broth to keep her from losing too much liquid."

The girl nodded without speaking as Phinehas watched. The room was warm. He looked to the fire and wiped his hands down his tunic.

The maiden was a Hebrew, for not one boil marred her beauty. Her lowly birth showed in her hand-woven tunic and sandal-less feet. She was a Hebrew serving Egyptians. Why?

Phinehas was Hebrew, but he would not call what he did for the Egyptians serving. He took as much of their wealth as he could get. Many Egyptians requested his swne skills, because they believed his grandfather's training gave him special powers. Phinehas added the spells and chants that the Egyptians expected. He could then ask for any payment that he wished. He dined with the rich and was favored by their gifts.

He used his swne position to speak directly to this maiden. "Help me drain some of these wounds."

She nodded.

Ptah's wife winced, crying for the help of her gods. Her tunic was drenched by her sweat.

Phinehas stood over the maiden as she applied pressure through the hot cloth. "Here, like this." He pushed gently on her fingers. "Start in the middle of the boil and push the evil to the edges. See how the cloth absorbed the evil?"

She nodded. Her fingers quivered under his touch.

Phinehas found another boil on the woman's arm that required draining. "Here, try this one." Again, he lightly touched her fingers as she applied pressure to the sore.

Ptah's wife screamed.

The maiden instinctively pulled back, but Phinehas's hand held hers over the wound. She turned to look into his face.

His face was right beside hers as he leaned over her. He looked into her eyes.

She blushed.

Phinehas saw her turn crimson as he continued to hold her hand longer than was necessary for the boil to drain. "You are doing fine."

She looked back at his fingers still holding hers.

He reluctantly let go, almost laughing at her innocence. He had been to many dinner parties for wealthy Egyptians whose entertaining dancers left nothing to the imagination but gave him great pleasure for his memories. He shook his head as he stepped away from her, blushing as well. Her blush came from innocence, his from a stained past.

Even as he stepped back, he wanted to know this maiden. "What made you help this woman?"

She touched her throat and stroked it. Moving the cloth to another area, she answered, "The swne asked me to help."

"My saba? How do you know my grandfather?"

"Aaron's your saba? But he is Hebrew."

Phinehas laughed at her puzzled expression. "He is Hebrew, yes, and so am I."

She hesitated before saying, "The swne is Hebrew, but you look Egyptian."

Phinehas smiled. "My training comes from my saba. He gives me the secrets of his God that help me to treat the wealthy with success."

Shaking her head, the maiden responded, "The swne succeeds, because he listens with his heart."

Never had a woman corrected him. Phinehas studied her. "What gives you strength?"

She tipped her head to the side. "Could you be the swne's grandson and not know? It's why I help."

Studying her face, he wished to hear her say more. Her words showed an active mind. He grew weary of Egyptian maidens who spoke of imaginary gods with no power. He thought to speak again, but Ptah's wife moaned, interrupting their conversation.

The maiden hastened to stir the fire and find more linen cloths.

Phinehas lingered, so that he could speak to her again, but the maiden slipped away. He had not even learned her name.

Zipporah longed for news about Moses. She spent her days watching the western horizon for any traveler who might tell her news of her husband. The brown hills that she could not leave before became a wall that kept her trapped.

She kept busy lest she fall apart. Why didn't any news come? Was Moses still in danger? Why did the Lord take so long to bring His people to worship?

She heard her father approach her doorway.

"Blessings, my daughter."

"Blessings on you, my father. What brings you here?"

"A merchant eats with us. I thought you'd want to listen. My servants will watch your herds. You're needed."

"Is something wrong?"

"Be at peace. We'll hear the news together."

After eating, they settled around the fire. Jethro sipped from his vessel. "Tell us what happens in Egypt."

Zipporah listened from the outer area of the fire where she and her mother quieted the children.

"You heard of the Nile turned to blood?" With Jethro's nod, the merchant continued. "All the fish died. I miss the fish. It will take many seasons for them to return.

"The frogs came, but when Pharaoh told Moses to take them

away, they just died. What a stench they made! I never want to touch the river again.

"Lice inflicted man and beast after that. We fought the cattle over water troughs to soak in." He chuckled.

"What could this God do next? I fled Egypt lest evil inflict me. I camped on the outskirts of town, catching news from all the merchants running from Egypt.

"A black cloud hovered the Egyptian town. I learned later that flies feasted on the blood exposed from the scratching of the lice. But no flies came to the land of Goshen." He paused in his recitation, chuckling. "Glad I missed that one!

"One merchant overtook me *without* donkeys. He'd lost all his livestock and donkeys. He ran from Egypt with whatever he could carry on his back. He said that he'd be safer in another country.

"Egypt's power is crumbling. Don't know how much more they can take. But Pharaoh still says no to the Hebrew God."

Zipporah listened. The Lord was doing great things. Moses was showing his people who their God was. Zipporah pushed her shoulders back and held up her chin. She wished to be with Moses, to watch this God do great things because her husband had obeyed.

Zipporah returned to her house. Moses's boys grew before her eyes without the influence of their father's gentle ways. Eliezer was walking. He did not hear his father's prayers. Could he even remember him? Zipporah stifled a sob. Her sob turned to a gasp as Eliezer toddled toward the cooking fire. She grabbed him harshly. "My son, how can you follow your father's footsteps when he's not here to show you the way?"

Tonight would be another long night. Tears flowed and her mind replayed the news of her husband. Moses still lived. Bless his God. But oh, it was hard to thank his God for the distance between them—not just steps apart, but gods apart.

Carmel entered Amunet's house. All was quiet. No servants moved. She remembered her way through the house. Had it been twelve harvests already since she had worked as servant here before her husband redeemed her? She entered the chamber where her former mistress lay on the bed. Reut hovered over her.

Carmel approached the bed. "Reut, when I heard about the boils, I had to know how you were. You don't have any?" She searched her daughter's face and arms.

"None. I'm not an Egyptian."

"How is Amunet? I didn't realize she was with child."

Their conversation was interrupted by a groan from the bed.

"Amunet, it's Carmel. Has the swne come?"

Reut answered for her. "Aaron didn't recommend tub soaks for her condition, but hot cloths. They cool quickly. It's hard to keep them hot enough to draw out the evil."

"Aaron came? Does she believe in our God? Have you told her about Him?"

Reut looked at her hands. "All the Egyptian swnes have boils. They hurt too much to help."

Carmel could not hold her excitement. "Does Amunet believe?"

"No, Mother. I don't know how to tell her. She doesn't know Him."

Carmel nodded. "Tell her. Time is fleeting. Father believes the time is short before we leave."

"What do you mean, leave?" Reut choked on the words.

"The Lord prepares us to return to the land of our fathers. Amunet could leave with us. Ask her when the time is ripe."

Reut looked at her feet.

Carmel held her daughter's arms. "You don't want to come?"

Reut shook her head.

"The Lord prepares all His people to be ready when He is."

Amunet groaned. Carmel reluctantly turned from her daughter to place a cool hand on Amunet's forehead. She wrung a cloth from the basin on the table by the bed and placed it on the sores. "Amunet, rest calmly in the arms of Him who can truly hold you."

Amunet turned to her side revealing more sores on her back and legs.

Carmel faced Reut. "Get hotter water. Let's draw the poison out before she awakes."

Reut hurried to obey.

Carmel watched her daughter's retreating figure, praying that Reut would be ready to leave when God called His people.

P hinehas passed Aaron on the street. "Blessings, Saba."
Phinehas paused and leaned against one of the craftsman's houses. "Saba, who is the maiden who helps Ptah's family?"

Aaron's eyes twinkled and he laughed. "You've met my angel of mercy. She helps me with my patients."

"Tell me about her."

"I removed her brother's leg; she nursed him back to health. In fact, I took a wood-carver to their house recently and fitted him for a wooden leg. He can now do things most take for granted." Aaron looked at Phinehas and laughed. "But I digress. You asked about the maiden. Because of her gentle ways, I've asked her help with these boils. She helps the family responsible for her brother's loss of leg."

"Why? I'd ignore their suffering."

Aaron looked at Phineas. "Would you?"

"How do you help someone who destroyed your life?"

"You obey the Friend of Abraham. Pain pushes you to God or drives you from Him. There's no middle ground. Either you trust in the God Who does not move or your heart becomes unmovable."

Phinehas nodded without understanding. Is that where she found her inner strength?

D inah and Salome returned to the banks of the canals to collect castor-berries.

Etania swung her basket in circles over her head. She ran

ahead to pick the lower berries. Looking at her fingers, she wrinkled her nose. "Ima, these stink."

Salome put Jabin on the ground under the tree. "That's the oil we'll boil from them."

"You mean we want it to stink?"

"We light the oil when we wait for Abba."

Etania resumed her picking.

Dinah started to pick under the tree. "Most of the berries are high and hard to reach."

A man spoke, "Here, let me help."

Dinah came out from the tree's overhanging limbs.

Moses explained, "I noticed others were harvesting berries, so I brought this cloth to help."

Ellis's words ran through her mind. She hesitated.

Salome emerged from her tree. "Shalom, Moses."

He gestured to the sheet he held. "If you spread this under the tree, I'll hit those high berries down with my staff."

Salome reached for it. "It'll soil the sheet."

At his nod, she spread it out. Clumps of berries fell as he beat the higher branches.

Etania jumped up and down. "It's raining berries!"

"Only better," Moses laughed. "You don't have to touch the smelly things."

Moses beat the branches with his staff. When no more berries fell, he stooped to lift one of the sheet corners. Dinah and Salome grabbed the other corners.

Etania ran through the berries to reach the fourth corner.

"Oh, Etania." Salome failed to stop her in time.

"*Ima*, I just made oil on my feet. Does that mean my feet will light the path where I walk?"

Dinah giggled while they all walked together beyond the tree's growth.

Etania grabbed her mother's hand. "We'd never have picked this many berries. Would we, ima? Not without Moses's help."

Salome nodded to Moses with a smile. "Never."

Etania chattered, "We must praise God in sending him our way, shouldn't we?"

Salome nodded. "We have much to praise God for sending Moses our way."

Japhet started to fuss. Dinah hesitated to take him off her back. She could not refuse Moses if he asked to hold him again. But she knew she would anger Ellis. Japhet cried louder.

"Does the little one want to be tossed in the air?" Moses asked, his eyes twinkling.

Etania jumped. "I do!"

Moses threw her up and caught her. She squealed with delight.

Dinah watched Moses's face. It glowed with pleasure. He did not squeal, but if that was acceptable he would have. Why was Ellis so angry at him?

Jabin laughed with his sister. "Me! Me!"

"Do you want a turn?" Moses turned to him.

His chubby hands reached toward Moses. Moses hugged him tightly. "You have the baby smell of growing up." He lifted him above his head.

Jabin giggled and squealed.

The laughter in Jabin's voice could not compare to the laughter in Moses's eyes. Dinah swallowed deeply and turned to take Japhet off her back. She could not allow Moses to hold him, but it would break her heart to refuse to do so.

After catching Jabin for the last time, Moses handed him back to Salome.

"You've reminded me of why I obey." Moses turned to look at Dinah.

She hesitated and held Japhet close to her.

He nodded but did not ask to hold him. "Toda raba," he said as he walked away.

Dinah watched him go with tears in her eyes. Why was it so hard for *her* to obey?

P haraoh summoned Moses and Aaron before his bed. He raised himself on his elbow and spoke. "Remove these boils from my people at once."

Moses could read Pharaoh's heart on his face, his fevered stare, his clenched jaw, and his squared shoulders. Pharaoh had not repented. Moses did not ask to worship.

As they walked home, Aaron mentioned his discussion about pain with his grandson.

Moses responded. "Pain has caused Pharaoh to turn away from God. What will that cost the Egyptian people?"

# CHAPTER 15

One cycle of the moon passed after the Lord sent the boils, but He did not forget His people nor their suffering. Moses entered Pharaoh's palace. He spoke the Lord's word. "Let My people go, so that they may worship Me, or I will send the full force of My plagues against you and your people. You will know that there is no one like Me in all the earth. For by now I could have destroyed you.

"But I have raised you up for this very purpose, that I might show you My power and that My name might be proclaimed in all the earth.

"You set yourself against my people and will not let them go. Therefore, at this time tomorrow, I will send the worst hailstorm that has ever fallen on Egypt, from the day it was founded until now.

"Order your livestock and everything in your fields to shelter, because the hail will fall on every man and animal. They will die."

The order spread before Pharaoh issued it. Those who feared the Hebrew God hurried to tell others. They remembered the boils, allowing pain to teach them. This Hebrew God warned them. They would heed. But some ignored the warning and left their slaves and livestock in their fields.

No one had waited for Pharaoh's command. Moses did not wait permission to speak. The rulers, when they heard what the Hebrew God said, did not wait to be told by him what to do. Where was the respect due his lordship? Where was the dependence upon his word? Pharaoh stomped out of his court.

He paced his chamber.

The vizier requested entrance. He bowed low. "Oh, mighty Pharaoh, what would be your favor on this matter of your servants in the field?"

"What do I care of the servants in the field? Don't my fields need to be watered?"

The vizier lowered his head. "Indeed, without water, the barley will wilt by midday."

"What is the state of the barley?"

"They have headed."

"And the flax?"

"They harvest in thirty days. "The question, oh, mighty Pharaoh, is not whether the plants need water but whether the Hebrew God will do what He said."

Pharaoh raised his voice. "Could it be so bad? It's not even the time for rains to come."

"Can we risk it if it comes?" countered the vizier.

Pharaoh stared at the vizier as if he was at fault.

The vizier stared back without fear.

Pharaoh used to make people tremble at his command, wait for his voice, listen to his orders. Now he was treated as nothing. His people did not wait for him to speak. His own vizier did not respect him. He turned abruptly from the vizier and stalked to a chair. He sat and pointed to another chair for the vizier to sit beside him.

The vizier suddenly stiffened. "You wish me to sit in your presence, oh Pharaoh?"

Pharaoh answered with a small nod.

The vizier sat on the edge of the seat and waited.

After a long moment, Pharaoh spoke in a defeated voice, "Tell me about my kingdom."

"What do you wish to know?"

Pharaoh slouched, resting his head in his hands. "Tell me all."

The vizier took a deep breath and drummed on the armrest of his chair for a moment. He began, "The army is all Hebrews, our charioteers unable to respond."

"How would Egypt defend herself from an uprising?"

"If these foolish people stopped asking and just went to worship, we could not stop them," the vizier answered flatly.

Pharaoh nodded. "What have you done?"

"Commissioned troops from Ethiopia."

"When will they arrive?"

"They should arrive any day now. But that is another problem."

Pharaoh sat up straight. "Yes?"

"All imports have ceased."

"All?"

"The Egyptian merchants fled Egypt after the livestock were destroyed. They do not come back. News has spread. People fear to come."

The vizier shifted in his chair, then continued, "I paid dearly from Egypt's reserves to replace the livestock. The livestock came just before the boils, along with the horses for your charioteers. No one enters our borders unless coerced by gems and a promise of protection. No one tempts the Hebrew God."

Pharaoh raised his head and looked directly at the vizier. "What does that mean?"

"If Egypt cannot grow her own food, she won't have any."

"So that brings us back to tomorrow. What we have in the field must live." Pharaoh stood.

"Yes."

Pharaoh finally answered the question that the vizier had asked at the beginning. "We cannot lose our crop. We must water. What choice do we have?"

The vizier confirmed. "We have none."

Pharaoh repeated with more conviction. "Then water."

The vizier stood.

Pharaoh turned his back to the vizier. "What if I let them worship?"

The vizier waited until Pharaoh turned to look him in the eye. "If you let them go?"

Pharaoh nodded. "Could Egypt be saved?"

"If you let them go, they will not come back. They will go to their own land. You will have lost your entire work force."

"And Egypt?"

"Will be no more," the vizier stated without feeling.

"Then what choice do I have?"

"You have none."

Pharaoh asserted again, "Then water tomorrow." He turned to the window.

The vizier began to leave again.

Before the vizier reached the door, Pharaoh spoke. "How would you stop this God?"

"Kill Moses."

"How would that stop his God?"

"He is His instrument."

"Do so."


The vizier sighed. Finally, Pharaoh would do something right. Pharaoh had not ordered Aaron's death, but the vizier would finish both messengers from this God.

He sent a messenger to the craftsmen section of town. He fidgeted at the window as he waited for the response, rubbing his hands with pleasure. This was something that he would enjoy. He could not think of when he had last felt so light and free. Maybe when his mother died...

The knock at the door did not startle him. He acknowledged the messenger at the door, but concealed his smile. He must not appear too anxious. He paused in his false perusal of parchments in front of him.

The tall man entered and stood, waiting before his table.

The vizier studied the man.

His cloak was askew as if he had grabbed it off the floor and thrown it over his body. His dark beard hid his facial features, although the look of his eyes spoke of darkness. After a careful examination, the vizier stood. "You know Moses."

The man nodded.

"Pharaoh wants him killed."

"Why not use Pharaoh's guards?"

"We cannot have an uprising of the people."

The man's gruff, deep voice demanded, "The price will be high."

The vizier held a small bag of gems in his hand. He shifted it from one hand to another, making it rattle. "It must be soon. Before the thunderstorms hit the land."

The man laughed. "What if the thunderstorms come without Moses to stop them?"

"You will not live to see the next day."

The man stopped laughing. "I will need to pay my assistants. That is enough for me, but what of them?"

The vizier loosened the tie at the top of the bag and shook the gems into his hand. Slaves cut the stones from Egypt's mines deep in the desert's hills.

The vizier watched the man's eyes widen. "It is enough." He gathered the gems, pulled the tie shut, and closed his fist around the bag. "Make sure he is dead. I do not want a second resurrection of this man."

The man's smile returned. "When I finish a job, it is finished."

The vizier turned his back to him. His hand rested on the blade at his side. Trust was not what he did well. "You may go."

The man started to leave. When he reached the doorway, the vizier stopped him. "While you're at it, kill Aaron, too." He looked out the window. He could feel the man's greed. "I will pay you well."

A dlai looked over his fields from the top of his roof.
Tamara bounded up the stairs. *"Abba,* you're home early!"

"The Lord spoke to Pharaoh again today."

"What will He do this time?" Tamara asked, excitement in her voice.

"The Lord will send the worst thunderstorm there has ever been in Egypt."

Tamara bounced on her toes. She looked over the fields that held their harvest. "Has it ever stormed this time of year?"

Adlai sighed. "Never."

"Will the storm bring enough rain to water without the *shadufs?"*

Servants irrigated his fields by using shadufs. They filled buckets from the canals, then swung the attached arms of the balanced buckets over rows and emptied the buckets. If canals were not close enough, brick reservoirs held water for irrigation. Many servants worked most of the day to water the fields.

"Tamara, I won't be sending my servants to the fields tomorrow."

"Why not?"

"The Lord said that the hailstorm would kill them."

Tamara's eyes grew as big as figs.

Adlai laughed at her expression. "Never fear, Tamara, they will be safe. The Lord has warned us and we will heed the warning."

"But what about our neighbors' fields? They are Egyptians. Will their servants be killed?"

"They have heard the Lord's words. We cannot make others obey."

Her voice trembled. "Will Reut be safe?"

"She will stay inside with Amunet." Adlai put his arm around her shoulders.

Tamara watched the fields of flax stir in the gentle breeze. She turned to Adlai. Her eyes gleamed excitement. "Abba, the storm will come tomorrow, right? It won't come early?"

"Yes." He studied her face. "What are you planning?"

She hesitated. "If the blossoms are going to fall off anyway, because of the hail, it wouldn't matter what I did now, would it?"

"What are you planning to do?"

She giggled. "Run through the fields of blossoms."

Adlai looked into her excited face and felt her bouncing on her toes again, just waiting to be released from his hug. "Tamara, I'll join you."

"You'd run through the fields?"

With his nod, she burst into laughter. "Let's go."

"On one condition," he said with all seriousness.

Her shoulders slumped. "What's that?"

"You hold my hand."

She laughed again. "Of course, Abba, but only if you can keep up."

As he concealed his smile, he said, "I'll do my best." He squeezed her hand as they hurried to his fields. Only a child of seven could see the blessing of today when tragedy stood in the wake of tomorrow. "You remind me to enjoy what God gives me today."

She giggled and began to run.

The mud of the Nile had brought forth the green vegetation of Egypt's plenty. Etania twirled. "The grass feels good after the hot sand of the streets." She followed Salome and Dinah to harvest wild radishes by the riverbed.

Etania paused. "Listen, Ima."

Salome tilted her head. "What do you hear?"

"Nothing. No birds sing. Why?"

Salome looked at Dinah. "Many left when the fish died. They have no food. But it's still too quiet. Can they tell of coming disaster?"

Dinah shrugged. She tapped the radish roots before putting them in her basket. "Now that Pharaoh gives less rations, how do you have enough to eat?"

"Some days Nathan brings home enough to feed one person. I

add water to take away the pain of hunger; it leaves the children fussy." Salome pointed to Etania. "Oh, honey, don't eat too many radishes, you will have a belly ache."

Etania stopped chewing. Her mouth was ringed with dirt where she had stuffed radishes in her mouth. "But I'm hungry."

Salome extended her hand for the remaining radishes. "Your belly won't like too many of those." She turned to Dinah again. "Nathan says they are rationing the food because they fear they won't have enough."

Dinah pulled more radishes. "Can we continue on short rations?"

Later that evening, Salome requested Aaron to come. A little girl had eaten too many radishes on an empty belly.

After treating her, he talked long into the night with them about God's works. He did not reach home until very late.


A tall man with a black beard and unkempt appearance knocked at Aaron's house.

Mack answered the door.

"I have an important message for Moses." The man spoke with confidence, yet his eyes were not direct.

Mack nodded, waiting for the message.

"I must speak directly to him."

"He is not here. Do you wish to wait?"

The bearded man shifted and fingered his sheath. "No, I will return. When do you expect him?"

"I don't know when he will return."

The man nodded and turned to go.

Mack began to shut the door.

The man turned back quickly and called, "I must speak to Aaron."

Mack shook his head. "He is not here. Do you wish to wait?"

"I will return."

"You wish to leave a message?"

"No."

The bearded man returned home and called a handful of men. Cheap beer flowed. He watched them partake, merely tasting his. He wished to remain clear-headed. He did not desire to share his gain with these men, but they must find Moses before the hail came.

His Jewish heritage did not sway him to believe this God of Moses, nor did the plagues change his mind. His merchant trips away from Egypt protected him during the blood, flies, and gnats. Now his Hebrew heritage guarded him. A smile crept across his face; his eyes gleamed.

He must find Moses and Aaron. The Hebrews did not have a temple in which to worship. Where would Moses petition his God for a storm? If he knew, he would not need these men. The riches would be his alone. He shook his head. He would take care of the men before sharing the gems.

One asked him, "Maessai, why haven't you left Egypt like the other merchants?"

Another interjected, "I've watched all of Egypt's merchants run without looking back."

Chuckling, another added, "They took only what they could carry on their backs."

Another scoffed, "Maessai is blessed by his God. Are his donkeys killed? He fears no evil from this God."

Maessai listened. How could he present the vizier's request? If he created hatred for Moses, then these men would comply willingly. Hatred motivated. He must be careful not to remind them of their fear of Moses's God. Fear would hinder them from doing the task. "Yes, my God protects me in spite of what Moses is doing to destroy your things."

He drank, and then cleared his throat. "All of you have been harmed by Moses." He paused, allowing his comment to settle in their thoughts.

He pointed to one. "Your little girl was killed by a crocodile." Maessai watched the man's eyes turn cold with anger and hate.

Maessai continued around the circle. "Moses's frogs made your great-grandfather sick."

The man nodded. "He struggled with the evil a long time."

Maessai looked at the next one. "You once had a herd of cows..."

"But now I have none, thanks to Moses." The man's eyes flashed anger.

Maessai spurred him to continue. "How have you been feeding your family?"

The man's eyes lowered. "It's a struggle."

Maessai prepared the men to receive his next words. "This Moses brought hardship and grief to you."

The men's nods encouraged him to continue. Maessai lowered his voice and leaned into the circle of men. "Moses must be stopped before another hardship comes to you. He has promised hail. If he is gone before tomorrow, the hail won't destroy Egypt's food. Are you interested?"

A fter leaving the palace, Moses felt restlessness. He had committed himself to obeying the Lord in this mission. But Pharaoh refused to allow God's people to worship yet again. Moses had not expected to be away from Zipporah this long. He paced his chamber. His restlessness increased until he left to walk the city.

Usually when he missed Zipporah or was frustrated with Pharaoh's delays, he would walk to the Hebrew slave village and watch the mothers and children working. Seeing them reminded him of his mission.

Walking the streets in the slave district, he sensed an urgency to keep moving. He could not walk fast enough. His heart could not find peace, even amidst his people. He looked to the desert beyond the village. The smell of sheep and goats, the feel of freedom compelled him to continue walking. He strode to the pastures where the shepherds protected their flocks under a ceiling of clouds. He found a boulder and settled to sit and pray.

He stayed long after the rays of the sun swept their colors across the western sky. He watched as the stars came out. He told the Lord his heart's cravings. He missed Zipporah and his boys. He asked for their protection as they worked and played. He wished for a way to tell them that he was fine, that he still lived. Eliezer would be walking by now, probably even talking. Would he even remember his father?

How long would Pharaoh delay? Moses's restlessness came over him again. He wanted to finish this mission. Pharaoh's refusals hindered him from seeing his family. Each time Pharaoh rejected his request reminded him that he himself had not obeyed God. Moses understood Pharaoh's rebellion. Pharaoh angered him, though, because he did not see his own people's suffering. Could he accept Pharaoh's denial another time?

He did not understand the oppression that he felt. He stayed under the stars, waiting for God to lift it. The night was far spent before he returned to Aaron's house to sleep peacefully.

Z ipporah kneaded the dough for the day's flatbread.

Gershom ran inside, holding the stick that he carried with him everywhere. He pinched off a piece of the dough and popped it in his mouth. "Does Father still live?" he asked abruptly.

"Of course." Zipporah tried to sound confident, but her voice broke.

"Has he forgotten us?" he persisted.

"No. He stays as long as his God tells him, not a moment longer." She stopped kneading to pat his hand, leaving a flour mark.

He studied it while she broke off a piece of dough to flatten. "If I can't remember what he looks like, does that mean I don't love him?"

She put her arm around his little shoulders. "You can't remember what he looks like?"

As he shook his head, tears flew out of his eyes.

"He's tall, taller than the tallest shepherd that lives in these hills. His beard grows thick so that he can tickle the most mischievous boy asking him questions." She glanced at him through tear-filled eyes, trying not to cry.

Gershom giggled.

"His hands are always ready to throw a boy into the air and catch him. But also gentle enough to help that boy cut the fleece off his lamb without nicking its flesh even when it wiggles."

He laughed again.

"He always has his staff close." She motioned to the stick in his hand. "Is that why you carry that?"

He nodded.

"Then you remember your father more than you think. He's not forgotten you. In fact, if I know your father, he's thinking of you right now." She squeezed his shoulders.

He grabbed another piece of dough to stuff in his mouth. "Thanks, Mother," he said as he ran out the door.

She wiped her arm across her face, pushing stray hair out of her eyes. Was Moses safe? What about those who wanted him dead?

Moses trained for great things. When he first arrived, he had mourned for his previous wife, Tharbis, even while she lived. Moses's Ethiopian princess wife would never have survived wilderness living. When Moses heard that Tharbis had died, he mourned her again. She had begged him to forget his other wife, but he could not.

Zipporah had known even when he first came that Moses was destined for more than watching sheep and goats. She had felt it. But now his first wife did not stand between them, God did.

Her thoughts took her to the last day with Moses. Even then, she could not control what Moses did. What God would take a man away from his family?

What woman would take a man away from his God?

She heard the question in her mind. She sat back on her heels and stopped flattening the dough. Moses was called for greater things, but she wanted comfort. She wanted Moses to fit into her life. She would not fit into his. But what would happen, if she did not bend? Would her life be like the Ethiopian princess, separate from her husband until she died? Could she accept that? Were safety and comfort worth being away from Moses?

Zipporah returned to her kneading with more force, but she could not find answers to her heart's questions.

At his usual time the next morning, Pharaoh prepared to worship Ra at the Nile River. The green vegetation along the beaches gave promise of the good harvest of the crops. He stood with hands loosely behind his back. He even smiled.

The Hebrew God threatened to steal the power from all the gods of Egypt: *Nut*, the sky goddess; Shu, the god of the air; Tefnut, the goddess of water and moisture; and *Seth*, the god of thunder, desert, infertility, and chaos.

Without Moses, what could his God do?

Badru arrived breathless, scanning the horizon and overhead. "Does the great Pharaoh desire a silent worship today?"

Pharaoh saw his fear and gloated over his power that would return. "No, the entire worship ritual will be expected. Proceed." He glanced at the sky. He frowned. The dawn's light did not come.

Badru hurried through the ritual, chanting the rites to the gods of the Nile and the sun. He stuttered as the sky turned blacker.

Ra did not shine. The sky darkened from gray to black. The wind pushed the clouds lower to the ground.

Pharaoh deepened his breathing, trying to calm himself. Had they not killed Moses before he called for the storm?

Egypt's thunderstorms came in the late afternoon or evening when the winds brought moisture from the coast, but only during the raining season. The raining season was long over. Never had thunderstorms split the sky this early in the morning.

Sudden winds bent trees in half as if they were flax in the field. Beyond the green of the Nile, sand whipped in circles, forming mountains before their eyes.

When Pharaoh looked around him, he noticed his attendants

and guards were gone. Badru alone remained with him. Thunder boomed, followed by a blinding flash of lightning.

Badru's eyes showed large against his ashen face. Without Pharaoh's permission, he scrambled toward the closest shelter.

Pharaoh ran after him. He reached a hut as the rains fell. He watched from the doorway as lightning struck where he had just stood by the Nile. He trembled and backed into the shelter.

The darkened hut, used by slaves when barges came up the Nile, smelled of musty palm leaves from the roofing. Once Pharaoh's eyes adjusted to the darkness, he glanced around its only room. Nothing lay on the dirt floor except an old reed pallet. The roof hung eye-level with Pharaoh, causing him to stoop. Pharaoh again looked into the storm, searching for a better shelter. He could see nothing beyond his arm's reach.

Badru quivered prostrate on the floor. "May the gods spare my life to allow me to worship them again." Every time the thunder rolled, Badru whimpered. "Seth, god of thunder, speaks. May he find pause from his speaking to listen to me."

The thunder resounded. Lightning rent the sky in two.

The thatched roof shook, sagging under the weight of the wind and rain.

Hail, the size of his fist, bounced into the shelter. Pharaoh hovered against the back wall. He felt the hail pelt him through the reed wall. He watched, mesmerized at the storm's power.

The temperature dropped. Pharaoh rubbed his arms. Normally, he needed no cloak in the hot season.

Badru, crawling toward the back wall, shouted over the wind, "Would Pharaoh like my priest's cape?"

Pharaoh grabbed the garment without a word and huddled under it.

When Badru looked at the roof, Pharaoh followed his gaze. An army pitching rocks at the roof could not have been louder. The added weight caused the roof to continue to sag even more.

Badru gestured toward Pharaoh as he covered himself with the worn-out reed rug, a discarded sleeping pallet from a slave. "Shall we cover our heads, oh great Pharaoh?"

Pharaoh stooped to sit beside Badru on the dirt. He had not spoken since the hail started. What if this God would not stop this storm, because Moses was dead? Beads of sweat, in spite of the cold temperature, formed on his lip and forehead below his wig. He wiped them with the back of his hand. Would the roof cave in before the storm stopped? Would he be buried under the matted, decaying palm leaves? The fear he saw in Badru's face mirrored his own. What had he done?

The vizier watched from his chamber window as the thunderous clouds hovered closer. He was grateful that he had not followed Pharaoh to the Nile River for the daily recitations of magic.

What would happen if Pharaoh did not come back? He had no heir.

The last time the vizier saw Nitocris, she was with child. They would have an heir, but in the meantime, he might control more decisions. How malleable was Nitocris to his influence?

He avoided Nitocris if he could help it. She held power, even greater than Pharaoh did. Rumors told of her rejection of Pharaoh when he called her. The vizier would not want to oppose her. Could he influence her?

He could no longer see his barn. Lightning split the sky, reaching the ground in front of his house. He stepped from the window opening. Hail pelted the window frame, leaving dents in the mud bricks. Some fell inside the window. He picked up one, the size of four fingers, more than one *span*. Even with the warmth of his hand, the ball of ice remained solid. How would Egypt fare against this? He wished Pharaoh had ordered his servants from the fields; re-training people took too long. Whatever barley had sprouted would be destroyed. The crop of flax would be gone.

He had not received word from his man. Had he succeeded in killing Moses? Would this God stop this storm without Moses's request? If they had killed Moses, would He be so angry that the storm would continue? Surely, a storm like this would not last too long with or without this God's word.

The vizier thought of Pharaoh's tombs. He would not go hungry, even if all of Egypt had no food. He would move the stored food in the tombs to a location for his own use.

As he thought about the tombs, he remembered Adlai's statement about Imhotep's bones. Perhaps, he could secure other means for his future. If he allowed Adlai to take Imhotep's bones, he could later accuse the Hebrews when those bones were missing. He would manipulate them. He rubbed his hands together and laughed. Things were looking hopeful.

C hike and Amunet sat together on their garden bench, watching the black cloud roll toward them. As it came closer, they took shelter inside.

Chike stood by the window until the lightning struck. He backed away. The thunder rolled, sending vibrations through the walls. He sat with Amunet. They watched in silence.

Amunet jumped, startled by the pounding on their roof.

Chike pulled her closer to him. He felt her shivering. "Cold?" He called Reut to bring her blue cloak and covered her shoulders with it.

She still shivered.

"Are you afraid?" he asked.

"Such power," she whispered. "Such destructive power. How could we appease this God of the Hebrews? What could we give Him that He doesn't already have?"

Chike leaned forward to hear her over the noise of the storm. Fear was not in her voice. She spoke with awe and reverence.

She continued, "How will this God change our lives? Each plague gets closer and closer to our own destruction. How do we prepare for it? What must we do to survive this God?"

W hen the hail did not stop and the lightning continued, Badru continued to tremble.

Pharaoh spoke, "Go find Moses."

Badru stared at him. Find Moses in this?

He glanced into Pharaoh's eyes. He saw murder in Pharaoh's expression. As Badru debated, he looked again. He saw fear also. That look brought him to his feet. Shaking off the pallet, Badru wished for his cloak. He would not ask for it.

At the entrance, he looked at the darkened world. The hail had not lessened. He took a deep breath and ran. He was pelted, bruised and sore before he reached an occupied house.

He entered the house with the authority of the chief high priest. "Pharaoh demands that Moses come to him."

"By all means." The host obliged, calling a servant to continue the journey.

Badru stayed at the house, shivering. He shook from cold, but more from fear. How close he had come to death.

The host stood by him at the fire. "Use this cloak to get warm."

Badru huddled under its warmth, reaching toward the cooking fire to warm his hands, stretching his feet toward the flames to still his pounding heart. If the gods that he adored would not respond to what he had to give, what more could he do? If Pharaoh was fearful, what was left? What could be done, but worship this God?

T he Lord protected Moses and Aaron as they followed the servant to the shack by the Nile.

Pharaoh held his head between his knees. The roof hung by a few reeds. He mumbled, "This time I have sinned."

Part of the roof in front of Pharaoh crashed to the floor. Dust flew from the floor before rain and hail poured through the opening. Coughing, he spoke again. "The Lord is right. I am wrong. Pray. I will let you go."

Moses studied the repentant man before him. Pharaoh's

confession reminded Moses of a child yielding only to avoid further punishment. He shook his head in disgust. "I will pray to the Lord. The thunder will stop. The hail will be no more. You will know that the earth is the Lord's. But you still do not fear the Lord God."

Moses left the shack and walked from the city. His heart was bent with the people's suffering. He lifted his hands toward the sky. "Lord, who can comprehend Your power? Your anger over wrong is beyond our understanding. How long will it be? Satisfy us with Your presence. May we see Your work and tell our children." His hands fell to his sides. His hair was drenched. His beard dripped from the torrent that ran down his face. "Lord, stop the hail."

The Lord did.

When the hail stopped, the silence left a hole nothing could fill. No bird sang. No animal ventured from its shelter.

As Amunet looked out her window, she rubbed her unborn child. The streets stayed empty. She feared to leave her home. She looked to the fields that previously held barley and flax to be harvested in a moon's time. Nothing was left but broken stems and mud.

How would Egypt feed her people? When would the struggle between God and their Pharaoh end? Why did Pharaoh not care enough to protect them?

"What happened?" The vizier stared at the assassin he had hired.

"Couldn't find him. He just vanished. Aaron, too. My men searched everywhere for them. Their God made them invisible."

"Try again tonight. We must stop them."

His assassin shook his head and wavered. "I didn't agree to fight God."

The vizier grabbed him and shook him. "You kill Moses, and no God will find you. I will make sure you are safe."

"Are you stronger than God? Somehow I don't see you bringing flies on me."

"Kill Moses. I'll make sure you have enough wealth to run from this God." The vizier let go of the man's cloak and stepped back.

Taking the bag of gems from his tunic pocket, he opened the drawstring and poured them into his hand. They sparkled from the sunlight flooding through the window. He caught Maessai eyeing the gems and fingering his sword.

The vizier snapped his hand shut.

Maessai swallowed and continued to stare at the vizier's closed hand. "I could try again."

"You will."


Pharaoh paced his chamber. How could his power be crumbling around him? His own people did not fear him?

He called the vizier to his presence.

The vizier bowed respectfully, already knowing what the Pharaoh wanted.

"Why is Moses still alive?"

The vizier looked him in the eyes. "My man thinks he fears this God. I have convinced him otherwise."

"So he will kill him before another mishap?"

"Most assuredly."

Pharaoh sighed, with satisfaction. "Then there's no need for them to sacrifice?"

"No need."

Pharaoh nodded. "Make it so."

The vizier nodded and left his presence.


Ra rose again the next day. The sun was oblivious to the

destruction that lay within its rays. Heat rose from muddied fields of a harvest that would not come.

Mothers and wives that had watched family work the fields yesterday, now searched for those who did not return home. The death wail split the air.

Slaves would not make bricks today nor work the stone quarries. They would dig graves quickly before the heat reached the bodies.

Ellis stooped to help Nathan lift a body. Their feet slipped in the mud under the added weight.

As they hauled the body toward the gravesite, Ellis said, "We suffer for Egyptians' disobedience."

Nathan said, "Others suffer because one disobeys. Doesn't your family?"

Ellis's face flushed. "What's God telling me to do?"

"Trust Him."

"Look at this destruction." Ellis's arm circled the field; several more bodies were left to remove. He shook his head. "I can't."

"Can't or won't?" Nathan went to the next body. "Ellis, you hold a grudge against God since your father was killed. God didn't kill your father. Evil did."

"But He could've stopped it!" Ellis shouted.

"Your father no longer suffers. Holding God at a distance won't punish Him. Don't you see how much you hurt Dinah and your son? You hold your hurt and it fills your heart with hate. Your arms are so full of it that you have no room to love your family. Cling to the hurt and you'll lose your family. Is that what you really want?"


A aron leaned back from the table, pushing his drink from him. "Do you ever think that Pharaoh will kill you if you go before him again? We bring bad news every time we appear before him. Aren't you ever afraid?"

Moses nodded. "Every time."

"What do you do with the fear?" Aaron persisted. "He makes me tremble in my sandals."

"This is God's work. If He wants me killed, that's His doing. I must obey."

"You've learned some hard lessons in the desert to bring you to this perfect obedience." Aaron shook his head and laughed. "I remember you as an arrogant general of the army who stretched the rules rather than obeyed them."

"The desert brought hard times, loneliness, and a threat to all I held dear," Moses responded. "I sent my wife home, against my vow that I wouldn't leave my wife again."

"It wasn't your rash behavior that brought you to Egypt this time," Aaron reminded him.

"No, but by trying to fulfill my vow apart from God, I nearly lost my family and my mission." Moses shrugged. "I can fear God's consequences because I disobey, or I can fear man's consequences when I obey. Which would you choose?"

# CHAPTER 16

The Lord told Moses, "Speak to Pharaoh, for his and his officials' hearts are hardened so that I may perform these miraculous signs. You will tell your children and grandchildren. You will know that I am the Lord."

Moses rested in the Lord's words. He would one day tell his sons about God's wonders. But his heart still ached for Zipporah to allow God to be truly hers. More waiting. More resting.

He sighed at the thought of approaching Pharaoh again. Initially, he could understand Pharaoh's stubbornness, but as Pharaoh's people suffered, Moses wondered how he could not concede. What kind of a selfish leader would allow his people to lose everything? What would it take for Pharaoh to acknowledge God?

God did not forget His people or His mission. He brought them together when He deemed best. No man could stand in His way.

Moses and Aaron once again stood safely before Pharaoh. Moses spoke, "The Lord says, 'How long will you refuse to humble yourself before Me? Let My people worship Me. If you refuse, I will send locusts into your country tomorrow. They will devour what little you have left after the hail. They will cover the ground so that it cannot be seen. They will fill your houses—something never before seen.'" Moses left the courtyard.

A full cycle of the moon had passed since the hail. Wheat and spelt would be harvested soon. If that were lost, Egypt would have nothing else left.

The vizier could remain quiet no longer. He yelled at Pharaoh, "How long will you allow this man to abuse us? Let the people worship! Don't you realize Egypt is ruined?"

"Call Moses back," Pharaoh demanded.

Moses was summoned and soon stood before him again.

Pharaoh queried, "If I allow you to worship, who will go?"

Moses stood before him. "All, young and old, with our flocks and herds. We will celebrate a festival to the Lord."

"The Lord be with you. But just the men may worship. Now be gone."

Moses shook his head.

The vizier watched him walk down the corridor and pause outside the palace on the top of the stairs. He stretched his staff over all Egypt.

The vizier hung his head and sighed.


The Lord made an east wind blow across the land. The winds blew throughout the day and night. The sand hovered in the air as thick as darkness. It blinded the eyes and scoured the skin. Everyone sought shelter.

Harvesting season had come. When these winds came during flooding season, the welcoming rains fell. But not now. These winds did not bring the cooling temperatures nor the promise of hope. Rains during the harvest could only bring one thing—loss.

The Egyptians looked to their fields of wheat and spelt almost ready to harvest and lost all hope.

Nathan and Ellis looked to the east and saw a dark cloud carried by the wind.

The overseer looked with them. "It's as Moses said. The locusts have come." He ran for the barn.

"Michael, come for safety." Ellis pointed to the swiftly moving cloud. They called their other team members and followed the overseer to the barn.

As they watched the cloud approach, they heard a sound like thunder.

Ellis and Nathan unhitched the oxen in the barn. They watched the locust cloud descend on the fields. Even from their distance, they could hear chewing and moving wings. They could no longer see rich, brown dirt, nor wheat and spelt ready to harvest. The fields moved as a black carpet that devoured everything in sight.

They left for their homes.

Nathan pointed as they entered their village. "Look. No locusts in the fields here."

"I still hear a humming in the distance," Michael said. "We are blessed to be God's people."

Ellis asked, "What makes us special?"

"God is the creator. He makes the rules," Michael stated.

"Is that fair?" Ellis asked.

"God never promised to be fair," Nathan said. "But God is just. And that's a crucial difference."

Michael looked into Ellis's face. "Our God is good. You can trust Him."

The conversation stopped as they went to their separate homes, but Ellis continued thinking. Who was this God Who knew and did right? Could death and destruction be right? What would this God do to him for his actions? He hung his head. Just this morning, he had left the house yelling at Dinah again. Her look of hurt tortured his conscience, but his response never changed. Why did he lash out at her? How would this God judge him?

Dinah was behind in making the flat cakes, even though she only had enough wheat berries to make a few. Why had she slept later than the sunrise?

Japhet was throwing their wheat over his head and giggling. How did Salome do it with two children?

"Quit that, Japhet!" She smacked his hand.

He sat still, his chubby face puckered in surprise.

Dinah watched his eyes fill with tears. She grabbed him and comforted him. "Ima loves you, Japhet. But you can't throw food."

Salome's words, spoken before Japhet was born, came to Dinah's mind. "You'll realize how much more you need God when you have children." Dinah used to think that she was patient and kind, but Japhet showed her that she was not. She understood Salome's words now.

A shadow crossed the doorway. She looked up and gasped. Her heart beat faster. "Ellis, you're home early. What's wrong?"

Ellis embraced her. "Locusts came to the fields. Nothing will be left to eat when they finish. Egypt will have no harvest."

Dinah stepped back. "Will God make us starve?"

Ellis shook his head. "I don't know this God enough to say what He will or won't do."

Dinah opened her mouth to speak, but shut it again. She bowed her head and spoke softly. "You speak so little of God. When you do, it surprises me." She backed away from him, immediately regretting her words. She cringed when he spoke.

"You are right."

She looked at him, surprised, but with a guarded expression. She saw tears in his eyes.

"If this God starved you, it would be my fault."

"Why?"

"Nathan said that another's disobedience could cause those we love to be hurt."

"How did you disobey?"

"I can't trust Him. How can I trust a God Who destroys and gives death?"

"How do you not trust a God Who gives peace and makes life?" She squeezed his arms.

"Can He really do both?"

"Only God can." Dinah searched Ellis's brown eyes for what kept him from trusting. She wished that she knew.

He stepped away from her and lowered his voice. "Trusting is hard."

"Not trusting is harder." She studied the ground rather than look at him.

"I must think." He walked outside.

This time he did not stomp off in anger. Dinah watched him from the doorway as he made his way toward the Nile.

Depending upon God to help her get the water and be nice to Japhet seemed little compared to what God was doing inside Ellis. But she knew that her God was capable of doing both.

A munet heard the buzzing, saw the room darken, and felt the ominous cloud descend like a blanket covering everything. When she looked out the window, she saw a living black rug creep over her windowsill and pour into her room with a ka of its own. When she actually saw what it was, she screamed in terror.

Reut came running.

Amunet jumped on her bed above the locusts. They climbed her bed after her.

Reut ran through them to stand by her on the bed. "God sends none to my people. Would you go to my father's house?"

Amunet swallowed the bile that came to her throat as she wiped her legs, still feeling their presence. "Yes, yes, Reut. We'll go."

The streets could not be seen. The locusts covered anything green, even rooftops where gardens grew. Chewing was the only thing heard.

Amunet stopped to catch her breath. Watching the movement at her feet left her head dizzy and nauseous.

Reut wiped away those stuck in her tunic. The women ran again.

When they reached the Hebrew town, it was like crossing a line between moving blackness and dirt, evil and good.

Amunet hugged Reut. "You have saved me. I couldn't have stayed there another moment."

"You are safe now. We can walk slowly." Reut brushed at Amunet's wig to dislodge a caught locust.

Reut's mother met them in the garden. Carmel hugged Reut tightly. "I'm so glad you came, Reut. You did the right thing. We watched that black cloud come over Egypt."

Amunet looked around at the green healthy plants. "My garden looked like this before the hail beat it down. Now, nothing will be left. My fig blossoms are gone. My dates..." She sighed. "I'm so tired of boils, lice, hail, flies, blood...What have I done for the gods to do this to me? I give them the best of my fields. Even my husband spends all his time fighting for the gods. What more can I do?"

Carmel rubbed her back. "Turn to the God Who controls it all."

Amunet shook her head. "I grow weary of all the gods."

"You seek the peace that only comes from the Friend of Abraham."


Called from teaching and informed of guests, Adlai hurried home. Who would visit during the day?

He saw the moving mass on the surrounding fields and heard the sound of chewing. His guests must be Egyptians escaping the locust. Which Egyptians would seek him?

He entered his house through the servants' door to gain information. He met his own daughters, Reut and Tamara. Reut recounted her flight with Amunet from the locusts.

Reut shivered. "I don't want to remember them. Every time I close my eyes, I see this black moving mass. I won't be able to sleep tonight."

Adlai kissed her on the head. "Maybe by nighttime Pharaoh will have asked Moses to remove them."

Tamara shook her head. "Pharaoh doesn't ask our God until he is desperate."

"Not too loudly," Reut shushed her. "Egyptians are here. Words like that can get Abba into trouble."

"Speaking of trouble, I must see to my guests." Adlai kissed both girls on their heads and headed toward the garden.

"The general will dine with you tonight. He was called for his wife's sake." The head steward spoke in a slight whisper as he walked with him. "The chief high priest and the vizier arrived early in the morning for an urgent matter."

"Did they arrive together or separately?" Adlai asked.

"They came at the same time but seemed upset at the other's presence."

He had arrived at the doorway to his garden. He would soon see why they had come.

B adru responded to Adlai's greeting, and then slumped against the back of the bench.

The vizier ignored them both.

Badru fidgeted. He answered Adlai's polite questions with short, hasty words and furtive glances toward the vizier.

After several awkward pauses, Adlai suggested, "If it would please the vizier, I could discuss a more personal nature with you in the house? Or would it please you to allow Badru so that he could return to his business?"

The vizier's eyes brightened. "Take what time you need. I prefer not to return too soon."

Adlai nodded, "Very well then."

Badru sighed audibly and rose to follow Adlai into his receiving area. He sat on the edge of the offered chair, his hands resting on his knees in front of him. He fidgeted with the hem of his tunic.

Badru took a deep breath. Perhaps he was too hasty to come.

He had not worshiped at the Nile this morning. Instead, he sent another priest to perform the duties. He feared being trapped, like when the thunderstorm had come. Would he be judged for it?

*Senehem*, the locust-headed god who protected Egypt from pests, would not win this new battle.

He must know what this God wanted. Would God strike him dead? He swallowed several times.

Adlai waited.

Badru stroked his hands down his tunic to wipe off the sweat, crossing and uncrossing his legs. Finally, he took a calming breath. "What can Egypt do to appease the Hebrew God?"

"Do you wish to know what Egypt can do or what you can do? Egypt must let God's people go. But I sense that you are asking, not for Egypt, but for yourself. Am I right?"

Badru hesitated, blinking rapidly, his brow furrowed. He was the high priest, after all. What would become of Egypt if the chief high priest did not appease Egypt's gods?

Finally, he nodded. "I want to appease the Hebrew God."

"Do you just want something from Him?"

Badru looked up. His eyes widened. Was he so obvious? "The Hebrew God is more powerful than Egypt's gods. Yet He is one God. The Hebrew God is more jealous of His people than Egypt's gods. The Hebrew God tells you how to worship. I don't know how." He wrung his hands and looked at his feet.

"Our God is the God of all creation, of all time, of everywhere. He is the only true God for all people. Because He made us, He can demand our loyalty, our allegiance, our worship. But we must worship His way."

"But what is His way?" Badru asked as he twisted the edge of his tunic in his hands. "Can we hope to do it right?"

"Are you familiar with Moses's writings of Hebrew history? He wrote them while he lived in the palace. He wanted the Hebrews to know the God of Abraham, Isaac, and Jacob."

Badru shook his head.

Adlai continued, "He spoke of God, the creator God, who made the sun and moon, the water and land, the plants and animals. He made man. He gave man a choice to obey Him. When the first people chose to disobey, He sacrificed a lamb to pay for their wrong choice.

"Your question 'Can we do it right?' is a good one. We choose to disobey. But God in His mercy redirects us back to Himself.

"You are not a Hebrew, one of His chosen. But God made a way for foreigners to worship, through circumcision. God commanded man to be separated unto Him for service. If you truly want to know the God of the Hebrews, circumcision would be the first step to worship."

"Egypt's gods hold much sway in me. I own their powers here." Badru held his hand over his chest. "Your God makes me consider. My heart wants to believe, but my thoughts won't give up my teachings. I'd lose control over everything."

"Do you *control* anything? Could you stop these plagues?"

Badru bowed his head but remained quiet, fidgeting nervously.

"You control nothing. The Evil One gives you just enough power to let you think that you control things. That is his lie. He controls you. He keeps you from knowing God."

"But all my incense, my spells, my incantations…"

"Are they more powerful than my God?" Adlai asked.

"I have much to lose if I give up those," Badru said.

"You have much to lose if you *do not* give up those."

Badru stood. "I must return to the temple. Worship calls."

"God calls you, too. Who will you hear?"


Adlai took a deep breath, requested more wisdom from God, and returned to the garden.

"Sorry to keep you waiting," he said. "What would you wish to discuss, Vizier?"

The vizier stood as he entered. "Scribe—"

"The name is Adlai."

"Yes, Adlai. I wish to discuss information that you need."

Adlai raised his eyebrows. "Yes?"

"Last time I spoke with you, you mentioned Imhotep's bones. I will help you."

"And *you* need information about..." Adlai prompted.

The vizier nodded, smiling. "About the tombs."

Adlai's brow wrinkled as he considered. "Perhaps the general of the army, who guards the tombs, or Badru could help you. I know nothing of the tombs."

The vizier shook his head. "What will your God do to the tombs?"

"You mean, will He destroy them?"

"Will the food stored there be safe?"

"Do you store food there?" Adlai asked.

"I've wasted my time. You do not wish for Imhotep's bones." The vizier turned to go.

"I do want his bones. I can tell you if something is against God's nature and, therefore, unlikely that He will do. But I am not God to know what will or will not happen."

The vizier faced him again. "Hasn't your God foretold famines? He must tell me what I need to know, so you can have those bones."

"God doesn't work like that. I don't demand of Him. I seek His desire, not my own."

"I suggest that you demand this information from your God so that you can get those bones!" the vizier shouted. He paced, his hands clenched at his side. "I petition no god. I demand what I want or someone pays. Who are you to withhold your God's help from me?"

Adlai stepped back. "God helps those He wishes. Perhaps, if we went to the tombs and you showed me the bones, I could hear the words of God to answer your questions?"

The vizier laughed. "You get what you need. What's my guarantee that I would get what I need?"

Adlai shrugged. "God may tell us. I do not know."

"I'd need the general of the army to attend us."

It was Adlai's turn to laugh. "He waits in my chamber. Today has been my day to receive important visitors. Shall we ask him to join us?"

R iding their horses west of the city, Adlai, Chike, and the vizier approached the step pyramid. The pyramid faced the setting of the sun, enabling the kings to live their deified lives upon their death.

Joseph had built this pyramid initially for grain storage during the seven years of prosperity. The pyramid protected the grain from theft, spoilage, and insects. Chutes built into the sides of the pyramid were oriented toward the stars of *Sah* on one side and the *Thuban* Star on the opposite side. After they used the surplus grain, Joseph redesigned the interior of the pyramid for Pharaoh Zoser's tomb.

When they approached the entrance, a guard appeared as if from the desert floor. The sun shone directly in his eyes. His face and exposed skin were darkened by the sun's rays.

Chike greeted him. "Fenuku, it is I, Chike. I bring the vizier and a guest to the tomb."

With a nod, Fenuku stepped aside to let them pass.

They passed a statue of *Meretseger*, a goddess in cobra form who blinded or poisoned any robbers of the tombs. Adlai noticed the vizier shiver as if he could shake off the power of the statue.

They entered the only doorway. The passageway was narrow, allowing one to enter at a time. They stood, allowing their eyes to adjust to the darkened hallway.

"Will we need torches?" Adlai asked.

"Most of the chambers are lit by candles on the walls. Should be enough," Chike said over his shoulder. The passageway grew darker as the sun's rays failed to penetrate.

Touching the cool stones for balance, Adlai followed. The air took on a closed, damp smell that sparked thoughts of being buried alive.

Coming to a fork in the passageway, Chike chose the upward path toward the middle of the pyramid.

Adlai felt weighted by oppression as they continued deeper into the hallways. He breathed deeply, reminding himself of the sunshine that lay outside.

They broke from the narrow aisle into a large gallery, well-lit and spacious. Instead of entering it, Chike turned to another passageway parallel to the ground.

Adlai felt that he had been cheated of the light, allowed only a glimpse before being led into more darkness. He could hear the vizier behind him breathing deeply, stumbling several times.

Chike stopped at the end of the passageway as it opened into a large, well-lit chamber. Shafts of sunlight streamed through channels facing the Thuban Star, the "indestructible star," and the stars of Sah.

Adlai gazed at the streams of light. The feeling of oppression, darkness, and evil fled before the presence of this outside light. He released a deep breath that he had not realized he had been holding.

The vizier fidgeted, eyeing the light. He rubbed his hands down his tunic.

Adlai asked, "Are you well, Vizier?"

The vizier nodded, rubbing the back of his neck. He cleared his throat. "Yes, fine."

Adlai tried to calm him. "Light is good after the dark passageways."

The vizier cleared his throat again.

Chike stood by the entrance, waiting for instructions. He shifted from one foot to the other.

Adlai noticed that Chike kept his eyes away from the light, a soldier ready to respond to the darkness. "Rather be in the sunshine sparring with your troops, Chike?"

Chike nodded with a smile, remaining at attention.

When his eyes adjusted to the light, Adlai saw in the center of the chamber a *sarcophagus*. Ceramic jars containing internal organs had been set beside the stone container, preserved and ready for the afterlife when this body would again need them.

The vizier paced in front of the sarcophagus. "Where's the

food? There's nothing." He scanned the chamber. "Where are the statues and amulets of gods to protect and deliver from the evil beyond life? Even Anubis, guardian of the tombs, isn't here. Whose bones are these that the Egyptians didn't give him the proper burial for the afterlife?"

"This is it," Adlai said with a wide grin and a chuckle. "This is Joseph." He peered inside the sarcophagus. Normally it would be sealed for the king's protection. This one was not. The plain rectangular box reflected the construction style of earlier coffins. The coffin inside was sealed. The body would face east on its left side to see the rising of the sun and the rebirth over the desert each morning.

"Look, the coffin tells the story of Joseph." Adlai fingered the carving of the images as he spoke. "See, here's the bread in red ink and cups in green. He interpreted the demise of the baker and the elevation of the cup holder to his original place of power. Those prophecies led to his appointment as vizier. Here's Joseph as ruler with Pharaoh."

Chike looked over Adlai's shoulder but kept his hand on the hilt of his dagger. The sunshine did not eliminate all presence of evil.

"How do you know it's him?" Chike asked.

"No gods were drawn on the coffin. There's no picture of Joseph's God. Not even His name was written." Adlai rested his hand on the cover. He recognized the sacredness of such an omission. No one had seen God at any time. He was not a god to be represented by an image. He was beyond what the eye could see and the mind could imagine.

"See, a man kneeling, beseeching God's favor." Adlai turned to show the vizier, but as he did, his excitement turned to alarm.

The vizier paced the room. His neck veins bulged. He stuttered to say something, and then stopped. He glared at Chike, but did not speak.

Adlai stood in alarm. "What is it, Vizier? What's the matter?"

The vizier faced Chike. "Where have you taken the tomb's provisions?"

Chike's mouth fell open. His body stiffened as he stepped back from the vizier. "No, your lordship, this is the first time since my preliminary appointment that I've been inside the pyramid."

"You knew the guard by name. He knew you. How is that, if you do not come regularly to steal?"

Chike shook his head but straightened his shoulders. "I know my guards. When I secure the tombs from entry, I make sure the guard is worthy of his calling."

Adlai interrupted, upset by this affront. "What's missing?"

The vizier did not even acknowledge him. He reached for his dagger in the folds of his tunic. When he found nothing, his frustration and anger showed.

Adlai breathed a sigh of relief. His own dagger lay back at his house, useless.

Chike suggested in a calmer voice, "If you seek riches, they're in the king's chamber. I thought you wished to see Imhotep's bones." He turned toward Adlai, keeping the vizier in his eyesight.

Adlai nodded.

Chike explained, "The pharaoh's tomb provides for the afterlife. This tomb, under Imhotep's request, was left empty. His God, he said, would provide for his needs in the afterlife. At least that was what I was told when I asked why he had no provisions to guard."

The vizier gulped and nodded. "Proceed to the pharaoh's chamber."

Chike re-entered the dark passageway.

Adlai tripped over a raised stone in the walkway as his eyes readjusted to the darkness. When they reached the fork, they walked upward to the antechamber.

Upon entering, the vizier sighed. He fingered the gems imbedded in the gods. He clutched one god, placed to protect the body, against his chest. He moved to another who preserved the pharaoh for his afterlife. He touched the gods as if he imagined their power were his.

Adlai breathed easier when the vizier became absorbed with the treasures. The vizier sifted through each jar of seed, grain, beans. The sounds echoed in the quiet room. He dug to the bottom of each pot as if to assure himself that it was full. Each pot held a power over him. His eyes glowed greedily.

As the vizier perused the jars' contents, Adlai backed into the king's chamber. The grander room allowed light from the heavens. Here he saw the pharaoh's sarcophagus. His life story was etched on the coffin with gods giving eternal hope, good life, and peace.

What could the vizier want from him? Did the vizier wish to steal from the tombs? If so, he and Chike could be in great danger.

Adlai returned to the entrance where Chike stood. He licked his dry lips. The coolness of the chambers now gave him chills as he watched the vizier.

Chike stepped closer to Adlai and whispered, "I fear for our lives."

Adlai nodded. Watching the vizier was like seeing a man possessed. Egypt's food sources had dwindled. Was the vizier contemplating stealing from the tombs? The vizier would not hesitate to demand Chike's assistance, then accuse Chike of the theft. Why did the vizier want him present, too?

Chike whispered again, as he touched the hilt of his dagger. "Don't stand too close. I will watch."

Adlai nodded and sighed. When was the last time that he had needed his dagger in defense? He licked his lips and waited, wishing to return to the sunshine and the air where he could breathe.

He now knew where Joseph's bones lay. Removing the bones for their trip to their land was achievable. He smiled. Praise be to God. Adlai's heart grew lighter. The oppression and darkness inside this tomb held no more sway over his thoughts. Even the threat of the vizier could not make him lose his peace.

After the vizier had studied everything in the tomb, he looked up to find Chike and Adlai watching him. He gave a weak little chuckle and a shrug of his shoulders. "Scribe…"

"Adlai. I am Adlai."

"Yes, well, Adlai, did your God tell you anything about what

He would do with the treasures?" The vizier spoke condescendingly, as if to a child.

Adlai hesitated to speak. "The treasures?"

"*These.*" The vizier pointed.

Adlai was still confused. He said nothing.

"Will I have food next year when no one else does? What does your God say?" As he spoke, he walked toward Adlai.

Adlai backed into Chike, who did not move. "My God tells me nothing about that."

The vizier laughed wickedly. "'My God tells me nothing'... Your God *is nothing*. I am ready now to leave."

The vizier said nothing more on their return trip until they reached the city's walls. There, he nudged his horse toward Adlai's horse. He pulled Adlai's reins until his horse stopped. The vizier stared Adlai in the face. "I do not forget. I demand an answer from your God."

"But Vizier, my God does not give answers by demand."

"I suggest, for your sake, that He does." The vizier reined his horse's head away from Adlai and kicked it into a trot.

Back at his own courtyard, Adlai offered, "Care to stay for refreshment?"

The vizier shook his head, but repeated his words, "I don't forget." He left.

Chike was quiet as he sipped his drink. "We are both in danger."

"Why was he willing to show me the bones of Imhotep?"

"He plans to extort something from you for those bones. Do not be deceived, my friend. He wasn't being nice. He has plans for you. Then he will eliminate you as a witness of today's lapse of control. Beware."

# CHAPTER 17

Pharaoh paced in his chamber. No one had ever spoken to him the way his officials did when Moses and Aaron had foretold the coming of the locusts. Did they not remember that he was god? What was wrong with these people? Could they forget what he did for them?

The last time Nitocris had come before him, some evil plagued her. How could a deity, like him, fear a woman? Perhaps, if he took her to the desert, away from these locusts, she would be more amiable toward him for his thoughtfulness.

He summoned her to his chamber, but when she came he did not recognize her. The boils had scarred her noble, fair complexion, once the loveliest in the country. Her delicate, slender figure was enlarged by the babe she carried. He was appalled. He would rather stay here with the locusts crawling over him than go anywhere with this ugly woman.

He did not touch her. The words of endearment that he so often spoke of her beauty caught in his throat. All he could say was the obvious. "Our heir grows. He will be worshiped."

She spoke not a word.

Her silence made him nervous. Why did she not say anything? He watched her feet as the locusts swarmed over them. Why did she just stand there? He grew brave and looked into her eyes. They had once held such worship for him, but now they revealed the same hatred that she had spewed forth the last time he needed her comfort.

He would find no solace here. He looked nervously down at her hands, thinking she might hold a dagger in them. There was none, but he shivered in fear anyway. She would not need one to do her damage.

He turned from her. "That is all. You may go."

He stood at the window, watching the locusts fall from the ledge to the floor of his chamber. He wondered at her cruelty. He was god, was he not? He expected worship; indeed, demanded it.

Nitocris had not left as he commanded. He grew angry at her disobedience and rejection. He thought to reprimand her, but she spoke first.

"Your arrogance has ruined all Egypt. You think that you are in control. You are wrong. You think that everyone worships you. You should hear what they say behind your back. They speak of killing you for what you have brought to Egypt. You think that you will outlive this Moses? You will die and he will have it all—Egypt, if he even wants this destroyed country, and all your slaves that you hold so tightly and won't let go." She spit out his name, emphasizing the wrong syllables, as she did when they were children and wished to anger him. "Phar-a-Oh Mer-EN-re Nem-TYEM-Saf II, you are nothing. And you don't even know it."

She stalked from the room.

After she left, he threw every container in his room and watched as they splintered against the wall. He looked for something else to vent his anger. There was nothing.

He must exert power over someone. But who?

Pharaoh summoned Moses. "Remove the locusts." He stood by his throne as Moses walked the distance to the outside stairs and stretched his staff over Egypt.

Just as they had arrived, so the locusts gathered as one and swarmed to the west.

Pharaoh settled back on his throne. The chewing, the crunching, the noise was gone. The silence came.

Why had the vizier not killed Moses yet? He turned behind him and saw no one but his guards. Where was his vizier? Even the chief high priest was not present. He must investigate this.

M oses looked at the pasture that had once held Pharaoh-esteemed cows and calves. He had admired their form and their build before the plague and had been saddened to see their death. Now he looked not at the livestock but at the land—brown, barren, lacking any green thing. The locust had devoured everything. He leaned on his staff and sighed.

A sound behind him startled him. He turned to see an Egyptian man. "Greetings."

"Why are you here?" the Egyptian spat bitterly. He stood clenching a dagger in his hand.

Moses glanced at the dagger but studied the man's face. "I've admired the livestock that grew fat on these pastures. They were fit for kings. I looked at the pastures rich in food for those cows. Now I mourn the owner's loss."

The man shifted the dagger in his hand. "Why? Aren't you the one who brought the destruction?"

Moses leaned on his staff. "I guess I could be blamed, but I do what my God instructs, just as you would follow a priest's commands if he told you the evil must be removed from your cow's leg in order to save its life."

"I have no cows to save. They are dead." The man's voice quivered with rage as he fought for control.

Moses looked away for a moment. "My God brings hardship in order for you to look to Him."

"I see only my barren field with no cows." His voice had gained control and, along with it, a hardness that made Moses look sharply at him.

"Do you kill the messenger who mourns your loss? Yet not see the God Who could give great riches?"

The man laughed without humor. "The God of slaves can give me riches? Bah! Do not think me a fool like the slaves that follow you."

"They do not follow me. They follow the God Who made them." Moses's gentle reply did not waver even when the man stepped closer with his dagger poised.

"If you had not come, I would still have my cows." He pulled back his dagger to strike.

Moses tensed but did not move his arm to defend the blow. "If you still had your cows, would you look to God?"

"I see nothing; no cows, no field. My life is gone." The man almost sobbed as his arm quivered.

"Then you will soon see my God. He is there for you." Moses reached to embrace him.

The man sobbed.

Moses held him as he lowered his arm. The dagger slipped through his fingers and dropped to the ground.

M aessai sat eating when one of his chosen men entered. The herdsman did not knock nor ask admittance.

Maessai did not invite him to eat.

"I won't do it."

Maessai stopped chewing his flatbread. "Why not? Didn't Moses destroy everything? Did you deserve it? Moses must be punished."

The man stared at Maessai a long time.

Maessai dropped his gaze.

"I will not do it," he repeated and walked out the door.

Maessai sighed, stuffing the rest of his flatbread in his mouth. He chewed as if he would kill.

T he man who had lost his little girl to the crocodiles followed Aaron to his house. Maessai had awakened his quest for revenge. His little girl had been only three harvests old when she was killed. He still had nightmares, watching her disappear beneath the flooded waters of the Nile's overfill into the jaws of the crocodile. She had been there one moment, then gone forever.

As he watched Aaron's window, he planned what he would say when the time came. He touched the dagger at his side.

As he waited, a messenger approached him, running. "Master!"

He sighed and turned from watching the window. "What is it?"

"Your wife calls, her time has come! The midwife needs help. The babe is stuck. I come for the swne."

The man spun back to Aaron's house and knocked at the door. The fear in his heart was enough to make him ask the man he sought to kill for help.

When they reached his house, the man paced outside his home, listening to his wife's agony, and hearing Aaron's calm voice dictating what to do. Listening to his wife's pain brought his life into perspective. How could he take another's life? Would that bring back his little girl? He bargained with any god to save his child and his wife. As he battled his thoughts, a baby's cries split the evening's silence. He was given new life.

The midwife called him inside.

He saw his wife cradling their new little one in her arms.

The midwife explained, "Without Aaron, we would have lost your wife and your baby. I couldn't make the baby turn, and your wife couldn't last too much longer."

He owed Aaron his family's lives. He shook his head. What would have happened if he had taken Aaron's life when he had stood outside his window?

Aaron smiled at the man. "The Lord has blessed you with another life."

The man agreed. It was more than another life, it was another chance to choose right.

M aessai bartered his wares in front of his house when the man approached. Maessai looked at him but continued to barter. Gems flashed before his eyes as he anticipated demanding more from the vizier. He hurried his transaction, placing his gold in his garment's side pocket. He turned to the man. His eyes dulled when he saw his expression.

"Maessai, I will not help you."

Maessai argued. "Don't you want vengeance for your daughter? Didn't you love her enough?"

The man's head fell. "Aaron saved my wife and baby's life. I will honor his service." He turned and walked away.

Maessai pounded the stand where his merchandise lay. How could he get those gems without this God's interference?

P haraoh called the vizier to his chamber.

When he arrived, he bowed lower than normal. "Oh great Pharaoh. You requested my presence."

"Why does Moses still live?" Pharaoh demanded.

"Moses's God makes him disappear when my men search for him."

"I don't want to hear about his God!" Pharaoh's neck veins bulged as he refrained from screaming. His face was hot. He could feel the pounding in his chest. "Call the man you hired before me."

The vizier started to leave.

"Stay here."

"As you wish." The vizier bowed again low.

A servant brought Maessai before Pharaoh.

Pharaoh studied him without speaking for a long time.

Maessai fidgeted from one foot to his other.

The vizier waited with hands clasped behind his back, his face blank.

Finally, Pharaoh broke the silence. "Moses lives."

Maessai swallowed and nodded.

Pharaoh picked up a vessel that a servant had recently delivered to his table. He took a sip. He paused again. "Why?"

Maessai did not look at Pharaoh. He cleared his throat.

Pharaoh grew tired of waiting. He threw his vessel over Maessai's shoulder.

Maessai flinched as the vessel barely missed him and splintered behind him on the wall. Shards hit him on his back.

"Why?" Pharaoh repeated.

"I sent men to kill Moses and Aaron. One by one they return to tell me they cannot do it. Their God protects them..."

The vizier interrupted. "You do it."

Maessai's shoulders slumped. He spoke, defeated. "I searched for them. Either they vanish by their God's power or crowds hinder me."

Pharaoh watched Maessai grow pale before his eyes. When he spoke, his voice was low and trembled. "Vizier."

"Great Pharaoh."

"Would the dungeon hold such a man as this who compares my greatness with a mere shepherd?"

"Sire, if he is confined, we may never rid your kingdom of this Moses. If all the other men have failed, who can we use? You cannot kill Moses openly, for even your people will rebel. We require this man's aid."

Maessai breathed deeply, gratitude showing in his eyes as he looked toward the vizier.

"Once he completes his duty, then you may do with him whatever you wish, since he has caused you so much grief," the vizier added, smiling.

Pharaoh nodded, also smiling. "Of course, there is always later for this man... But...!" he shouted. "I will wait no more for this deed's completion!"

Maessai nodded vehemently.

Pharaoh pointed to the door. "Go and do it."

Phinehas set the basket of figs down by the door. He rubbed his hands down the front of his tunic to dry his sweat. Would he catch a glimpse of her?

The door opened and he cleared his throat. "Greetings... Shalom."

"Shalom." A man stood in the entry and waited for him to state his business.

Phinehas coughed and cleared his throat again. He looked around.

"May I help you?"

"Yes, well, I..." Phinehas stuffed the basket into the man's hand. "I brought you these."

The man glanced into the basket. His eyebrows rose as he studied the man before him. "Toda raba." He continued to stand in the doorway.

Phinehas tried to see around him for a glimpse of her. "What I really wanted to know..."

"Yes?" the man was obviously confused now.

"Your daughter..."

Recognition came into the man's face as he nodded. "You are Aaron's grandson."

"Yes, yes." He nodded in relief. "Phinehas."

The man embraced him. "You have helped our people."

"That is nothing." Phinehas stood taller. "My Saba Aaron told of your son."

"Amos?"

"Yes, I've come to see how he heals."

The man stood aside and allowed Phinehas's entrance to his house.

Phinehas looked for Hannah but only saw the sparse furnishings. A low table pushed against the wall allowed passage through the small room. A lad of not more than thirteen seasons greeted him from a pile of cushions on the floor.

Phinehas tried to remember what Aaron had said of him. He could only remember about the maiden. "Do not rise. I wish to see my Saba's work." He squatted beside the lad.

"It is the Friend of Abraham's work that you must see." The father watched over Phinehas's shoulder.

"Your Friend must know my Saba well. The two of them have done a fine job with your leg."

Phinehas rested his hand lightly on the stump, feeling for heat and noting the color. The flesh had grown over the wound. "You heal quickly." He glanced around the room again not seeing the maiden. She should not be outside this late in the evening. He had made sure he came late enough. He squeezed the stump.

Amos winced.

"Sorry, lad." He patted him on the shoulder. Where could she be? Amos shifted away from Phinehas on the cushions.

Phinehas dug in his tunic pocket. "My Saba asked that I bring you more of this." He extended a vial. "How is your pain?" Phinehas looked again to the doorway.

At last, Hannah entered. "Sorry I'm late, Abba. Rachel's baby did not want to—" She stopped short when she saw Phinehas. She smoothed her tunic and patted her hair held back in a braid. "I didn't realize that you had a visitor. Sorry to interrupt."

Phinehas stood as she spoke and stepped toward her.

Amos interjected, "Don't be sorry, Hannah. He's been looking for you ever since he came. He didn't come to see Abba or me."

"Amos! Don't say such things," Hannah reprimanded, a blush spreading across her face.

Hakeen laughed and tried to lighten the awkwardness. "Phinehas brought a basket of figs."

"How thoughtful." Hannah took the basket her father handed her. She glanced at the figs, and then at Phinehas.

"I thought, well, many do not have fruit after the locusts have come."

Amos corrected him. "We are Hebrews. The locusts did not come here."

"Yes, you are right." Phinehas nodded, looking from Hannah's face to her hands. He felt stupid at the correction.

"Perhaps you have not eaten?" Hakeen questioned Phinehas.

He tore his gaze from Hannah. "Umm. Eat? No, I haven't eaten yet."

"Perhaps you would join us for our meal?" Hakeen asked.

"Yes, I could do that," Phinehas responded without thinking.

Amos snorted, looking down to conceal a smile.

Hannah put the basket down by the hearth and began stirring the coals under a pot.

Phinehas realized that he had agreed to eat, yet wondered if he could swallow a bite. He followed Hannah to the hearth.

Hakeen stopped him. "You may sit here with Amos, Phinehas. We will wait for the meal here."

"Yes, of course." Phinehas shook his head and tried to focus on the man's words. What was the matter with him? Proper manners would dictate that he talk to Hakeen. No girl from the rich houses of Egypt had ever caused him to act so stupid. Why could he not even think in her presence?

"Would you like a drink?" Hakeen settled on the cushions beside Amos.

Phinehas only answered in monosyllables. Why had he come? Hannah's father must think him a fool. He could not formulate a complete sentence. He glanced at Hakeen. Had he asked him a question? "I'm sorry, my mind was somewhere else. What did you say?"

Amos stifled a laugh and handed Phinehas a vessel of water. "Take this. It'll give you something to choke on."

"Amos!" Hannah reprimanded again.

Phinehas did not hear. He sipped from the vessel. The coolness felt refreshing to his dry throat. He licked his lips. He dragged his eyes from Hannah and tried to engage in conversation with her father. What had his saba told him? "You apprentice with whom?"

Hakeen's face blanched and he spoke softly. "Ptah. He sculpts for the temple gods."

Phinehas looked at his vessel. Of course, how could he forget? That was how Amos had his accident. He was not doing well at impressing Hakeen. He tried another means of conversation. "The gods, which do you value the most?"

Hakeen gulped, choking on his water.

Amos burst out laughing. "Are you a Hebrew or an Egyptian?"

Phinehas looked at Hakeen to find what he had said wrong.

Hakeen completed his swallow. "Amos, that will be enough. Not all Hebrews know the Friend of Abraham."

Phinehas looked from one to the other. This was the second time they mentioned this Friend of Abraham. "Who is this Friend of Abraham that you mention, and where does He live? I must visit Him sometime."

Amos started to speak, looked to his father, and held his tongue.

Hakeen nodded. "You will not visit where He lives, for He lives in the lives of those who seek Him. Our people first learned of Him through our Father Abraham."

"Oh, you mean *that* Abraham." Phinehas blushed crimson. "Of course, I know of him."

Hakeen continued, "God told Abraham to leave his home and go to where He told him."

"Why would he do that?" Phinehas asked, hoping this subject would not further embarrass him.

"God gave him a restlessness that made him search for Him," Hakeen explained.

"Why? Wouldn't that make him unhappy with life?"

Hakeen nodded. "Life without the Friend of Abraham is empty. Nothing has much meaning."

Phinehas looked at Hannah as she added spices to the pot. He could smell the fragrant stew bubbling. His insides had stopped fluttering around like bats in a stable. He was feeling comfortable in this house. He could probably eat now.

His life would have meaning with Hannah at his side. He would not correct Hakeen, but life was fine without this Friend. When he ate with the rich Egyptians, he saw what life could really be like. He would not depend on this Friend of Abraham to give him meaning. "I enjoy life without knowing this Friend."

Hannah gasped.

He watched her until she looked at him. What had he said that disturbed her?

# CHAPTER 18

Then the Lord told Moses to speak to Pharaoh again. He did not want to go. The Egyptians had already suffered so much. He did not want so many people to suffer because he obeyed, but he did not want to know what would happen if he did not obey.

In the morning as the dawn began to lighten the sky, Moses stretched his staff toward the sky. Darkness spread over Egypt—darkness that could be felt.

Total darkness covered all Egypt for three days.

The vizier awakened from a restless night. When the sun gave a weak glow before it went dark, he remembered what Moses had promised. He had not imagined such darkness. The darkness was like fog, sweeping around him. He felt it. The air was thick. It covered him as if it could grab him. He felt confined. He could not think. His chamber seemed too narrow. It closed around him. The air grew hot. He breathed faster. His heart raced. Could someone die from darkness?

Badru gulped air to calm himself. He wrapped his arms around his body. His chin trembled. The Hebrew God now threatened their key god, Ra, the sun god and ruler of all other gods.

Sacmis approached him as he remained in bed. "Why aren't you worshiping at the Nile? Has Moses promised another calamity?

He nodded. Badru could not share his thoughts with Sacmis. She belittled his fears and told him how much more he should do. What more could he do?

She blamed him for the lice, as if he caused them to crawl on her. Did he not also scratch himself raw?

She cursed his inability to rid her house of the locusts. The sound of chewing still echoed in his head, making him shiver.

She accused him of causing the plagues by failing to feed the gods enough, as if they were pet dogs.

Should he tell her why he wished to be inside when the darkness came? Darkness brought evil. Did not the light battle with evil every night? He always blessed his gods when the sun arose again, for evil had not conquered, and the sun had won another day.

"What calamity did Moses promise?" Sacmis asked. She would nag him until he told.

He sighed. How could she blame this on him? "Moses promised darkness for three days." He glanced out the window. The dawn did not brighten the sky; in fact, the sky looked darker, as if twilight was coming.

"Why can't your gods fight the darkness away?" she demanded.

He wished he knew. The sunrise dimmed and suddenly all was darkness. He could not see his wife. He could only hear her, as he sometimes heard her in his sleep, droning on and on without a purpose.

"I want power, prestige, position. With you as high priest, I had that, until Moses came. Do you know what people say? That a new chief high priest would appease the gods better and keep Egypt's power."

Was he responsible for hanging the moon in place? Badru looked through his window for the moon or stars. He could see none. Day had come, but the blackness was like the darkest night.

His wife's droning continued beside him, for she could not see her way out of his chamber. A nightmare without hope of waking had begun. It would not end for three days. He sighed in anguish.

He could not please the gods, he could not please his wife, and he could not pretend to sleep for three days with her in the room with him. He felt her sit beside him.

She touched him.

Her touch used to bring comfort, respect, and satisfaction. Now her stroke made him shudder. What more would she say that he should have done differently?

Adlai's suggestion about circumcision came to his mind. What would she do to him if he did that? He grunted.

"What's so funny?" she demanded as she tightened her hold on his arm.

If he could make her quiet, he would feel better. This darkness concealed much evil. An accident could be believable. If only he had planned better before the darkness. What could he do with her body if he stopped her talking now? Why had he not planned better? He shivered.

"Don't think you can make me quiet!" Her voice pierced into his thoughts, as if she could read them in this darkness. "Do what I say, and this Moses wouldn't bully you and the gods so much."

He turned over and tried to sleep. Her presence made it impossible. She would be with him for three days and three nights. He moved to the edge of his bed, avoiding touching her, and shut his eyes.

Phinehas started treating more Hebrews instead of Egyptians. He was challenged by the Hebrews' injuries, but not because he sought to improve his swne abilities. His attention was consumed by a certain Hebrew maiden, who was like an angel to those hurt. She could charm a viper from striking. Indeed, Ptah's wife changed from complaining to thanking her.

He forced opportunities to cross her path. Thoughts of her consumed his head and heart. Her name was Hannah. That information alone had caused his heart to sing.

"Why are you smiling?" Aaron asked as he mixed herbs.

Phinehas tried to stop smiling but could not.

Aaron laughed. "My angel shines light to glow in your heart."

Phinehas tried to concentrate on the tonic he distilled with oil. "Life would be good with an angel."

They worked in silence for a time.

"Saba, why would having the Friend of Abraham as my Friend mean so much to Hannah? She avoids me, but I know it's not because of coyness. She's too innocent for that."

Aaron stirred the contents of the vessel in his hand. "The Friend of Abraham requires total control. If you do not allow Him control, you won't understand Hannah. She will become a thorn in your side, not a balm for your wounds."

"She could never inflict pain to me," Phinehas defended her.

"By her presence, she will show you a peace that you do not have. Your insides will be torn until you make things right."

"My insides fight to have her," Phinehas responded angrily.

"Then she does well to avoid you. She cannot make you happy, Phinehas. Only the Friend of Abraham can do that."

Phinehas shook his head. He wished for more time with the angel of mercy. She did bring peace to his searching heart.

Nathan and Ellis arrived with the other slaves at the work place as normal. They waited for the Egyptian overseers. None came. Instead, they saw Moses approach.

"I come from Pharaoh's palace. The Lord sent three days of darkness on the Egyptian district. No one will be moving from his house. No overseers will be coming for three days." He smiled as exclamations erupted at the prospect of three days with no work. "I don't know what more the Lord has planned for us, but I do know our time here is short. We must prepare to sacrifice to our Lord as He directs. Pharaoh's heart continues to be hardened. But the Lord's name will be glorified, even as it has been this past year.

"Many times the added suffering has caused you to wonder if God has forgotten you. I prayed for your burden to be lighter. Now the Lord brings one more plague. Before, you were protected without doing anything. This last plague requires you to choose. Look to your elders for instructions."

Nathan spoke for the group of men. "Toda raba for speaking to Pharaoh on our behalf. We are grateful."

"It's God's message. I'm just His messenger. If I had not obeyed, He would have used someone else. My brother Aaron also speaks for Him. Do as He commands. God's ways are best."

The men began to go home to tell their families the good news, but Ellis remained.

"Moses." Ellis went to stand beside him. "I don't know if you remember me. I was the one who yelled at you when we had to find our own straw for our bricks. I, well, I..."

Moses chuckled. "Nothing need be said. I was angry as well."

Ellis looked into his eyes and saw compassion. "I've been so angry at you, at your God, at Pharaoh. I want to be free."

Moses met his gaze. "If your heart is bound by anger, you can never be free. True freedom does not come from what you do, but Whose you are. If you are a free man, but only live for yourself, you will become angry when things do not go your way. If you live as God's man, you will have true freedom. Anger holds your heart where God seeks to hold. Let God hold those wrongs done to you."

"Has my wife been talking to you about me?" Ellis squinted, anger rising in him anew.

Moses laughed and shook his head. "I used to live with anger. I killed an Egyptian overseer for beating my fellow Hebrew. Was it right to be angry? Yes. But I allowed my anger to control me, and I did wrong. I had to flee Egypt.

"God worked on me for forty years in the desert. I learned to give my anger to Him, every time. Do I forget? Yes, but I'd like to think that I don't forget so often. Now I have freedom by allowing God to be in control."

Ellis listened intently. "How do you start?"

"Give every thought, every wish to God. Every time you get angry, give it to God. Tell Him that He is in charge. If anger seeps in, you stop, and give it back to Him. The more you do it, the easier it gets. When you forget, He reminds you. You will find the burden lighter when He carries it. And you are happier, because you are free."

Ellis extended his hand in friendship.

Moses accepted it and embraced him.

Standing this close to him, Ellis realized how tall Moses was, not just in stature, but also in character. Here was a leader that he could follow. "Toda raba."

Moses let go of him. "God bless you as you choose to give Him control."

Ellis returned home with a lighter step. His anger would no longer control his family. He would give God his hurts and allow God to control his wishes.

After three days, the sun returned to shine. Pharaoh summoned Moses. "Go, worship the Lord. Even your women and children may go with you, except leave your flocks and herds here."

Moses shook his head. "We must sacrifice to the Lord our God. We will leave no hoof behind us. We use them in worshiping our God."

Pharaoh erupted in rage. "Get out of my sight! Make sure you do not appear before me again. The day you see my face again, you will die!

"Just as you say," Moses replied.

The vizier called Maessai before him.

Maessai entered, wearing the same dirty cloak. This irritated the vizier. Could he not make himself presentable? He drank from his vessel before meeting Maessai's eyes. "Why isn't Moses dead?"

Maessai recited his rehearsed words, "His God protects him even from Egyptians who do not know his God. My most loyal help have returned with a change of ka. I will not fight a God."

The vizier paced. "Moses must die! I cannot take another plague!" He pushed his hands through his wig. Suddenly, he turned and glared at him. "You are not motivated enough." He reached in his pocket and threw the bag of gems at him.

Maessai caught it. Without looking at the contents, he slipped the bag into his tunic's pocket. He slid his arm to his sheath.

The vizier hissed the words slowly. "I want no more plagues to torment me. No God will control me. Take care of him."

# CHAPTER 19

M oses told Aaron, "The Lord brings one more plague on Egypt. Pharaoh will refuse to listen so that the Lord's wonders will be multiplied in Egypt. After that, he will let us go."

Aaron asked, "Should we go before Pharaoh again? He said he would kill us."

Moses did not answer.

Aaron fidgeted. "I know what you are going to say. 'We obey.'"

Moses nodded and headed toward the palace.

As they walked, Aaron asked, "Do you ever wonder if someone will try to kill you for all that you've caused Egypt?"

"They have."

Aaron stopped. "Someone's tried to kill you? When? Why didn't you tell me?"

Moses walked faster. "You didn't need to know. We will never know how many times God shields us from harm. We live our lives as if He's not around. If we saw what He did every day, we would worship and not fear."

"Moses…" Aaron shook his head and hurried to walk beside him as they entered the palace.

Pharaoh saw Moses enter his court. "Guards, seize him!"

Moses raised his hand. "I warn you of one final plague."

Dismissing the guards with a wave, Pharaoh settled back on this throne to listen.

"About midnight on the fifteenth day of the month, the Lord will go throughout Egypt. Every firstborn son in Egypt will die, from your firstborn son, to the firstborn son of the slave girl, even all the livestock's firstborn. All of Egypt will mourn, but among the Israelites, quietness will reign; not even a dog will bark. Then you will know that the Lord distinguishes between Egypt and Israel. After that we will leave."

As he spoke, Moses watched the Pharaoh for signs of softening, but there were none. Pharaoh's face was as unreadable as stone.

He clenched his teeth, anger surging through him. How could a leader watch his people die when he held the power to stop it? "I worked with your father, Phiops II. He protected, guarded, and built this kingdom. I served as general of his army. I would have given my life for his kingdom. But you, you don't even know what your kingdom is. Your people cry for mercy, but you do not hear. Your priests tell you of the true God's works, but you do not acknowledge. Your land lies ruined, yet you do not know. Who will be left to worship you when all is gone?"

The Lord outlined each step of the coming days to Moses and Aaron. They relayed the details to the elders and the people.

The plan was complete. The people would be ready. God would accomplish His mission.

Moses would soon see his family, God willing.

Zipporah… had she claimed the Lord as her God? He thought often of writing her, but no one could read it to her. The chasm between them deepened.

He wanted his sons to be raised Hebrew. They must see God. He wanted their young minds trained to acknowledge Him.

Pharaoh might be close to letting God's people go, but Moses wondered if Zipporah would ever let go of her sons, so that God could truly have them.

He went to his chamber, not to pray for the Hebrew people to be ready to leave, but for his wife to be ready for what God would do for her. He needed her.

C hike felt the change in his men.
The vizier had come to watch the training. "How are they?"

Chike shook his head. "If situations were different, I'd be pleased with such ambition and focus. They prepare as if for a campaign." He lifted his hands in a gesture of hopelessness. "My footmen practice to win. They have a leader, numbers, and now a reason to fight."

"How are the horses from the Hittites?"

Chike explained, "My charioteers can now train again, but they are not to full glory."

"How are the Egyptian recruits?"

Chike sighed. "Too soft. None see the need or the danger."

"What about those from Ethiopia?"

"Our army coerced them to enter our borders. They fear associating with the Hebrews, lest a plague fall on them. My army is divided."

The vizier listened, his brow furrowed. "Could we dismiss the Hebrews?"

"And allow them to unite against us?"

The vizier answered with a small nod. "What would you suggest?"

Chike sighed dejectedly. "If I knew, I'd be doing it."

As they watched the maneuvers, Chike pointed to a man on the ground. "See that, the Ethiopian soldier was supposed to protect the Hebrew soldier in that drill. He did not. That's why the soldier is down."

"That's not necessarily a bad thing." The vizier tapped his chin as he considered.

"That kind of thinking will destroy an army; all must present a unified front," Chike corrected.

"But fighting within the army would destroy the Hebrews' strength."

"Too many good soldiers would be lost."

"But you could strengthen the army afterward," the vizier countered.

"You are suggesting that I fight my own soldiers. I can't do that."

They fell silent.

Chike looked at the vizier out of the corner of his eye. Would he still have his life after his defiance? He stood his ground. "When the Hebrews leave to worship, do you think they'll come back?"

The vizier looked directly at him. "Why would they?"


A servant in the doorway startled Zipporah. "Is there news?"

The nod was enough to make her heart race.

"I'll be ready in a few moments."

The trip to her father's house seemed longer than normal. What news would the traveler bring? Why was Moses taking so long to return? Was he alive?

She rushed to greet her mother and father. News was precious. She would have taxed the donkeys if the servant had not slowed her down. "What news do you hear?"

Jethro hugged her. "We'll all hear at the meal. Let your heart be at rest."

Let her heart be at rest? When her husband could be dead? She breathed deeply to calm herself.

The meal dragged. The traveler enjoyed eating and did not hasten the meal.

Zipporah refilled his vessel many times during the meal. She wished that he would finish, so that her father could ask for news.

Finally, the man finished eating. He settled back on the cushions and made himself comfortable.

"So you come from the land of the Canaanites?" Jethro prodded at last.

The merchant nodded as he sucked juice from the fig that he had taken from the bowl in the center of the table.

Would this man ever stop eating? Zipporah shifted the cushions against the wall.

He took his vessel to drink.

"What news do you hear?" Jethro prodded again.

"Interesting. We don't often hear of Egypt except of her riches and glory, but lately..." He paused.

Zipporah held her breath.

"Lately, we do not hear of anything but Egypt."

"What do you hear?" Jethro encouraged.

"A ship's captain told me that Egypt sent for Ethiopia's entire army to come to her city."

"Is Egypt preparing for battle?" Jethro asked.

"Normally, the captain said, they would keep an army in Ethiopia to keep those people subservient. To remove their army could lead to an uprising in Ethiopia, but..." He lifted his empty vessel toward Zipporah for another filling. "Times must be bad in Egypt if they need the army there."

"Why would Egypt need Ethiopia's entire army?"

"Since the merchants all left, news from Egypt has been scarce. No one ventures into her borders. This moving of the army created quite a stir. Even the officers did not want to go to Egypt. Egypt sent part of her army to escort this army into her border. I don't even know how they are feeding all these soldiers. You heard about the livestock plague, right?"

With Jethro's nod, he continued. "After the livestock died, Egypt replaced its stock from neighboring lands. They purchased horses for their chariots from my neighbors. Their horses are good.

"The livestock arrived in time for the next plague—boils on man and beast, but only on the Egyptians. The Land of Goshen was spared." He chuckled.

Zipporah found it hard not to be angry. What about Moses?

"After the boils, when everyone finally healed, hail came. I'm not talking little bits of ice."

Gershom, who had been sitting by Zipporah, whispered, "What is hail?"

The traveler glanced to the corner where they sat. "Chunks of ice fall from the sky during a rain storm. That's hail. Guess you'd never see one here. Egypt only receives that kind of storm in her rainy season, but never like this and never now. She's in her dry season. Her flax and wheat were ready to harvest. Any rain at this time ruins a crop.

"When this hail fell, it was the size of a large grapefruit. Do you get grapefruit here?"

When Jethro shook his head, the man paused. "Let me see your hand." He grabbed Jethro's hand. "If you cup your hand, the hail that fell from the sky was that big."

Gershom's small voice burst out, "Like heaven fighting earth. Remember Father telling us of Lot running from the city before God hailed fire and boulders? Why is God angry with Egypt?"

"God wants Egypt's attention." Jethro glanced at Gershom.

The traveler agreed. "If this God doesn't have Egypt's attention yet, He will soon. Now Egypt has two armies to feed, plus their slave labor with no fish or game birds, no livestock, no wheat...

"But that's not the last of their problems. Locusts came. They ate everything, even the bedding made of flax. I can't imagine what the people are eating now. And with two armies to support?" He shook his head.

Jethro wondered, "Why would they bring a second army?"

"I can only speculate. Some say they fight themselves. What else could happen when you mix Hebrews with Ethiopians? No one can even guess.

"Most don't know why Pharaoh won't allow the Israelites to worship—not that I'd want my work force to leave. I like my comfort." He leaned back on the cushions and belched, extending his vessel again to Zipporah.

She held back a sigh as she refilled it for him.

He waited until he drank half before speaking again. "Even if

Pharaoh allowed his slaves to worship now, there's no hope for Egypt. Egypt is destroyed. Her power is gone."

Zipporah wanted to interrupt and ask about Moses. The merchant had said nothing about him. Was he even alive? The silence lingered and she chewed her lip. She gulped some water, trying to keep from blurting out her questions.

"Know something interesting about all of this? Moses has become a leader, not just to his people, but to the Egyptians. Many listen to his words. Some forsook their own gods, believing in the God of Moses. Even if the Egyptians do not follow him, they do respect his God. Guess any one would after seeing all those plagues."

"So Moses is still there?" Jethro asked.

The man picked another fig from the bowl in the center of the table and took several bites. He wiped his arm across his lips before speaking again. "He's preparing those slaves to walk away from Egypt and never look back. Pharaoh really has no choice—if he lets them go, he's finished. If he does not, he is finished. If I were him, I'd look to this God and do what He says, but... we'll see what happens."

Zipporah thought long into the night about what the traveler had said: "I'd do what He says." Would she? Was she *allowing* God to use her husband in His mission? Or was she still resenting the mission given to Moses and fighting God over where Moses should be?

Sacmis watched the entrance of the temple until the guard left the gate for his rounds. Then she stole through the doorway and down the hallway, glancing into rooms and passageways. "Badru, Badru, where are you?" Her whispers echoed in the hollow chambers.

Sconces in the hallways occasionally lit the dark interior. She felt the evil grow the farther she tiptoed into the temple's depths. Following the smell of incense, she found her husband sitting behind a table with papyrus papers surrounding him. "Badru, how thin you are! Why have you not come home?"

He raised his glazed eyes to meet hers. "Why are you here? How dare you contaminate the temple!" His voice was gruff, as if he had not spoken for days.

"Badru, you've lost weight. The leopard skins hang on you like limp rags. Have you slept? Have you been drinking too much? Your eyes are bloodshot. Why don't you come home?"

He stroked his chin, usually beardless, but now after weeks of neglect, quite full. He stared at her. "Why have you desecrated the temple by coming?"

She twisted the gems on her collar and fidgeted as she stood. "You haven't come home in weeks. What is wrong, Badru? Tell me. What's Egypt's future?"

He mumbled like one possessed. "He shares His power with no one. He is a jealous God. He won't give me control." He shuffled parchments on his desk, searching for something. Had he forgotten that she was there?

She looked over his shoulder. She saw scribbles. Ink spills pooled, waiting to be soaked.

She shook him. "Something is going to happen to Egypt, I feel it. You cannot help the gods anymore. Just come home and help me."

He tore from her grasp and shook his head, mumbling. "He has left no god alone. He laughs at even the small gods. He humiliates all of them. My gods are powerless, defenseless.... They are nothing. I trusted them." He dropped his head against the table.

Sacmis shook him again. "If you have lost faith in the gods, what is left for Egypt to believe?"


S acmis stumbled through the temple, losing her way in all the chambers leading to secret worship places. Reaching the outside gate, she paused to recover her breath. An assistant priest started to close the gate.

"Wait!" Fearing being locked inside, she darted through the gate.

He called to her in warning. "Why were you here?"

Ignoring him, she ran, seeking to forget the emptiness she saw in Badru's eyes. Had the gods taken over her husband's mind?

She entered their house and sat, panting on a bench inside the door for a long time before she gained her resolve. She would pretend that he was fine and all things were well. Things must be orderly and organized. No Hebrew God would destroy what she had built for herself. If she ignored it, Badru would heal and come home. She just knew it.

D inah helped pound grain into flour, while Salome made flatbread. "Ellis seems content lately. Do you think he's found peace with God?"

Salome paused in her kneading. "That's what we've prayed. Has Ellis told you?"

"No, I'm afraid to ask, lest it break the spell."

Salome shook her head. "God doesn't work magic like the evil one. He is all powerful, but not through magic."

Dinah nodded. "Sometimes it's difficult to separate what is truth from what is not."

Salome placed the flattened bread on the pile with the others. "As we listen and obey, God tells us. You'll be eating lamb with us on the fourteenth, won't you?"

"Perhaps Ellis's change is only because of the coming freedom. He acts as excited as a child, full of energy, chattering as if he can't hold it inside. I hope it's more than just freedom that's caused his change. How can I tell the difference?"

"Does he speak of God or just freedom?"

"He leads the evening prayers. His face does not hold the hardness that it did. As he carries Japhet, he tells him of God's power over Egypt's bondage."

"You already know. Are you afraid it won't last?"

"Maybe that's what it is." Dinah finished grinding the flour in the indented rock and gathered it together in a bowl.

"If it is from God, it will last."

"His excitement makes me so happy. It makes me want to sing." With that, she scooped Japhet in her arms. "I must get home before he does. Shalom." She went home humming.


The vizier noticed that Pharaoh had stopped worshiping at the Nile during the sunrise. Was Badru the cause? He had not seen him at the palace in weeks. Pharaoh did not even ask about him. Did Pharaoh know where Badru was and what he was doing?

The vizier went to Badru's home to investigate.

Sacmis met him in the inner chamber.

"I came to see the chief high priest."

"Badru's not here." She rubbed the amulet on her neck and did not look at him.

"Where is he?"

"The temple."

"When was he last home?" he asked directly.

Sacmis hesitated. She glanced at the doorway, clearing her throat. "Just before Moses's last visit to Pharaoh."

The vizier nodded and studied her for more information.

She fidgeted and picked at her collar.

"So I could find him at the temple?"

"Yes." She seemed relieved that he would leave. She walked toward the door.

He followed. What was she hiding? He would return after he went to the temple.

As he was leaving, she quickly added, "Don't go to see him. He is not well. Wait until he is better."

He smiled as he left. He went directly to the temple. He would find Badru. Something was not right. He pushed past the guard at the temple's gate. He barged down the hallway, searching. He heard mumbling and followed the voice to a dark room.

Badru sat at a small table strewn with papyrus sheets.

"What are you doing here?" The vizier took a step into the room, wary about why there was only a small candle lit.

Badru looked up.

The vizier took another step and looked into his eyes.

Badru did not acknowledge even seeing him. He slurred, "All the gods are against us. We are without hope." His voice broke. He burst into tears and sobbed.

The vizier watched in silence. When Badru stopped weeping, the vizier asked, "What are you doing?"

At his voice, Badru looked startled. "No god should have that much control. He wants it all. He can't have it all! I want some! He should share it with me. I want power, too..."

The vizier studied Badru's eyes. Their far-away, glazed look told the vizier that the chief high priest to Pharaoh had lost his mind. He would be no use to Egypt.

Not taking his eyes from Badru, the vizier backed out of the room. No wonder Sacmis had not wanted him to come. She was humiliated to have a mindless husband. He chuckled as he walked home.

This God changed everyone whom He touched. Some changed for evil. Some changed for good. Once He touched them, could anyone return to who they once were?


A dlai and Carmel visited Chike and Amunet.

Adlai began without hesitation. "We ask you to obey the voice of God. You can be spared on the night the Lord passes through Egypt."

Chike's face was firm. "I have heard. We will stay within our house."

Adlai grabbed his arm. "It won't be enough to stay inside. Death will come to all who don't have the lamb's blood painted on the doorpost."

Amunet gasped and touched her belly as her baby kicked. "Egyptians don't handle sheep or blood."

Carmel begged her, "It's the only way for protection, Amunet. We want you safe. Won't you do this?"

Chike held the door open for them to leave. "We appreciate your concern, but we are Egyptians. We cannot do this."

Adlai hesitated. "Wouldn't you do anything to keep your son alive?"

Chike looked at Amunet.

She hugged her belly.

Chike shook his head. "We are Egyptians."

Adlai turned to leave. "We won't detain you. If you change your mind before five days bring word to me. You may stay with our family."

Chike followed Adlai outside. "Your other request will be done in four days. You may obtain the requested item from the desert. I will honor Imhotep's request for his bones."

Adlai embraced Chike. "Thank you, my friend. I wish that I could be trusted as your friend."

As they walked home, Carmel swallowed hard. "Will God have mercy on them?"

Adlai shook his head. "Their hearts do not lean toward God. They are comfortable in what they know and do not want to change."

"But they don't have a hard heart against God. Look at all the gods they worship."

"Carmel," Adlai placed an arm around her waist. He swallowed the lump in his throat. "Worship must be acceptable in God's sight, not our own. He makes the rules."


Adlai walked outside the sheepfold, examining the yearlings. Tamara followed close at his heels. Bleating filled the air. Dust rose, as the lambs circled, trying to stay with the flock.

Tamara pointed. "I like that one, Abba."

Adlai rested his arms on the top rungs of the fence. The Hebrew shepherds had separated out their firstborn male lambs at the beginning of the month. They walked among them, selecting lambs for each household. "Is that the one you want?" Adlai pointed to the lamb.

One of the shepherds brought it to the fence. "Not a problem with this one." He passed the lamb through the gate to Adlai.

Adlai gave it to Tamara. He spoke to the shepherd, "I will take one more for my brother's family."

Tamara held the lamb in her arms. "Will Reut come home for the feast?"

Adlai nodded. "Chike granted permission."

He approached the owner of the flock. "Would tunics or cloaks be acceptable for exchange?"

The shepherd started to shake his head, but Adlai laid out the tightly woven rich Egyptian garments on the fence.

The shepherd extended his hand to touch the fabric but then stopped. His sheepskin cloak looked dirty and worn in contrast to the woven cloak's construction. He dropped his hands rather than touching the rich fabric with his soiled hands. He smiled.

Tamara held the lamb firmly on her lap as they rode in the wagon to deliver Nathan's lamb. "The feast day seems a long time away, but it won't be. I like lamb meat, but killing it will be hard."

Adlai remembered Chike who would not change his beliefs to be protected by the lamb's blood. "Sometimes, obedience is hard."


The four days between the tenth day of the month and the fourteenth passed slowly for Ellis. He could not wait to see his son growing as a free man.

Dinah was cleaning when he returned from his day's work. She rose from her knees. "Shalom."

"My busy one, what are you doing?" He took Japhet from her side as she struggled to stand.

"Moses said we must have no yeast in the house. I've been cleaning."

"But do we ever have yeast in the house?"

"No, that's why I make flatbread, but I guess other Hebrew

houses have it. Salome thought maybe we'd feel more a part of the feast if we cleaned."

Ellis looked not at the house but at Dinah. "The house looks clean and yeast free."

She laughed.

"I can always tell when you've spent time with Salome."

"How?"

"You're renewed like I feel with Nathan, now that I don't argue with him. What project do you have for tomorrow?"

"We'll dig horseradish and look for parsley along the canals. That will go well with the lamb, don't you think?"

Ellis jiggled Japhet on his lap. "I can smell the lamb already."

Dinah began serving beans from a pot over the coals. "What will freedom be like, Ellis?"

He thought before speaking. His eyes studied the stream of moonlight that reached inside their hut. "I used to think freedom was doing whatever I wanted, but now... I think freedom is holding the peace of God in the palm of your hand. And being able to do what He wants to keep it there."


Adlai wiped his sweaty palms on his tunic as he held the reins. His horses waited, harnessed to Aaron's wagon. His servants sat in the wagon bed. Why did he feel like a thief, when he had asked for the bones? What would he do if the vizier showed up? Planning in his head was different from actually doing it. He clucked to the horses and shook the reins before he lost his resolve.

He reached the step pyramid without difficulty. As before, he strode to the entrance, instructing the servants to stay close to him. Had Chike prepared the guard? Would they be able to enter? Adlai walked to the doorway. The guard was absent, and they entered without difficulty. He hurried, hoping he remembered the right passageways. Oppression and impending doom clung to him.

When they reached the chamber with Joseph's bones, Adlai,

breathless from hurrying, paused to instruct, "We'll bring just the coffin, not the sarcophagus."

The servants worked under Adlai's guiding hand. The stone-top sarcophagus was heavy. All the servants lifted together, grunting under its weight. The scraping stone echoed off the silent stone walls. They lowered the top to the ground.

Adlai looked at the coffin. "We'll lift the coffin from the sarcophagus and place it by the door."

They each found a place to lift. They retraced their steps, returning the stone cover onto the base of the empty sarcophagus.

Adlai released a sigh. The chamber's air was dead, silent, and still.

They next turned to the coffin at the doorway. The servants prepared to carry it.

Adlai instructed, "All ready? Lift."

He led the way through the narrow passageways. The weight of the air seemed heavier, the silence greater. Their breathing echoed in the passageways. When they reached the final door, he paused.

Looking at the sun, he was conscious that more time had passed while inside the pyramid than he had anticipated. He rushed the group to the wagon. Jumping into the wagon seat, he clucked to the horses to gallop toward Aaron's house.

Adlai breathed deeply of the hot desert air. He had left the oppressive evil behind him. He slowed the horses to a trot after his quick start. He took deeper breaths.

Moses and Aaron were waiting for him outside their home. He greeted them.

Moses tapped the wagon frame. "You've done well. Only your diligence enabled us to honor Joseph's request."

"God stirred me to obey."

Moses nodded. "This year has brought much stirring. It's always best to listen to His leading."

What will tomorrow bring?

# CHAPTER 20

The fourteenth day of the first month of the Hebrew year had come. The Egyptians feared Moses and his God, allowing the Hebrews to do no work except food preparations. They closed their shops and markets. The entire Hebrew district was quiet.

The day before, women had gathered hyssop from the canals and hauled extra water. No house held any yeast.

What did the future hold?

When twilight came, the Feast of Unleavened Bread began. They saved the lamb's blood and painted doorways up and down the streets of Goshen. Some doorposts remained unpainted. The occupants of those houses would share their meal with another family.

In the Egyptian district, Hebrews were conspicuous as they painted their entryways. Egyptians watched from their windows, afraid to step beyond their dislikes to protect themselves from what they knew was coming.

Adlai approached Moses. "Can an Egyptian partake of the feast? May they leave with us?" His training had already told him the answer, but he hoped there was another way to save his friend Chike.

Moses confirmed his fears, "No uncircumcised male may eat. If they are circumcised, then they may eat."

Adlai nodded, understanding the separation of their people from others. Chike would not be protected. He would never agree to circumcision.

R eut stayed with her own family. She helped Tamara care for the lamb one last day.

She did not feel part of all this Hebrew preparation. She would stay with her family tonight, as instructed, but she would check on Amunet when permitted in the morning.

This Hebrew feasting was restrictive and full of rules. She liked the freedom she had at Chike's house to do what she wanted until Amunet needed her. Was this Hebrew God worth all these rules?

Did she want to remember what this God had done? Amunet had told her that if the Hebrew God was really so powerful, He should free His people without Pharaoh's permission. Pharaoh must still be stronger, if the Hebrew God must ask him.

Reut did not know what to believe; what she had heard from Amunet or what her parents taught her. Amunet did fine without all this blood painting and flatbread. Reut might be only eleven, but she saw that Amunet and Chike lived so much better than her family. If that were any indication of how this God treated His people, she would rather stay with Amunet than go with her family.

E llis could already taste the feast planned for that night. Had he even had lamb before? He could not remember.

Nathan, Michael, and Ellis shared a lamb among their families. They would all eat at Ellis's house. It was closer to the edge of town, where they would join their clan in the morning as Moses commanded. The men painted their doorways, top and sides. They prepared the meat for roasting. They would not boil nor eat it raw, in accordance with Moses's directions.

Salome and Dinah had all the other requirements ready: the flatbread without yeast, the parsley with the salt-water dip, the horseradish mashed into a paste for the meat. Adlai sent apples, wine, nuts, and spices that were mixed together to provide a contrast to the bitter horseradish.

"Why the blood?" Ellis asked as they washed the area.

Nathan had been painting, but stopped and handed the hyssop to Michael. "After God created man and woman, they disobeyed. The Lord restored them through a blood sacrifice. God uses blood somehow to make us acceptable. I don't understand it all, but I just know that is what we must do."

Ellis responded. "How do you know that you've done enough?"

"It's not about doing, it's about being His. When you are His servant, you obey because you love Him. His desires become yours as you obey," Nathan said.

Ellis nodded. "Then I will be content today. Tomorrow may be a bit harder."

Nathan added, "God keeps us focused on what we are doing today. He takes care of tomorrow."

They washed from the jar by the door before entering their home, which they would not leave until morning.

As the head of the family, Hakeen gave the blessing for the feast. He stood over the meal. His cloak tucked into his belt and his sandals were ready to leave quickly. He stood before his family and another family whom they had invited.

They paused for the blessing, then ate with heartiness. Hannah and the other women served while the men ate. Amos, only thirteen years old, joined the men.

"Your cloaks are new, aren't they?" their guests asked.

Hakeen responded, "The Lord blessed us and prompted Ptah

to give to our family." He pointed to Hannah as she blushed. "Hannah served them while they had boils."

The visiting family said, "We, too, have been given gifts: gems and precious stones our own people mined from the desert hills. The Egyptians insisted we take them."

Conversation slowed to enjoy the flavor of the meat. They grew silent, each lost in their thoughts of what tonight would bring.

They finished the meal, spreading their pallets across the floor. Women placed theirs in the back, close to the hearth, ready to prepare the quick meal for the morning. The men settled near the door, as protectors from what the night might bring. All anticipated what God would do.

T he vizier watched as the Hebrews prepared for the night. Painting with blood! This confirmed that they were dogs. Their God had changed water into blood, and now they painted with it. Blood was no god to him, nor would he paint his doorway for any god, no matter how powerful.

The twilight turned to darkness. He continued to look over the city from his rooftop. All was quiet, unusually quiet.

He was still uncomfortable in the dark after the three days of darkness. He had felt trapped, confined, suffocated. Those three days had seemed to last for many seasons. When he had left his chamber after the light returned, he saw his image in the fountain's reflection. He had aged in those three days. His hair had turned gray. His face took on the look of his father overnight.

His father had lost his position as the pharaoh's vizier by failing to manipulate. Now he, also, could not control the pharaoh with his advice. Pharaoh no longer consulted him for anything. He doubted that the pharaoh even knew that the Ethiopian recruits did not compare with the Hebrew army that he would lose.

He watched the town prepare for darkness. Silence wrapped around his body. All sensed the coming doom. The wealth of Egypt had poured into the hands of the Hebrews, as if they were praising Moses for what he had done. The vizier felt a stab of jealousy. Moses possessed more power than he did. Moses controlled a people, even if it was just Hebrews.

Who was he? Merely the vizier, and not even that, if Pharaoh refused to listen to him. He was second to Pharaoh, but he hated his position. He might as well be a slave.

He suddenly remembered the tombs. How could he have forgotten to watch Adlai, and the bones? He had been preoccupied. He grabbed the railing around his roof in frustration. What could he do now? Adlai probably already had the bones.

A snort from his stables interrupted his thoughts. His horses, acquired from the Hittites after the livestock plague, were restless. He glanced down, expecting mischief. Nothing seemed amiss. He heard his horses shifting restlessly. He would check on them. Then he remembered what night it was.

He would send a servant. He would stay inside until morning. He dared not tempt the Hebrew God by venturing outside the safety of his house.

Chike was reclined in his chamber when Amunet found him. "Can't sleep, either?" she asked as she sat on the bed beside him.

"A heavy weight lies on me tonight," Chike responded. "Why can't you sleep, my Kitten?"

She shrugged and shook her head.

"What's wrong?"

"What if Adlai and Carmel are right? What if the Hebrew God attacks tonight?"

"And kills every firstborn male? Amunet, that's me. Look at me." He took her chin and turned it to her face toward him. "I am fine. I am not dying."

She lowered her eyes and rubbed her unborn child. "Would a God take so many lives just because He wants control?"

"How could He do it? We are safe here at home." Chike

covered her hand with his own, feeling the babe kick and squirm. "You are feeling fine?"

She nodded. "But there have been so many unexplained happenings. None of our gods could do anything that the Hebrew God has done in one year. Our gods did not protect us from anything. What would happen to me if you died? I cannot lose you, Chike. What would I do without you?"

"Oh, Kitten." Chike moved behind her, embracing her. "You worry over too many things. The little one makes you nervous. You try to hold the future in your hand. Just rest in the moment. Tonight was made for us." He turned her to face him. "We will be together as one for the night and let the gods fight in another house."

A dlai and Carmel finished their feast with those whom they had invited. All rested in their chambers, waiting for the sun to rise. Adlai and Carmel lay in their bed, but did not sleep. Carmel reached over to Adlai's hand to hold it.

"You are anxious, Carmel?"

She responded with tears in her voice, "Reut has become very Egyptian. She has accepted the Egyptian gods and does not know God. Didn't we teach her well enough?"

"She is young. Tomorrow, she will see the salvation of the Lord. Her ka will turn to Him."

"What about all those gods that she's embraced?" Carmel asked.

"They will fall away when God is all she sees."

"Have we failed to teach her?"

Adlai said, "We planted the seed. The Lord will make it grow."

"Then we need to ask Him to take away the weeds, quickly, for we leave tomorrow."

Silence ensued for a time, as their hands rested in each other's.

"Adlai," Carmel spoke softly.

He answered, almost sleep, "Yes?"

Until My Name Is Known

"What of Amunet and her baby? Would God take the babe if it hasn't been born?"

He turned to face her in the dark and spoke gently. "Could we stop Him if He did?"

"No, but... she has so much to lose."

"I know, my love. God is good. He will do what is best. We cannot stop Him, nor do we want to, do we?"

"I guess not." Her voice drifted off, but her mind did not. It would be a long time before sleep came. She would spend the time telling God her thoughts and hoping to understand His.

A ll Egypt waited, restless, anxious. Tonight was the promised night. Could they believe God?

Those watching the herds sensed unrest among the animals on this night. These flocks, brought from the southern slave lands after the livestock plague, needed tending even if there was no pasture. The cattle were nervous. The herdsmen remembered Moses's words. They felt for their daggers by their sides and looked for their distant companion on the hillside. Tonight was not a pleasant night to be alone outside.

Egyptian houses did not experience the feasting that the Hebrew homes did. They recalled the promises already fulfilled by God over the past year. Fear crept into their kas, grabbed hold of their minds, and would not let them go. Where could they hide from this God Who controlled the water, the earth, and the air?

# CHAPTER 21

Pharaoh lay in his chamber, restless, unable to sleep. He wanted to call Nitocris to his chamber but feared rejection. He did not want another outburst like last time. Perhaps, enough time had passed to make her pleasing again. As he deliberated, he walked toward her chamber. The palace was big, and he would decide how to approach her when he reached her room.

The entire palace seemed deathly quiet. With fearful anticipation, he walked quickly to dispel his eerie thoughts. His sandals echoed in the hollow passageways. He reached her chamber and entered quietly. It was dark, but he could see her in the moonlight from her window.

She was not in bed but sitting on the floor by the window.

"Nitocris," he whispered. He walked toward her. Should he embrace her?

She did not rise in respect of him, nor even acknowledge him. Her hand rested on her unborn man-child.

Pharaoh sank to his knees beside her and placed his hand over hers. He could feel the movement of the child within. "You are well?"

She did not answer but grabbed his hand.

He could feel the tension within her.

She gasped, squeezing his hand.

The tenseness across her belly relaxed.

She released his hand.

He touched her face softly. "What is it?"

She looked at him without speaking.

Another tightness, another contraction, another squeezing of his hand.

Her body tightened in pain, and she held her breath. When she let go of his hand again, her whole body relaxed.

"What is it, Nitocris? Tell me. Is it the baby? It is too soon. Should I call the swne or the midwife? What do you want me to do?"

She looked at him. Her eyes were hollow and lifeless. The pain replaced the emptiness in a moment and she grunted.

He would rather that she screamed out her pain. He would feel better, but she remained silent, stoic, sharing only the barest of touches, only when her pain was the greatest.

He wished to hold her, to make the pain disappear. He did not know about these things. He felt helpless. Should he get help against her wishes? He debated.

She squatted.

He embraced her from behind, supporting her.

She leaned on him as she pushed. Her head lay against his shoulder. She grunted again and fell back weakly against him.

He tried to see her face. The moon hid behind a cloud. Darkness surrounded them.

He held her as she pushed again. He could feel the baby as it fell between her legs. She lay back, unmoving. He remained where he was, holding her body like dead weight, feeling the blood and mass spread by his feet.

What should he do? He held her silently, wishing for wisdom.

She continued to bleed.

The mass did not move, nor did she.

"Nitocris, my love." He shifted to look at her.

She did not breathe. She was dead.

He carried her to her bed, covering her with the sheet. His arms were numb from holding her. The numbness did not compare to his ka, which felt lost.

She had spoken no word to him.

He did not hear his wailing, but the entire palace heard when he screamed, "No! Not her!"

A servant rushed into the room. She found the baby and the blood by the window where Nitocris had delivered her firstborn son, dead.


The Death Angel had begun his work. Fear that crept into the Egyptians' kas before twilight changed to a grief the world had never known. Death started, leaving no comfort.

Egypt's gods did not help.

They did not care that the Lord was a jealous God. Could wrong beliefs demand such judgment?

They were not Hebrews. The Hebrew God was not their God. This year had not convinced them that God wanted their worship. They had refused Him. They did not know God.


Sacmis despaired of Badru's well-being. But on this night, she wished that he were with her. Something was not right. She could feel it. Sleep would not come.

She planned for her son. Surely, if her son became the next chief high priest, she could save her reputation. As she planned, she walked the halls.

Walking by her son's chamber, she heard a noise. She called at the doorway, waiting before entering. Sensing something wrong, she ran to his bed.

He was dead. His death crushed all her plans to stay in power. Whom could she control now? Her tears were not for her son who was gone, but for the power she never had.

A munet felt Chike shudder at midnight. She turned toward him.

He did not move.

She felt for his breathing against her cheek. She pulled his head forward to look into his eyes. Her panic turned to anguish.

He was dead.

She screamed. She held his head in her arms against her breast. "Oh, Chike, you said you wouldn't leave me. I cannot sing without you. You are too strong to die..."

The contractions from her womb came, but she did not feel them. Her ka broke over her husband's departure. She cared for nothing else. The pain eased and flowed, but she felt it not. The anguish in her ka did not stop. She did not feel the gush of blood nor the baby that left her, as she continued to wail.

When her tears were gone, her voice was hoarse; she sensed the blood and looked. Her son was gone. New tears flowed. She cradled her son in her arms as she lay beside her husband until morning. No Egyptian god could make them live again. She was alone with no god to comfort her, only the promise that God had kept His word.


R a had risen. No one greeted his morning rays. Egypt had spent the night in mourning.

"Why are you here, Reut?" Amunet demanded as she sat on her bed. "Shouldn't you be leaving?"

"I've come to say goodbye. Come with us." Reut saw the bundle in her arms and gasped. Amunet still held her dead baby. Reut tried not to look beside Amunet where Chike still lay unmoving.

"I have nothing anywhere. Your God would kill me, just as He did everyone else that I love. Why do I still live? I wish I had died, too. I am tired of your God's wrath!"

Reut swallowed. Amunet's hopelessness was hard to watch. What words could bring comfort when everything was gone? "Come with me."

"I will appease Jackal, watchdog of Isis. He is angry. I must appease him before I die, so my baby and my husband will be protected and live happy in the Land of the Dead." Amunet placed her baby carefully on the bed, as if it was still alive.

She searched frantically, wildly, until her eyes settled on the golden cup before her shrine for the *Lady of All*. She thrust it into Reut's hands. "Let me appease your God before you leave."

Reut's eyes widened. The gift was immense. Amunet worshiped the goddess for her love, beauty, and joy. She avenged Ra and nourished the dead. "You will need this for the coming days."

Amunet shook her head. "My goddess won't need it. She didn't keep my husband alive." She roamed the house.

Reut followed, wringing her hands. Amunet's denial of the gods' help frightened her. Where would she find hope?

Amunet ripped a *menat* from her neck. The gold beads gave immortality and the amulet made of precious stones invoked divine favor. "Take this. It didn't help me last night."

Reut looked at it. She had watched the Hebrew silversmith make it for Amunet to ensure an heir for Chike. She swallowed. Amunet's heir was no more. She put it in a pocket in the folds of her tunic.

Amunet threw more statues off the table from their shrine. "Take these!"

The shrine to *Sa*, god protecting pregnancy and birth. "What faithless gods!" Amunet cried.

Reut bent to pick the statues from the floor. Her arms grew heavy with the offerings.

Amunet continued to view the room with the wild-eyes. "Here." She handed Reut a linen bag for the statues. She noticed her cloak of royal blue on the bench. "Take that, too."

"I couldn't."

"I couldn't wear it without..." At last, she broke down and wept.

Reut dropped the bag and embraced her. "Come with us."

"He said he wouldn't leave me. He promised. Why didn't the gods help?"

Reut held her.

Amunet pushed from Reut's embrace and ran to her chamber.

Reut grabbed the bag and the cloak, and followed not knowing what else to do. When she found Amunet, she had thrown herself onto Chike's body, clinging to it.

"You cannot leave me! Who will protect me from the God that killed you?" She began hitting Chike's chest. "You promised to protect me!"

Watching Amunet's outburst, Reut felt torn in two. She must return to her family, but how could she leave Amunet now? As she watched Amunet sob, she knew no words would help. She could do nothing to give her peace.

If this God would separate a couple who loved each other more than life, Reut didn't know if she could trust Him. She bent to pick up her gifts, and backed slowly from the room. At the doorway, she whispered goodbye, knowing Amunet would not hear her.

Reut left, weighted not only by her gifts but also by the meaning of them. She said goodbye to the only life she knew. She would no longer be a servant, though her service had developed into a friendship of a sort.

Should she not feel free? She laughed almost bitterly. Instead she felt like a nursing child without his source of food. What would she do? She did not want to sacrifice to this God. She only knew Him by what He had done to Egypt.

What else could she do? As she walked, she saw ugliness. This God had destroyed Egypt. Nothing lived. Nothing of beauty remained. She kept her head down as she hurried through the streets.

From every house, she heard wailing. The people mourned the loss of their heirs, their firstborns, their reason for power. How much grief could a nation take?

When Reut reached her family's courtyard, they were packing.

The wagon was loaded with blankets, clothes, tools, vessels of food, and her father's scrolls.

Carmel looked from the bundle she was packing. "Reut, will Amunet come?"

Reut shook her head, trying to hold back her tears.

Her mother's eyes rested on her arms, laden with treasures.

Reut extended the bag for her mother to take. "She wished to appease our God. Her husband is gone, even her baby."

"I wish..." Carmel shook her head and sighed, then straightened her shoulders. "Pack those with the blankets. We must finish before your father returns from his errands."

As Reut tucked the cloak under a worn blanket, Tamara ran to her side. "What did you bring, Reut?"

"Some gifts from Amunet." She hid the shiny items from her sister's view.

Adlai entered the courtyard, leading a horse.

Tamara jumped up and down. "Abba, what a beautiful horse!"

"Yes, the Egyptians turn with favor on us. This mare was given to me."

Carmel came from the house with another bundle. "Adlai, could we allow Nathan to use the horse with that extra wagon?"

"Our wagon is loaded?"

With Carmel's nod, he continued, "Good. Let's go to Goshen. Moses demanded haste."

He harnessed the horse to an empty cart and handed the reins to a servant. Reut watched him help her mother into the wagon. She scrambled with Tamara into the back. Her father shook the reins and started northward.

She looked at her house for the last time. She held the menat, hidden in the folds of her tunic, to reassure herself that she was not losing everything of Egypt.

As they left the city, they heard wailing from every house not painted with blood.

Tamara looked at Reut, wide-eyed.

Reut patted her hand. How could she appease this God?

The noise of the streets turned from wailing to busyness. Carts and backs were loaded with belongings, including unleavened bread made according to the directions of Moses.

Seeing the bread, Reut felt her stomach rumble. Since she had slipped to Amunet's house in the early hours before the sun rose, she had not eaten. She scrounged in one of the baskets in the wagon and found flatbread. Biting into it, she settled against the blankets to watch the streets, wishing to forget the sorrow in Amunet's face.

Tamara jostled beside her. "Shalom!" she yelled to their cousin Seth.

At Tamara's greeting, he waved. He was guiding his donkey loaded with tools of his father's silversmith trade. Seth's father manipulated silver into any god the Egyptians desired. Reut had watched him when Amunet requested amulets or statues.

Reut closed her eyes. She fingered the menat in her pocket. Would it protect her? She would need protection from this God.

Moses glanced in the wagon where Joseph's bones lay tucked beneath a sheet. He looked over at Aaron. "Ready?"

With Aaron's nod, they moved out, taking their first steps from Egypt toward freedom for their people.

Moses's insides felt like they held butterflies. He had not been able to eat this morning. Were they actually leaving with Pharaoh's permission?

When Pharaoh had summoned Moses in the middle of the night, grief lined his face. His red eyes showed desperation.

Moses had stood silently waiting before him.

Pharaoh swallowed several times before speaking. His voice cracked from deep emotion. "Go and never come back."

God had finally broken Pharaoh's ka. Restoration could come after all the other plagues—the blood changed back to water, the lice and flies left, the livestock had been replaced. But with this plague, no amount of pleading could make death less permanent. Nothing could bring back lives from the dead.

Moses sighed. He wished no harm to the Egyptians. Why did the people suffer for the sins of the leader?

Moses walked among the people, hastening them. Pharaoh's consent would not last long. Moses had a nation to deliver from Pharaoh's hands before he changed his mind. Grief would only last so long before Pharaoh realized he depended on the Hebrews for everything.

The excited chatter of the people rose around him. Moses preferred the solitude and quietness of Zipporah's mountain and the flocks. He shook his head and thanked God that his mission was ending. God's victory stirred his ka. He would see Zipporah and his boys soon. If Zipporah could see his people now, walking into freedom, surely she would accept God.

A aron nodded to Mack who drove the wagon holding his swne supplies, their belongings, and the bones of Joseph.

Mack raised his arm in salute. "No more suffering."

Aaron shook his head. "We aren't with Abraham yet, Mack, but the suffering should be lessened."

"That it should."

Aaron moved among the people, assisting the frail to find wagons to ride, greeting people whom he had treated during his ministry in Egypt. The people energized him. Their suffering would end. He reminded them to keep moving; they were not out of Egypt yet.

E llis held Dinah's hand as they walked side-by-side. Custom did not allow touching in public, but today was a day to celebrate. He carried a bundle on his back, almost all they owned, but his ka was free.

Ellis carried cloaks given to them, as well as bedding that would keep them warm during the cold desert nights.

As he walked, heading north toward the *Reed Sea*, Ellis glanced back to see Egypt growing small on the horizon. His servant's life was falling from him, like sand off a sandal.

Ellis looked at his feet. He wore sandals, the first time since birth. Egyptians, attempting to appease gods, had given them to him and Dinah. How nice they felt walking without the heat of the sand baking his feet through his callouses.

Ellis felt like a child waiting to receive his blessing from his father. What would God do? What would freedom be like? Ellis would raise his son without slavery, and suffering.

God had seen the sufferings of His people. He proved faithful. He did what He said He would do. He gave them freedom, real freedom, both inside and out. Ellis's anger that had held him captive had fallen from him when he gave it to God to hold. Ellis must continually give it to Him. Sometimes, his anger would surface and he would remember that he had taken back control.

He smiled at Dinah. She had blossomed through her friendship with Salome and her trust in God. They shared such happiness now. His peace was full. He did hold the peace of God in his hand.

Dinah glanced at Ellis and smiled. She found contentment in giving God her worries every day. When she forgot, she knew it, for the contentment would fly with the wind. What a difference a god made! No, what a difference God made!

She carried Japhet in a wrap around her front. Salome had been right. A child did make her depend upon God every day. But sharing that dependence with Ellis had brought harmony to their home. Dinah's heart was full.

Salome squeezed Nathan's rough, callused hand in hers. Their children bounced in the wagon, chattering like magpies.

She was thankful that she would no longer experience the sufferings of Egypt. It was good to obey. God had brought them through so many struggles, especially this year. Their hardships might not be over, but as she glanced at Nathan's back, covered now with a cloak, she thanked God that the beatings were behind them and the threat of oppression was past. God was good. They were blessed.

N athan caressed Salome's hand.
The wagon ahead of them held all they owned, driven by Adlai's servant.

Nathan's family knew God as Friend. God truly was a Friend for all times.

A wagon pulled beside them as they walked. Adlai called out, "Like a ride? There's room."

Nathan shook his head. "I want to leave Egypt on my own feet and feel the freedom that God has given us." He looked at Salome. "Did you want to ride?"

She shook her head. "My place is with my husband."

A dlai clucked to the team. He thought of his own story of fulfilled prophesy. Joseph's bones lay hidden with Moses's possessions. God heard the desire of a man and granted it four hundred and twenty years later. If he ever doubted God caring about the details, he would remember this.

Carmel sat, crying beside him on the wagon bench. Her concern over Amunet kept her from enjoying the excitement of her people. Adlai rested a hand on hers. "God may bring her to Him yet, Carmel."

She nodded, wiping her fallen tears. She inhaled a deep breath. "Reut came."

He nodded and patted her hand. "Look forward and rest in the Lord Who knows best—for Egypt, for Reut and for His people."

Adlai glanced to the back of the wagon where his two daughters sat together. Reut sat serious, mourning, and quiet amidst the excitement and jostling Tamara caused. Tamara bounced like a whirlwind of sand and wind that left a person wondering what hit them.

Adlai squeezed Carmel's hand. "God has begun His good work to take His people to their own land. He will finish it."

Phinehas drew his wagon beside Adlai. "Shalom. Have I reached the Levi tribe yet?"

Adlai answered, "Shalom. We are of the tribe of Judah. Levi travels in front of us."

"Toda raba," Phinehas replied. He had helped Hakeen and Hannah pack their belongings, now he hastened to his tribe.

Hannah drew him like flies to honey—he shuddered at the picture. The memory of flies he could do without, but Hannah was like honey. Perhaps on this journey, he could find the strength she had.

Amos chirruped the horses as they fell in line with their tribe of Judah. The wagon and horse had been a gift from Ptah. He cautioned Hannah after Phinehas had left, "Beware of that one. His intentions are written on his face, and his desire is in his eyes."

Hannah laughed. "He must first convince Abba, and I'm not sure he's interested enough to brave that fight."

"I'm glad Abba protects you, but so will I." Amos followed the dust of Phinehas's wagon with his eyes. "Abba's sight seems faulty since Ima died."

Hannah watched the dust as well. "Today is cause for celebration. We are free from the bondage of Egypt's gods."

He propped his wooden leg on the wagon's frame. It already throbbed from use. The scars of Egypt's gods would remain on his body, but Amos walked free of their power. "No Egyptian god will take my ka."

Hannah cautioned him, "Our strength may not be enough for the days to come, but like Aaron told me, we can rest on the God Whose power is as deep as it needs to be."

# CHAPTER 22

THE EXODUS: 2450 B.C.

P haraoh paced the roof of his palace. The garden, that had once flourished, was no more. No leaves offered him shade. He looked over his kingdom. Instead of seeing fields ready to harvest, he saw barrenness. Instead of his people bustling around the marketplace, the streets were absent of life.

Mourning magnified the hollowness of his life. He ate nothing. No servant attended his needs. The once-proud leader felt loneliness, rejection, and destroyed hope. Pharaoh Merenre Nemtyemsaf II knew the pain of having it all and losing it. He had fought the Hebrews' God and lost.

The week that had passed allowed the numbness to wear away, but in its place, Pharaoh burned with an unquenchable desire to control this God Who brought him pain.

He returned to his counsel room to begin business for the kingdom. He sat on his throne and listened as Egyptian supervisors reported.

"Pharaoh, your people fear to leave their houses, lest the Hebrew God still remains."

Another servant approached. "Oh Pharaoh, your stone quarries are silent."

Another bowed low. "Mighty Pharaoh, no bricks can be made. Your temple lies unfinished."

Pharaoh felt the triteness of these reports. What importance was his pyramid if Nitocris was gone? Why would he need bricks if he cared not for any temple?

He almost did not listen to the next messenger.

The servant bowed as he disclosed his report. "Bodies are rotting. No slaves are present to dig the graves."

The priests came behind him. Pharaoh noticed that the Chief High Priest Badru was not among them. They did not look into the Pharaoh's face. "Who will wash and prepare the bodies? Who will make the statues that protect their life afterward? Will the Land of the Dead hold all these bodies?"

Pharaoh turned to speak to his vizier. Where was he? He spoke with irritation, "Get the vizier."

An Egyptian servant returned promptly. "He is dead."

Pharaoh tapped his fingers on the armrest.

No one moved.

Pharaoh stared at the distant doorway. "Find them. Find Moses and his people."

Messengers bowed and ran from his presence.

Pharaoh stalked from his throne and slammed the door of his chamber.

The messengers returned and reported, "The Israelites wander in confusion. They went from Rameses to Succoth, camping at Etham. They follow a cloud that leads them. Then they turned back near Pi Hahiroth. Now, they stay by the Reed Sea, hemmed in by desert and mountain on either side."

"Prepare my army."

A messenger bowed low. "Chike, the General of the Army, is dead."

Pharaoh ran his hands through his wig. He rubbed the back of his neck. "I will lead the army. I will recover these Hebrews and Moses. Bring six hundred of the best chariots. Prepare for battle."

Did he have an army left to lead? What had the vizier said

about the state of his army? He held his breath until he heard the horse hooves of his charioteers beat through the empty streets.

He breathed deeply. His power was still great.

He mounted his chariot, grabbing the reins from his shield bearer. "Onward!"

The trumpet sounded the command.

This God would not win.

E llis pointed. "What's that dust in the distance?"

Others turned to look.

A cry broke among the people. "It's Pharaoh! He comes with his army to kill us!" Panic spread.

The people crowded around Moses. "Did you bring us here to die? Couldn't we be buried in Egypt?"

Watching his freedom disappearing, Ellis panicked, shouting from the back of the crowd, "Didn't we tell you to leave us alone?"

The people muttered to each other. "We should have stayed in Egypt, if we're just going to die in the desert."

Moses walked higher up the mountainside, and raised his arms. The crowd quieted as he spoke. "Do not fear. Stand firm. The Lord will deliver you today. You will not see the Egyptians again. The Lord will fight for you. Be still." He raised his staff over the sea.

Ellis watched as the cloud of the Lord, which had led them through the desert, rose in front of them. It thinned and filtered between the people. He saw nothing but the mist, felt only the damp drops of the fog, heard nothing of those around him. He was alone within this great group of people. The thickness rested on him like a blanket, wooing him to calmness. He could not see his hands held in front of him.

The cloud thinned. Those around him took shape once more. He was not alone. The air was still, and full of peace

Ellis searched for the dust of Pharaoh's army but saw nothing except the cloud. He stared in wonder. The fear and anger at the sight of Pharaoh was gone; calmness remained. Could a mist protect them from the power of Pharaoh?

How quickly he accused God when problems came! God already knew his problem and the solution. Ellis bowed his head in shame. He looked at his hands, remembering his words to Dinah: freedom is holding the peace of God in the palm of your hand and being able to do what He wants to keep it there. Ellis did not have to *do* anything for God's peace, he just needed to watch God work.

That night they camped between the mountains and the sea. An easterly breeze swept down the mountain and over the sea.

Many could not sleep, but watched through their tents' flaps. Memories of past beatings lent fear of what Pharaoh would do to an escaped slave. They listened for the hoof beats of Pharaoh's mighty chariots coming to crush them as they slept.

Those who looked to the glow of God's fire, which led them at night, received comfort.

When morning came, Etania snuggled between Nathan and Salome on their pallet in their tent. "Listen, Abba, do you hear anything?"

Nathan paused to listen. "What should I hear?"

"I don't hear the waves. Last night they calmed me to sleep as they lapped against the sand. This morning they aren't there."

They stepped outside the tent, looking toward the west. The Reed Sea was no more. In its place, a dry seabed stretched toward the horizon. An Invisible Hand held the water back on both sides of the path. They felt the ground pulsate as the force of the piled water moved up the wall.

Nathan stared. "Give thanks to the Friend of Abraham!"

Etania reached for her father's hand. "A path for us to walk!"

Nathan squeezed her hand. "A path to safety."

She looked into his face. "Is God going to keep us safe?"

Nathan studied the cloud that stood between them and

Pharaoh. He looked back at the path in the sea and nodded. "He will, indeed."

A s Dinah and Ellis took their first steps onto the dry seabed, Dinah grabbed Ellis's hand.

Ellis looked at the walls of water. "Afraid?"

She nodded.

"Fear turns me to God. Fix your eyes on the cloud, Dinah."

Dinah turned to see the cloud. She patted Japhet who rested wrapped to her chest. The sun's rays peaked over the mountain, glowing through the cloud. She shivered in spite of the cloak that she wore. "If we don't walk through this sea, we face death by Pharaoh. If we do walk through the sea, we walk toward God. Which is more dangerous?"

Ellis breathed deeply of the cool morning air. "The danger of God is the only place for peace." He held her hand tightly as they began to walk through the seabed.

N athan and Salome broke camp and followed the masses. Salome wrapped Jabin on her back as Etania twirled around them collecting small stones smoothed by the waters.

When they were almost across, Salome looked around them. "Where's Etania?"

"She was just here." Nathan's eyes caught the movement of a small figure walking from the crowd toward the wall of water. He ran to her. "What are you doing?"

"Don't you want to touch the wall, Abba? What makes it stand straight without bricks?"

Nathan took her outstretched finger and squeezed it firmly in his own hand. He breathed deeply from his run. He glanced from the wall of water to the dry seabed and then to the sky that hovered over them.

"Don't you want to touch the power of God?" Etania persisted.

Nathan shook his head, still breathing deeply. He studied his daughter. Could he have the faith like his little daughter, so strong in what God would do? Could he really touch the power of God?

Etania wiggled as she waited for his answer.

He nodded.

Together they walked to the wall.

He watched Etania out of the corner of his eye as they walked. She did not hesitate. She swung her hand as if she was going to get water at the Nile. She turned to smile at him.

Nathan saw the excitement, the twinkle, the love of knowing God. He squeezed her hand tighter. Did it take a child to trust God that much?

They stopped before the wall.

Etania wiggled her hand in his. "Let's touch it together." She raised their hands toward the wall.

Nathan hesitated. "Wait."

She looked at him with her child-like faith, questioning.

He swallowed, held her hand tighter, and nodded. "Ready?"

She smiled. "Yes!"

They touched the wall together. Nathan did not know what he expected to feel. He could feel the power pulsate through the water as it traveled up the wall. He swallowed as he looked to the top. He could see no spray. The power behind the wall felt moving, growing, intensifying, like it was alive.

Etania exclaimed, "God doesn't allow even a drop to hit us!"

"Our Friend of Abraham knows how to keep us safe."

"Why do you call Him Abraham's Friend, Abba? Why can't we call Him, my Friend?"

Nathan put his arm around her shoulders. "He's Abraham's Friend, but yes, we can call Him our Friend. And with power like this, we will want Him for our friend."


Phinehas sat in his wagon on the bank before the seabed. His fear did not lay with Pharaoh's army. No overseer had ever whipped him. He had eaten and drunk with high officials.

His fear lay before him. Would his wagon wheels sink? Should he follow this people to their land?

The people glanced behind them at the cloud, then stumbled into the bed as if that was the least of their fears.

He looked at the cloud. It held no power over him.

As he waited, the danger lay in standing still while this mass of people around him kept moving. He watched other wagons. Their wheels rolled without sinking. Was that Hannah's wagon further ahead?

He could not allow this opportunity to pass. He would overtake Hannah to offer her courage. Clucking to his team, he slapped the reins. He squeezed his wagon to the edge of the people and raced along the side to catch her.

He felt the firm surface beneath him. His wheels rolled as if on an Egyptian street. He slowed his wagon again to maneuver back into the movement of people to arrive beside Hannah. He coughed. "You are well?"

Hannah turned at his voice. Her smile and shining eyes told him more than her words. "God is preparing the way for us!"

He nodded without comment. What else could he say? She did not need his false courage; she had a strength that he did not have. How did he get that strength?

M oses had stepped first into the seabed and walked across. He stood on the rise of the opposite beach, waiting for the last person to cross.

The people had celebrated their freedom the last few days as they had traveled. Now at the first sign of difficulty, they accused him of bringing them to their death. How quickly they changed, like the wind-tossed sand.

The trials of the year seemed small now that they were leaving. Moses had chosen God's side and His people. How would God take this people from knowing only bondage to a people to defend God's honor?

Moses turned his face toward Egypt. He had grown weary of

Pharaoh's fickleness, his hardness. How could God show mercy to one so stubborn? Pharaoh's sorrow had not taught him.

Moses's eyes lingered on the cloud that stood between them and the Egyptian army. The noise and jostling of the people diminished. He looked beyond what he could see. His longing to know God consumed him.

Aaron's touch and voice startled him. "Will you stand here all day? The people have crossed."

Moses shook his head to clear his thoughts. He looked to the cloud. It was distant again. All the people waited with him on this side of the sea. Moses stretched his staff toward the cloud.

The cloud lifted.

The people gasped as they saw the army waiting.

P haraoh's thirst for revenge so consumed him that he did not see the walls of water. He saw only *his* slaves huddled on the other side of the seabed. He would finally conquer this God Who had brought so much heartache to him.

Commanding his trumpeter, "Sound the call to advance."

Pharaoh led the attack. His army followed. Reaching the center of the seabed, his horse began to sink. He whipped it harder. Although stuck up to its hocks, with sweat glistening from his neck, it could not advance.

Pharaoh peered over the side of his chariot. His wheels spun buried to the axle in the soft sand. After hearing a cracking, he was jarred to a stop. His wheels splintered and broke.

Pharaoh heard his footman yell as they retreated, "Run! The Lord fights for them!"

Pharaoh jumped out of the chariot. "Stop! We must fight! We will win against this God!"

He ran after his shield bearer who was running away.

"Wait! Stay here! I must win against this God!"

Moses watched from his post. At the first sign of the army's confusion, he stretched his staff over the sea.

The walls broke. The sea roared into its place, engulfing everything in its wake.

The people watched the wall of water fall with a mighty roar. The waves resounded to regain their territory.

The path they had just walked was no more.

No soldier's retreat succeeded. Leather straps ripped from horses. Bodies tossed in the torrents. Water engulfed chariots, horsemen, archers, and footmen as if they were mere flies. Bodies, mangled and grotesque, spoke of a power that would destroy.

No one survived. It was as if the army never was.

The Israelites watched silently. They had just walked through those walls that held such power. They had touched the same ground and safely reached the other shore by the power of their God. They had witnessed Egypt's great army destroyed.

They stared in fear and wonder. What God had they decided to follow? Were they safe?

The roar resounded in the people's mind, but the sound of wave following wave was all that remained.

No longer would Pharaoh command their obedience. No longer would he hinder their worship. No longer would the power of Egypt's gods hold them. They were free. Pharaoh was defeated.


Then Moses and the Israelites sang to the Lord.
*The Lord is my strength and my song;*
*He has become my salvation.*
*He is my God… And I will exalt Him…*
*The Lord is a warrior; the Lord is His name…*
*Your right hand, O Lord, shattered the enemy…*
*The enemy boasted, 'I will pursue, I will overtake them…'*
*But You blew with Your breath, and the sea covered them.*
*They sank like lead in the mighty waters.*
*"Who among the gods is like You, O Lord?*

*Who is like You—majestic in holiness, awesome in glory, working wonders?...*

*In Your unfailing love You will lead the people You have redeemed.*

*In Your strength You will guide them to Your holy dwelling.*

*The nations will hear and tremble;*

*Anguish will grip the people of Philistia.*

*The chiefs of Edom will be terrified,*

*The leaders of Moab will be seized with trembling,*

*The people of Canaan will melt away;*

*Terror and dread will fall upon them.*

*By the power of Your arm they will be as still as a stone—until Your people pass by, O Lord...*

*You will bring them in and plant them on the mountain of Your inheritance—*

*The Lord will reign for ever and ever."*

God looked down from His throne. *"I have raised you up for this very purpose that I might show you My power and that My name might be proclaimed in all the earth."*

# EPILOGUE

Thus, the Old Kingdom of Egypt ended. God had indeed shown not just Egypt, but the world, that He was the Lord. News reached throughout the civilized world of Israel's God Who had shown Egypt His supremacy. The nations heard and feared. The world proclaimed His Name.

The great world-renowned Egypt had fallen. They fought the battle with God. God had won. It would take over four hundred years before Egypt would again become a leader, recognized by the world as a threat for ultimate power. But their time in 2450 B.C. had come to an end.

Historians and archaeologists puzzle over the location of Imhotep's bones. They look in the wrong country and the wrong year.

God continues to desire His name to be proclaimed in the entire world. It will again be proclaimed at the end of time, when He will rule as King of kings, Lord of lords, the Great I AM. He will no longer seek friends; He will demand total allegiance. At that time, just like the time of Egypt, no one will question His authority. He will reign as the one true King.

# SUMMARY REMARKS

I desired to weave the biblical account with archaeological and historical records to tell the story of the Hebrew exodus from Egypt. Any discrepancies were not intentional, with the exception of Nitocris. History shows that she ruled alone for a short time after Pharaoh's death. I altered this.

A careful reading of the Bible and other research reveals details that may be different from some readers' recollections of the biblical account. Consider the following.

Moses and Aaron maintained vitality in their eighties. Moses's children were young, as seen by Zipporah circumcising them. They aged differently than we do today.

Josephus, a historian, documented Moses's first wife.

Zipporah rode a donkey through the desert in the Exodus, not a camel.

Archeologists find stone homes during this time in Jethro's land, not tents. This may be due to predictable pastures and less desert-like conditions than the present. (Much can change in four thousand years.)

The timing of the Exodus is essential to biblical chronology. Until recently, the wrong date was assigned. This wrong date kept archeology from substantiating the biblical record. Many scholars doubted the reliability of the Bible because the stories could not be proven. If Egypt was destroyed by ten plagues, history should show it. If six million people wandered in the desert, archaeology should demonstrate it, but it could not. People doubted the Bible.

Dr. Gerald E. Aardsma's date of 2450 B.C. for the Exodus brings cohesiveness to the biblical and archeological accounts. No historian could explain why the Old Kingdom of Egypt disappeared without a trace. Aardsma's research answers why. Archaeologists found an unknown people wandering the desert during this time. The Exodus of the Israelites explains them. Aardsma's research gives answers. Further details regarding his findings can be found at www.BiblicalChronologist.org.

*Yam Suph* from the Hebrew Bible/Old Testament has been translated Red Sea. More recently, a better translation of Sea of Reeds or Sea of Seaweed has been suggested. The location for Israel's crossing substantiated by archaeological records lies not in the modern day Red Sea area but at Lake Bardawil, close to the Mediterranean Sea. This Lake Bardawil, walled in by mountains, trapped the Israelites with no escape. Aardsma gives depth calculations substantiating the number of people crossing in the given amount of time.

Several editors have corrected my capitalization of God and the pronouns for Him. According to the current standard, God's pronouns, (i.e. Who, His, He) and His body parts (i.e. hand, finger) should not be capitalized. When those words have referred to little gods, I honor that standard. But for the sake of respect for God, as well as clarity in the text, I have chosen to capitalize them regardless of the standard. I trust the reader was not overwhelmed by the 'mistake' of this choice.

The Bible tells the story in Exodus chapters 1–15. Read it for yourself with preconceived notions aside.

I pray that you not only enjoyed the book, but saw God better through it. Let me know at www.sonyacontreras.com.

*Map of the North Sinai peninsula showing the route of the Exodus (dashed line) which the archaeological data imply. Open circles mark the location of archaeological sites, solid circles mark modern towns.*

# ACKNOWLEDGMENTS

The New International Version by the International Bible Society, Zondervan Bible Publishers was used when the Bible was directly quoted. Scripture used in Chapter 6 is from Hebrews 11. Scripture at end of the book is excerpted from Exodus 15:2–18. The story-line was taken from Exodus 1–15.

Without the research of Dr. Gerald E. Aardsma, this book would not have been possible. His research in Biblical Chronology changed the date of the Exodus to synchronize biblical and secular chronologies of Egypt. His research in the area of the Exodus is explained in his book, *The Exodus Happened 2450 B.C.* Further research in the area of Biblical chronology can be viewed at www.BiblicalChronologist.org. Aardsma researches from a conservative Christian perspective, assumes historical integrity of the Bible and shows the sacred and secular data harmonize without difficulty when the date of the Exodus is right.

*The Works of Josephus* by William Whiston provided crucial scenes to supplement the Scriptures, particularly those of Moses's years as General of the Egyptian Army and his marriage to the Ethiopian princess.

No book comes together without much help. Bob Rutherford's

prayer support kept me focused through the book's many revisions. Thank you.

My boys listened to problems that I had to solve. Their quietness while I finished a thought and their enthusiasm for the plot allowed me to write and edit until they memorized the scenes and saw God in their sleep. I thank you, Joey John, Josiah, Jonathan, Jonas, Jacob, James, Joshua, and Michael.

Technology overwhelms me. If it were not for my son Joey John and his wife Rachel, I would have lost my entire manuscript several times and never found it. Joey's patience as he solved formatting problems helped me believe that my book would be finished. His skills were indispensable. Time sacrificed during school cannot be measured but is appreciated. Rachel's ability to reduce redundancy and correct awkwardness in the flow of the story helped sharpen the message. Thank you, Joey John and Rachel.

The Holy Spirit is the comforter, but if there was anyone who could be personified as the comforter, it would be my best friend and husband. He came beside me when I doubted whether I could write a book. He read the book in its roughest form and said, "It is good." He provided the funds for several editors. He rejoiced with me when the chosen cover designer consented. He prayed me through the printing process. He celebrated its completion, assuring me that the sales would come. He reminded me of my purpose—for God and God alone. The words "thank you" are not enough.

# GLOSSARY

- *Abba* Hebrew, term of endearment for father
- *Apis* god, protector of dead, renewer of life; symbolized Pharaoh's courage, strength, and virility
- *Belladonna* very toxic plant used for pain relief and anti-inflammatory
- *Chevon* goat meat
- *Cubit* unit of length, distance from the fingers to the elbow; 17 to 21 inches
- *Fathom* unit of length, distance of a man's outstretched arms; 6 feet
- *Geb* god of earth; depicted by ram, bull, or crocodile; personified earth; freed dead from tombs
- *Heqet* goddess of childbirth and fertility; symbolized by frogs; represented fruitfulness, new life
- *Horus* god of sky; falcon or hawk-headed; stood for wholeness and renewal
- *Ima* Hebrew, term of endearment for mother
- *Imhotep* Hebrews' ancestor: Joseph, son of Jacob, Egyptian patron of wisdom and medicine
- *Isis* goddess of medicine and peace; protector of dead; goddess of children

- *Jackal* god of death; watchdog of Isis, guarded tombs
- *Ka* spirit
- *Khepri* god of resurrection, creation, movement of sun, rebirth; beetle-headed
- *Lady of All* goddess of love, beauty, joy; avenged Ra, nourished the dead
- *Lotus* plant harvested near the Nile River
- *Menat* amulet worn to secure divine protection and fertility
- *Meretseger* goddess in cobra form; known as 'she who loves silence'; poisoned robbers of tombs
- *Nun* god of fertility of the Nile; controlled flooding of Nile
- *Nut* goddess of sky, mother of all; nightly she swallowed sun giving birth to it in morning
- *Oy vey* Hebrew, exclamation of dismay, grief, or exasperation
- *Ra* god of sun, creator of the universe, gods, and first people; ruled world until end
- *Reed Sea* commonly mistaken as Red Sea; Hebrew literal translation "Sea of Reeds"
- *Sa* god shielding young children against evil; used as amulet or good luck charm
- *Saba* Hebrew, grandfather
- *Sacmis* goddess protecting pregnancies and birth; warrior goddess
- *Sah* companion star to Orion; father of gods; guided the king
- *Sarcophagus* a stone coffin displayed above ground
- *Sekhmet* god preventing epidemics; protector of Pharaoh in wartime
- *Senehem* god of pests; locust-headed god; protected Egypt from pests
- *Seth* god of thunder, desert, infertility, and chaos
- *Shaduf* watering system: pole mounted on a seesaw, buckets pivoted from water to plants

- *Shalom* Hebrew, greeting for meeting or parting; means 'peace' or 'completion'
- *Shu* god of air; calmed, reassured
- *Span* measurement in ancient times from tip of thumb to tip of middle finger
- *Swne* Egyptian, doctor; pronounced sunu
- *Talent* unit of mass, equivalent to 60 pounds
- *Tefnut* goddess of water and moisture
- *Thoth* god of magic; head of ibis or baboon
- *Thuban* North Pole Star in ancient times; star from Draco constellation
- *Toda raba* Hebrew, thank you very much

# BIBLIOGRAPHY

Aardsma, Gerald E. *The Exodus Happened 2450 B.C.* ARP Aardsma Research and Publishing, 2008.

*Ancient African Medicine, Egypt (Khemit) and the World.* africaresource.com. Web. Accessed April 22, 2014.

*Ancient Egyptian Medicine.* En.wikipedia.org. Web. Accessed April 22, 2014.

*Atropa belladonna.* En.wikipedia.org. Web. Accessed April 22, 2014.

*Baby Girl Names.* Babynamesworld.parentsconnect.com. Web. Accessed 2013.

Bailey, Ted. *The Sinai Peninsula.* Testimony-magazine.org. September 2003. Web. Accessed April 16, 2014.

Bellair, Lynn. *History of Egyptian Medicine and Philosophy.* Realmagick.com Web. Accessed April 22, 2014.

Bowden, Hugh. *Mystery Cults of the Ancient World.* Princeton: Princeton Univ. Press, 2010. pp. 156–159.

Chiddingston. *Egyptian Calendar.* Chiddingstone.kent.sch.uk October 2012. Web. Accessed 2013.

Chosen People Ministries. *The Meaning of the Passover.* Chosenpeople.com 2013 Web. Accessed 2013.

Clayton, Peter A. Chronicle of the Pharaohs: Reign by Reign

Record of the Rulers and Dynasties of Ancient Egypt (2686–2181 B.C.). Thames and Hudson, 1994. pp. 30–67,.

Dollinger, André. *Ancient Egypt: Brick Makers.* Reshafim.org. 2010. Web. Accessed 2013.

Dollinger, André. *Ancient Egypt: Fruits and Vegetables.* Reshafim.org. April 2010. Web. Accessed 2013.

Dunn, Jimmy. *Defensive Equipment of the Egyptian Army.* TourEgypt.net 1996–2013. Web. Accessed 2013.

Dunn, Jimmy. *Labors of Pyramid Building.* TourEgypt.net November 14, 2011. Web. Accessed 2013.

Dunn, Jimmy. *Military Man in Ancient Egypt.* TourEgypt.net 1996–2013. Web. Accessed 2013.

*Egypt Weather and Climate.* Touregypt.net August 21, 2011. Web. Accessed 2013.

Emotional and Psychological Trauma: Symptoms, Treatment and Recovery. Helpguide.org. Web. Accessed April 22, 2014.

Eyewitness Travel Guides: Hebrew Phrase Book. NY: A DK Publishing Book, 1999.

Gower, Ralph. The New Manners and Customs of Bible Times. Chicago: Moody Press, 1978.

Harri, Macdonalds. *How to Treat for Shock During First Aid.* Wikihow.com. Web. Accessed April 22, 2014.

Harris, Geraldine. *Gods and Pharaohs from Egyptian Mythology.* NY: Schocken Books, 1982. pp. 51–52.

Hassan, Fekri. *The Fall of the Egyptian Old Kingdom.* Bbc.co.uk, 2010. Web. Accessed 2013.

Heinrichs, Ann. *Egypt: Enchantment of the World.* NY: Children's Press, 2012.

Hill, Jenny. *Old Kingdom: Egypt.* Ancientegyptonline.co.uk 2010 Web. Accessed 2013.

Hill, Jenny. *Queen Nitocris (Neterkare or Nitikrty).* Ancientegyptonline.co.uk 2010 Web. Accessed 2013.

*How to Make Baskets.* wikihow.com Web. Accessed 2014.

*How to Make Incense.* Scentsofearth.com. Web. Accessed May 7, 2014.

Hurdman, Charotte, Steele, Philip and Tames, Richard. *The*

*Illustrated History Encyclopedia: The Ancient World*. Southwater Annes Publishing Limited, 2000. pp. 72–130.

Jackson, Kevin and Stamp, Jonathan. *Building the Great Pyramid*. Fireflybooks, 2003. pp. 32–100.

Lambert, Tim. *Life in the Old Testament*. Localhistories.org. Web. Accessed April 14, 2014.

Lockyer, Herbert Sr. *Nelson's Illustrated Bible Dictionary*. NY: Thomas Nelson Publishers, 1986.

Locust and Other Migratory Pests Group. *Food and Agriculture Organization (FAO) of United Nations, Rome, and Italy*, fao.org. 2009. FAO 1994 Desert Locust Guidelines (5 Volumes) Rome: FAO

*Lonely Planet Phrasebooks: Hebrew*. Australia: Lonely Planet Publications, 2007.

Long, Terry. *Ancient Egyptian Burial Customs*. Chicago: The University of Chicago Press, 2009.

Mai. *Ancient Egyptian Armies*. Ancientmilitary.com 2009–2012. Web. Accessed 2013.

Meeks, Dimitri and Favard-Meeks, Christine. *Daily Life of the Egyptian Gods*. London: John Murray Publishers Ltd., 1996.

Memon, Mohammed A. *Brief Psychotic Disorder Clinical Presentation*. eMedicine.medscape.com, September 3, 2013. Web. Accessed April 28, 2014.

MummyFriends.com. *Common Egyptian Phrases*. 2004–2011.

Philip, Neil. *Annotated Guides: Myths and Legends*. NY: DK Publishing Inc., 1999.

Putham, James. *Eyewitness Books: Mummy*. NY: DK Publishing, Inc., 2004.

Shanks, Hershel. *Ancient Israel*. Washington D.C. Biblical Archaeology Society, 1999.

Taylor, John. *Death and the Afterlife in Ancient Egypt*. Chicago: The University of Chicago Press, 2001.

*Ten Egyptian Plagues for Ten Egyptian Gods and Goddesses*. inthedoghouse.hubpages.com. April 9, 2012. Web. Accessed 2013.

Thompson, James C. *Medicine in Ancient Egypt*. Womenintheancientworld.com. July 2010. Web. Accessed 2013.

Thompson, James C. *Mistress of the House*. Womenintheancient-world.com July 2010. Web. Accessed 2013.

Thompson, James C. *Women in the Ancient World*. Womenintheancientworld.com July 2010. Web. Accessed 2013.

Thompson, James C. *Women's Clothing and Fashion in Ancient Egypt*. Womenintheancientworld.com July, 2010. Web. Accessed 2013.

*Three Levels of Slave Labor*. Jackmack.net Web. Accessed 2013.

Wagner, Jordan Lee. *Daily Blessings: Eating Meals*. Home.comcast.net. 1998. Web. Accessed April 16, 2014.

Wilkinson, Richard H. *The Complete Gods and Goddesses of Ancient Egypt*. London: Thames and Hudson LTD, 2003. pp. 70-71, 84, 101-102, 111-112.

Wong, Cathy. *What is White Willow Bark?* Alternativemedicine-about.com May 23, 2014. Web. Accessed April 22, 2014.

*Works of Josephus, The*. Translated by William Whiston. MD: Hendrickson Publishers, Inc. 1987.

# THERE'S MORE

The series *Tell of My Kingdom's Glory* began with Book One, *Until My Name Is Known*, where God brought all to see Him. The Israelites escaped Pharaoh's control and left Egypt's gods.

The series continues with Book Two, *I Have Called You by Name*.

The Israelites are not ready to be God's people. They wish to reach their promised land, but God has other plans for them. They find God seeking them. Some do not want His restrictions. He is jealous and demands their obedience. Others find safety in those boundaries. All depend upon God to reach their land.

The Time: 2450–2409 B.C.
The Place: The Sinai Desert
Becoming a nation is more than just freedom.
*I Have Called You by Name*
Brings Israel from the Exodus
To the entrance of the Promised Land.
See God's glory.
Learn God's law.
Feel God's judgment.
Know His care.

> *I Have Called You by Name* brings all to know
> The one true God.
> Read it to know Him.

# KNOW HIM

Knowing about Jesus is not knowing Him.

We could never satisfy a holy God's requirements. We fall short of what God wants. So God prepared the way for man to enter His presence. His Son died, a substitute for us. His justice was then satisfied. Our judgment can be removed.

Please do not hesitate to accept His Work in your life. Tell Him you fall short of His holiness. Recognize He paid for your sin. Ask Him to remove your sin. His requirements are satisfied. Thank Him.

Know Him and be His.

# ABOUT THE AUTHOR

Growing up with five sisters, Sonya Contreras asked God many questions, even when she did not like His answers. Graduating from Cedarville University and Institute for Creation Research with a Master's Degree in Science Education did not stop her questions. Marrying her best friend and homeschooling their eight sons, she found that dreams do come true, in spite of unanswered questions. Trusting God, Who knows all answers, she shares questions that matter weekly at www.sonyacontreras.com.

## IF YOU LIKED UNTIL MY NAME IS KNOWN, READ THIS FREE SHORT STORY

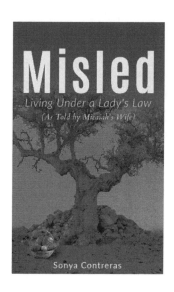

Available Here

http://sonyacontreras.com/misled-free

# ALSO BY SONYA CONTRERAS

*Tell of My Kingdom's Glory Series* tells the love story between God and His people.

In **Book One:** *Until My Name Is Known,* God brings His people to see Him as He frees them from the bonds of Egypt.

In **Book Two:** *I Have Called You by Name,* God draws His people to know Him, as He provides safety through the demands of His Law and teaches dependence upon Him to reach their Land.

In **Book Three:** *I Am with You,* God reassures His people that, as He had been with Moses, so would He be with them. He brings them into the Land promised them, giving rest from their journey.

*He Has Not Forgotten Series* tells why man needs God, as the short stories tell of the judges.

### In **Book One: But You Have Not Obeyed Me**

God's people forget God. They scarcely survive, crushed by their own choices. When they cry to Him, He restores truth through judges. These six short stories show their cycle during the judges: sin, suffering and salvation.

COMING SOON: In **Book Two: Remember Me** the series continues to tell of Jephthah, Ibzan and Samson and how God helped them remember Him.

### *Expecting Jesus*

See Jesus through the eyes of those who met Him. Most expected Him. Only a few were ready for Him.

Short stories showing how people were changed when they met Jesus.

### *Faith Like a Mustard Seed: Wisdom for Your Walk*

Cultivate that mustard seed faith by knowing the Savior. See how others' faith has grown by looking to Christ. Take your everyday needs and struggles to Him, and find your faith held secure in His hands. And Watch the mountains move.

### *Our Story of His Lessons: Twenty Years of Christmas News*

People ask about our boys and how we do it. The yearly letters found here give you a glimpse into those answers.

We've lived in the foothills of the Sequoias for over eighteen years. Almost half of the boys were born in the house. We've set down roots, not only in our garden and with our animals but in our hearts where the land has helped us settle. We share memories on a yearly basis of what God teaches us, thus the chronicles of the Christmas letters.

### Let Her Hear: Parables from a Mom

These parables (devotionals) are not a substitute for careful, study of the Word. They give a starting point to focus on where God wants you to be all day, a help to see Him even while doing the mundane, routine, necessary, "mom" things in life. They remind you of the heavenly realm that's part of the earthly walk.

They were taken from articles previously written for my website and made into book form.

### How Suffering Shows God's Love: A Paradox Explained

Pain opens the heart to search for meaning. We ask God, "Why?" and find He is silent. We question His goodness, love, and sovereignty. These questions bring us to Him.

By coming to Him, we learn the deeper answers. We find the love we crave. We discover the God Who wants us to know Him.

This collection of articles leads us to find that meaning, learn those answers, and see our God.

For a complete and current listing of books with excerpts see
www.sonyacontreras.com

Made in the USA
Middletown, DE
08 September 2021

47910346R00179